DON'T LOOK DOWN

MATTHEW BECKER

aethonbooks.com

DON'T LOOK DOWN

Aethon Books
www.aethonbooks.com

Print and eBook formatting: Kevin G. Summers. Cover art: Steve Beaulieu.

Published by Aethon Books LLC.

ALSO BY MATTHEW BECKER

RUN

DON'T LOOK DOWN

Want to discuss our books with other readers and even the authors?

JOIN THE AETHON DISCORD!

For Sarah

Thanks for all the adventures you promised, and all those still to come.

PROLOGUE

Late night, March 4

He ran, panting and stumbling, through the trees of Theodore Roosevelt Island. With only eighty-nine acres, this spit of land on the Potomac River across from Washington, D.C., was not nearly large enough. He needed distance, or cover, and it did not provide enough of either. Moonlight and the distant glow of the Kennedy Center were the only illuminations guiding him, and his wingtips narrowly avoided divots as he ducked branches, not brave enough to look behind him and gauge the distance.

He knew his pursuer was still there.

The gym did not prepare him for this. The quadriceps muscles that looked so strong when squatting were not built for action. They, like all his muscles, were solely for show. For the first time in his life, he wished he'd gone on more runs.

He jumped onto the raised walkway, trying to gain some speed. As soon as he felt he had, he hopped back down into the marsh. He ducked behind a fallen tree, sucking in breaths far faster than his lungs could handle. The sticky air coated his throat, and he could hear the shrill buzz of some nearby insect.

How had it come to this? How was he—*of all people*—shrinking himself behind a box elder tree, hoping to avoid a mystery assailant for just a few more hours? Just long enough for the sun to start peeking over the horizon. The signal that soon the myriad of outdoor enthusiasts in the D.C. area would once again make their way across the footbridge onto the island.

Surely, he'd be safe then.

He inhaled and closed his eyes. The air grew still and the only sound he could hear was the river softly lapping against the dirt and trees. He had persevered and survived much more than this. He would continue to do so. Once old Andy put his mind to something, no one could stop him. That winning line one of his Senate buddies loved to trot out whenever he spoke on the floor.

I will not die this day.

How could he have been so naive to think this source was going to provide him 'explosive dirt' on his enemies? The trail of drip-fed details had been just salacious enough for him to throw caution to the wind and meet under cover of darkness.

Mary.

She would be waiting patiently, trusting that, like always, he knew what he was doing. That being gone for hours in the night was a mere quirk of his job. Midnight is when the real power brokers work, he had told her. Some of the time, that had been true. More often, he had used that excuse for other, less upstanding, excursions.

He tasted the salt in his sweat as little streaks cascaded down his face. He couldn't tell if there were tears mingling with the sweat.

He had never in his life considered death. Sure, people he knew had died. Older relatives, an acquaintance from high school, that one incident years ago. But death was for other people. Not him. Not for a man of consequence. That teenage invincibility had never worn off.

But that wasn't the truth of it.

As he peered around, trying not to move lest the mud squelch too loudly beneath him, he knew the real reason.

He was terrified of death. He told himself that if he didn't face it, if he simply convinced himself of his own immortality, then he wouldn't have to confront the crippling fear.

What happens to us after we're gone? What really happens?

He couldn't answer, and it petrified him.

Time was moving too slowly. Where were the intrepid early morning runners? Where were the park police, coming through to make sure no riffraff were hanging about?

He couldn't wait. Salvation wouldn't come. He needed to find it. That was who he was, after all, wasn't it? A man who, when presented with a problem, got off his ass and found a solution.

Make a move.

The Potomac wasn't too wide here. He could get to the water and then swim across to Washington Harbor. Someone would be awake there, hear the commotion, and he'd be safe. This assailant wouldn't jump into the water. He wouldn't shoot into the water, either. This was it. He would be safe.

He didn't have to fear death today. He would go home to Mary, like he always had before.

Tomorrow would be another day.

A small cough scattered a pair of nearby ducks.

He opened his eyes, and his breath caught in his throat. The barrel of a handgun stared down at him. He raised his head, following the arm up until his eyes locked onto his assailant's, the rest of his face covered by a balaclava.

"But... why?" His mouth couldn't form any more words. His tongue was dry and cracked.

The assailant cocked the gun. A small smile emerged from the mouth hole in his mask. "Yes, you do deserve an answer, don't you?" His voice was high-pitched, nasal, with an almost song-like quality.

He watched as the assailant slowly removed his face covering. The man paused halfway through, only his eyes still covered. The grin grew until it overtook his entire face, and he pulled the balaclava off with a flourish.

"You!" The word came out as a croak. His heart started to thump even louder, pulsing fear through his veins at an alarming rate.

"Me," the assailant bobbed his head up and down. "You recognize me. I like that. That means," he cocked his head and looked down with a pitying smile, one corner of his mouth ever so slightly raised. "You know why I'm here."

"I... now just wait a minute. It wasn't my fault, you have to believe me, it wasn't my fault!" The man's chest heaved up and down, the sweat on the front of his once-crisp button-down almost touching the widening circles under his armpits.

"No, no no no. You don't get to talk your way out of this one. You and everyone else who was there that night." The assailant's smile turned rueful. "This is exactly what you deserve." He paused, before he spat out the final word. "Senator."

His finger squeezed the trigger. Just a twitch. A loud bang followed, and Senator Andrew Billingsley slumped forward, the blood pouring out of his head reddening the moss and honeysuckles as one last breath escaped his lips.

CHAPTER 1
VERONICA

Morning, March 5

"Look, Ben, what do you want from me?" I shook my head as we began the same daily argument that had plagued us ever since I was let go from my position as a mathematics professor at Georgetown University four months ago. "I wasn't exactly hirable. Why shouldn't I have taken a chance on this?"

My husband raised his hands, a gesture meant to calm me down that he knew only riled me further. His palms were the whitest part of him, which took some doing, considering his pasty Boston Irish complexion. "I just don't get it, V. You spent your whole life running from your childhood. Why would you want to bring that back?"

We stood on opposite ends of our too-cramped kitchen, a concession you make when you live in a historic townhouse in Old Town Alexandria, Virginia. Built in the shape of a corridor, long and thin, the kitchen had a little room on one end with pantry space along with our washer/dryer combo, and a door out to the back patio on the other end.

"And what part do you think I'm bringing back?" I could feel the heat and anger rising inside me.

I knew what he wanted to say. He wanted to tell me—*once again*—that he was not comfortable with my past. That those loving words, those affirmations he gave me when I was lying in the hospital, having just won the fight for my life, now rang false.

That's the thing about your childhood, though, isn't it? It's not like you get a choice. No one asks for your consent to be born into the family you do. I knew that better than just about anyone else. I was born Alessandra Portillo, and for years I wore my surname like a prized jewel around my neck. I was a *Portillo*, no one could touch me. No one would dare mess with Yancey Portillo's flesh and blood. I believed that in my core. Right up until someone proved just how wrong I was when they sent a hailstorm of bullets straight through the body of Kelvin, my older brother.

Then I was Alessandra. Alex. Thrust into the role of the youngest *and* the eldest sibling. A young girl growing up with as much normalcy as possible when her father was San Salvador's most notorious crime lord.

But I had a secret.

A history of some light murder on my father's behalf. No one except our inner sanctum knew. Yancey Portillo's Secret Weapon.

The thing was, he didn't ask me to. It was an initiative I took completely on my own. He just jumped aboard a freight train already steaming ahead.

Even though no one outside our compound's walls knew who I was, everyone in the city knew of my deeds. My actions rang out, if not my actual name. The assassin who slipped in and out, never seen, never heard. But if there were a dead mobster with a missing finger, you could be sure who was behind it.

I killed bad people. That was my *raison d'etre*. Were they, in hindsight, not that different from my father and his organization? Sure, but that was not for a young girl to decide. I was protecting my own. With mom dead from cancer and Kelvin gone, all I saw was my family falling apart in front of me. I was not going to let anyone hurt any more of my people.

Then one day everything changed. I lost my own pinky in a botched kidnapping, and I ran and never looked back. Veronica Walsh it is now, and I'd never been prouder of my own name.

But when you don't look back, you don't realize just how quickly your past is closing in on you.

Ben didn't say the words I could see circling his brain—*you killed people, you tortured people, you're a monster*—each of the accusations he defended me against for the past five months. I couldn't pin a specific moment when I realized that he was defending me a little *too* vehemently, but once I knew, I saw it every time someone made a negative comment in public. He wasn't chivalrously backing his wife to the supermarket clerk who'd mumbled that I should be "sent back where I came from." He was arguing with his own thoughts. The clerk was just a proxy.

"You're going to be around dangerous people again," he finally said, leaning his elbows onto the granite countertop and burying his head in his hands.

"Do you think I can't handle that?" I asked, lunging forward and grabbing the saltshaker he had unwittingly sent rolling toward the edge of the counter. "Have the last months not at least taught you that is not a concern?"

Simultaneously thwarting a would-be president's murderous plan and exposing his role in the current president's assassination attempt as a couple was one of things that's supposed to bring you closer.

Shared experience, shared trauma. The bedrock of successful relationships.

Of course, that only works when one party doesn't blame the other for the trauma.

Ben put his hands on his head. "Jesus Christ, V, *I'm* not cut out for this! How am I supposed to go along every day, not knowing what you might be up to? What about the kids? What happens when Nico and Maria get caught in some inevitable crossfire?" He stalked off into the living room without waiting for an answer.

There it was. It always came back to this. Ben was a thoughtful, decent human being. But he was a man, a well-off white man from the northeast at that, and he had never faced real hurdles before.

Haven't you considered how this will affect me?

That's always the real question. It's not their fault, they can't help it.

As ever, the struggle was internal. He knew that if I hadn't intervened, Jeremy Wiles' plan would have likely gone off without a hitch, and we'd all be worse off for it. You can't plan an assassination and then end up the President of the United States. Not yet at least, in this country.

But Ben also blamed me for it, since if I hadn't, my childhood would have never resurfaced—or so he told himself at least.

I did get shot in the neck by Jeremy Wiles for my troubles. If my crime was exposing the truth of my past, I wasn't convinced the punishment I received—weeks in a coma in the hospital—really fit the crime.

Life was different than he expected it to be. Congresswoman Moore kept him on, of course, but he watched his role diminish. No longer the reliable chief of staff. He knew that if she had any presidential aspirations, he'd get thrown overboard quickly.

But what of me?

My career was over, that was for sure. Academia, for all the right-wing media claims about socialists and communists running the show, is a pretty conservative place. Sure, professors tend to lean progressive, but administrators, provosts, and presidents very much do not. And more than anything, they are risk averse. Keeping a professor who has a—might as well call it what it is—murderous past, well, what else could we expect than me getting fired as soon as I was out of the hospital?

I don't know how he did it, but my birth father, Yancey Portillo, convinced the Salvadoran authorities not to seek extradition for my crimes. I would have fought it, and with scant evidence besides my word, which I was not willing to give in a courtroom, I didn't think they'd have a slam dunk case anyway.

I didn't like to dwell on how he persuaded them.

So, without criminal charges looming over my head, my prolonged stay in the United States was my main concern. That went away when, one day, Ben came home and announced that my immigration status was cleared up, and that it was made abundantly clear to him, in a very private meeting with Congresswoman Moore and a couple others he would not name, that was already more than we could have asked for, and not to ask more questions. I still didn't know exactly what went on behind those closed doors.

I was sure I could find *a* job, but I wanted to do something meaningful. I had spent my entire adult life teaching and engaging minds. That, more than any of the research, was what got me up in the morning. What could do that now?

I had no interest in going back to my previous life. My father's persuasion of—well, whomever he persuaded—made that very clear. I don't think he realized that by keeping me out of prison, he'd slammed shut the path toward any reconciliation. Yes, we had a brief reconnection in the hospital in the days after, but unless he turned away from his entire life, I was done with that. I couldn't be the person I need to be here in America, with my family, if I got sucked back in. He would just have to understand.

On the other hand, with my childhood friend Francisco Orellana staying in D.C., I figured why not lean on some resources but stay on the legal side, and start my own private investigation business? I wouldn't have to get involved in whatever he was up to, but he could be an assistant, consultant even, for when I needed help.

Plus, private investigators don't actually spend their days in grave danger. They spend it on marital disharmony and finding lost pets. I'd be fine.

So that's what I did. Made a little website, just bare bones contact info. I didn't need to put any references. People already knew too much about what I could do.

We moved to a new house, still in Old Town Alexandria, but kept our name off of public documents. Not exactly witness protection, but just an attempt to keep the crazies from the door. A historic Alexandria townhouse. Exactly what we both wanted, if not the kitchen size we hoped for. I couldn't advertise my location for work, so I just used a bedroom as a home office and met clients at coffee shops nearby. Not *too* nearby, though. Can't be too careful when you live in a country full of people with strong opinions and easy access to guns.

I wasn't sure what public reception I'd get. I assumed it would be polarized. That was my life now. On the macro level, though, I was grateful for the level of public support I ended up receiving.

I hadn't expected that in the slightest.

When I woke up in the hospital my first thoughts were keeping my family safe and stopping Jeremy Wiles. Only when that was over did I allow myself to think about the long-term effect that my truth would have on me and my family.

I never would have guessed that the public would rally around me. An organic groundswell of positive public opinion, starting on social media, pushed the narrative that I was an abused child, who only acted the way I did because of emotional—and physical, they speculated inaccurately—abuse at the hands of my father. He became public enemy number one, not that he ever wasn't. But I became a symbol of resilience to, frankly, far more people than I ever imagined. I was a survivor.

They got that part right at least.

The clerk whose comment Ben took exception to? He was decidedly in the minority. Even more reason I didn't need Ben defending me, as if we needed to have unanimous public support for my actions.

The President even made a statement. I imagine he saw public opinion and cynically decided to harness it, but he said something about how impressive I was. I didn't pay much attention. I knew he didn't actually care about me. After that, Ben let slip that he was the one behind closed doors who put his hand on the scales and tipped them toward letting me stay in the country. I was grateful, but it wasn't about me. With men that powerful, everything is only ever about themselves.

Did this support help me keep my job? Absolutely not.

But the faceless hordes on the internet managed to make someone's life better for once, turning me—almost overnight—into a sympathetic character. Men and women alike projected their struggles onto my own, sending me messages about how my strength in difficult circumstances allowed them to believe in their own strength. I didn't really understand how that worked, but it seemed that "stan" culture had turned its eyes on me.

That was the second reason we had to move and become unlisted.

The well-wishers. They were almost scarier.

I had more requests to my private eye business than I could handle.

Most were asking me to kill someone on their behalf a couple hundred miles away. I flagged those down and passed them on to the appropriate people, but when the first of my "followers" was arrested, many blamed me for my perceived hypocrisy. After that I just ignored any messages unless they were local, accessible cases.

I thought Ben would be happy about this. I really did. A job with flexible hours, more time with the kids, a home office. In this post-pandemic world, who needs their private eye to have a shabby old office in a run-down building with a rickety sign on the door when work-from-home culture has inexorably changed the fabric of our work/life balance?

What's that line about sharks? They have to keep swimming, or they die? I couldn't look back anymore, I had to move forward.

CHAPTER 2
MIKAELA

Evening, March 5

"*May our tears be turned into dancing.*"

As her own tears spilled down her cheeks, Mikaela Alonso's mind drifted to the line from that boppy Catholic song she heard at Mass as a kid. She had never understood it. How does a noun—this physical thing—turn into a gerund, a verb of motion? Do the tears sprout legs and start dancing? Does she, a woman with tears pooling on her cheekbones, eventually end up dancing and forget about them?

And how quick is the transformation, anyway? When will she be dancing again?

The police officer, a brute of a man with an unfortunate unibrow, stood above her, his heavy black sneakers treading the fibers of her oriental carpet down to the floor. He reached down a tree trunk of an arm and tried to put a hand on her shoulder. As if the physical touch from the man who just destroyed her world could possibly help. She shuddered it away, shrinking deeper into her couch.

Their—ahem, *her*—house did not have much that anyone would call noteworthy. Especially not any of the neighbors in their little Stanton Park district of Washington, D.C., all of whom worked for this or that Congressman or think tank and aspired to levels of grandeur and power unheard in ninety-five percent of the world.

But what they did have was this couch. A Sixpenny, now years old and worn down by use so that each seat was perfectly fitted. A soporific wonder when required, a cozy retreat when the world became too hard outside our walls. The place where Tony and Mikaela made every life decision together, a place of comfort, even their favorite love-making spot—not that they mentioned that to their visitors.

Now forever sullied. No longer would any of those memories stick, only the current soul shattering tragedy. *Where were you when—?*

"Mrs. Alonso?"

She looked up and into the officer's eyes. They were flitting around, trying desperately not to make eye contact. In this moment he was rethinking every life choice that led him here, telling a thirty-two-year-old woman that her husband was gone. Because why else would he be here?

"I just need to confirm a couple things with you, and then I'll be out of your hair." He shuffled his feet, each instance of eye contact lasting a mere nanosecond.

"Mikaela." She took a long, deep, breath, as if the extra oxygen would somehow give her the strength for what was to come. "Please, call me Mikaela."

The officer—his name plate said Duncan—nodded, his eyes now concentrating far too intensely on the throw pillow beside her. "Mikaela, your husband is Antonio Alonso, correct?"

She waved her hand dismissively, not bothering to answer a question they both knew to be true.

"You and your husband own a Toyota RAV-4."

That one wasn't even a question.

"Your husband carries an Italian leather wallet."

"For the love of God! Get to the point and then get the fuck out of my house!" She grabbed the pillow and shoved it onto her lap, forcing him to look at her.

She knew how she looked. Her hair was knotted and stuck to her scalp, her mascara running down her face.

Her amber skin alone caused enough confusion. She heard all the whispers—*what's her deal? Is she black or just really tanned? I thought she was Latina! Her husband is, so it's not weird I thought that.* Nope, just a child of a black mother and white father, something entirely unremarkable yet remarked upon by seemingly everyone, especially all the kids in foster care growing up.

"Mrs.... Mikaela. We found your husband's car parked in the breakdown lane on the Woodrow Wilson Bridge. The car was still running, and his wallet was on the driver's seat." He at least had the decency to not look away while he said that.

She squeezed her eyes shut, as if that could stop what was coming next.

"We received several calls from drivers. They said a man looked like he was about to jump. But by the time we got there, there was no one on the bridge." Now he was wringing his hands together. Somehow that was worse than looking away.

"You think my husband jumped?" she asked, no emotion in her voice.

"We don't know for sure, but we are doing our utmost to find out."

But she already knew. She knew from the moment she answered the doorbell and stepped out onto the front stoop. There was only one answer they would find. One truth to be uncovered.

Her husband didn't cause his own death.

She did.

CHAPTER 3
EMILIA

Morning, March 6

Detective Emilia Brown liked to say she enjoyed the tough ones. The cases that took all the brainpower. The satisfying solves. That's what people wanted to hear.

But, when you are a homicide detective, things get graded on a curve. There are no happy endings. Easy, quick solves don't provide that much more joy. No one rejoices when a murderer is put away. They might breathe a sigh of relief, feel glad justice has been served, or even celebrate a victory for the good guys, but it's all hollow. The victim is still dead. The act was final.

She thought about her current case.

Leonard Barry, what has happened to you?

She stared down at her notes, several pieces of paper hastily stapled together. Witness statements, thoughts while she rode the metro, all jotted down on whatever loose paper she had with her in the moment. Should she have a dedicated notebook, maybe one for each case? Perhaps. But that wasn't how her mind worked. And they hired and promoted her specifically for her mind. As long as she always had something to write on within reach, she didn't care what it was.

She re-read every page.

Missing but presumed dead, called in when he didn't show up to work. Middle-aged, lived alone. No family. Resume consisted of odd jobs, none full-time or particularly long-lasting. Wouldn't have made his way to her desk if it weren't for the dried blood on his pillow. Enough to warrant the presumption of wrongdoing.

One prior arrest for heckling a politician too loudly. A drunk in public that he pled guilty to and paid a small fine for.

But besides that? Nothing. No one saw anything. Neighbors had nothing of note to say. Friendly enough guy, always kept to himself.

Time to dig deep. Find those connections who each unwittingly has a single piece to the puzzle. Stack them all together and unveil the truth. *Leonard Barry, I will find you. Nothing will stop me—*

"All hands on deck!" Chief Branaman called down the hall.

"Oh, come on. Right now? I've got my own case here." Emilia rolled her eyes toward her partner across the shared cubicle. "I guess this one just isn't as important?"

"When I say, 'all hands', that includes you, Brown!" The chief hollered.

"No way he heard that," Emilia said.

Martin Fahey grunted. "Come on now. You've lived in this city just as long as I have. You know the drill." He shifted his massive frame, wedged sardine-like into his little chair.

"I know, I know. I just thought maybe we'd have a little more time before this whole thing took over." Emilia shook her head and sighed, looking down at the file on her desk. "All right, then. Leonard Barry, I'm sorry, but we'll just have to find your killer later."

Emilia straightened out her purple mohawk and joined Fahey and the rest of their colleagues trudging along toward the conference room. Fahey took his customary spot in the front row, Emilia in hers the closest to the door.

"You all know the situation." Chief Branaman started things off. "Senator Andrew Billingsley went out for a drive late two nights ago. His wife says that she thinks he was meeting with a contact but doesn't know any more details. Who is that contact, and where is the Senator's red Cadillac Escalade now? I don't need to tell you all that we need these answers yesterday."

He began to delegate tasks, and Emilia thought about what she knew— and had hastily learned since seeing the news report yesterday morning. The Republican senior senator from West Virginia, he was in his early sixties but took great pains to look decades younger. His closely cropped haircut and rugged muscles suggested to his voters a past service record that did not exist in reality. Married, divorced, and remarried, now pushing close to twenty-five years in the Senate. There were ongoing rumors swirling about him running for higher office, the question of which he always answered 'no comment' with a glint in his eye.

A few unsavory bits of legislation aside, there was nothing that jumped out about his profile. Knowing this city as she did, though, Emilia would be shocked if he wasn't hiding something, either personal or professional.

"All right, let's move," Fahey said as he ambled past. "Up and at 'em."

She gathered up her stack of papers and strode alongside him, a considerable task when he took up almost the entire hallway. Their task was to retrace his steps, see if anything he did the day that he disappeared might shed some light on this mystery drive he took late at night.

"Check it out." Fahey pointed at his phone, where he had the senator's schedule on the screen. "Recognize someone? Looks like we might be talking to your boy."

CHAPTER 4
MIKAELA

Morning, March 6

This is not what was supposed to happen.

Mikaela hadn't meant to push him over the edge.

She knew she had said some hurtful things to Tony and knew there was a strong possibility they were words you don't come back from, but this was never on her mind.

Tony jumping off a bridge? Killing himself? She might not have physically been there, but, sure as the rising sun, she gave him the final push. Now she would have to live with that forever.

It might not have even been his fault they couldn't conceive. They hadn't done all the tests, the studies. The anxiety as you wait for a diagnosis, a reason, anything that explains why what seems to come naturally to everyone else in the world isn't happening for you.

Why the thing you want the most in life is maddeningly just out of reach.

It's easy for others to claim they understand the hardship, but no one truly knows until you go through it yourself.

Her generation was getting better at talking about infertility. Just like miscarriages, it was becoming less of a taboo, a stick to beat the mother with, and more of a shared journey that women—*and their partners*—could take together.

But how to make others understand just how much being a mother —and having a family—would mean to her? How it had driven her every move from as far back into her childhood as she could remember. When you never know your own mother, never get to feel the overpowering warmth of maternal love, how can it not be all you want to give in this world?

A foster home in North Dorchester, just south of Boston, is not the childhood any girl should have. Especially when it became clear that her parents weren't both dead, just simply had no interest in raising her.

She remembered the first time, at age thirteen, when she heard that there were monthly payments from her father coming into the home.

"You are an ungrateful little wretch; you know that right?" Missy, the group home administrator, had said. "Do you not know where you'd be if I didn't have it in my heart to house and feed you?"

Mikaela had said nothing, just stared down at the uneaten bowl of pea soup in front of her, trying her best not to inhale any of the stench for fear she'd vomit.

"Your heart." Missy's husband Greg chuckled from the head of the table. "You mean our wallets, more like. And don't give her any ideas —we need that fat check from her daddy each month."

Missy saw my eyes grow wide. "Greg! What the hell?"

But she couldn't put the horse back in the stable. Mikaela never knew anything about her real parents. All she knew was that her mother had dropped her off and never wanted to see her again. As a child she wondered every day about what it was about her that her mom didn't like. What characteristics could she fix, and then get her mom back. She was left as a baby, so was it that she was ugly? Did her mom take one look at her and say nope, not for me? Or did she cry too much? Was her mother maybe a loving woman who just got too overstimulated and cracked?

Her father, though. He was alive and accounted for. He could have all the answers. And she had a lead to find him. She would just have to figure out how computers worked first.

Two decades on, with a computer science degree in tow, and she had to admit, knowing who her father was, and what he did to her mother, did not make her life better. That's what they don't tell you, those people who claim 'closure' is always healing.

Sometimes the truth doesn't help, sometimes it just makes your entire life worse.

Since then, she had been dedicated to living the life her mother should have. The nurturing, the caring, the raising of *at least* one child. A good life. A Godly life, with a good man.

Well, up until yesterday.

CHAPTER 5
VERONICA

Morning, March 6

I never liked the idea of a spouse.

Not in general—I'm not a monster—but for me. When I ran away from home in San Salvador, I knew that emotional proximity to anyone would be dangerous. And everyone knows when you start a relationship with a lie, no matter how well meaning you are, it will eventually blow up in your face. And boy, was mine a big one. My secret body count was not a string of one-night stands.

So, I didn't think it was worth it. Boyfriends and flings, absolutely. Long-term relationship, not on your life.

Then I met Ben.

In my defense, he was supposed to be just a fling. I was a graduate student and needed to blow off steam, so together with a couple of girls from my program at MIT, I got dressed up in my best going-out top—and by that, I mean a friend's because in the moment I decided I hated all of mine—and headed off into the night.

He'll tell the tale differently, but the truth is I spotted him first. We were in the basement of a club somewhere in Cambridge, and I could feel the thumping music like a second heartbeat. First thing I noticed was just how pasty white his skin was. The white of a boy who'd never worked outside a day in his life. A boy of privilege.

It's always the eyes, though. People will insist otherwise. They'll claim their partner's best attribute is their lips, shoulders, or butt. But nothing compares to the eyes. His were perfect. Playful, intelligent, engaging.

I knew I was a catch. Pretty face, olive skin, and a mysterious missing finger—I didn't cover it up until after college—that was like catnip to the Boston boys. The small clavicle tattoo—*deus nobis haec otia fecit*, God has given us these days of leisure—that I liked to show off didn't hurt either. Their eyes always caught on it. There is, and was, a lot more to me than just that, but I knew the rest was just icing on the cake to them.

I swooped in and he folded.

We ended up back in his dingy little apartment, panting in a jumble of sheets and sweaty limbs at three in the morning. The exact end of the night I had planned.

Except the night didn't end. He didn't roll over, give me some awkward compliment in the morning, and then avoid eye contact until the next time we drunkenly stumbled into each other at a party. He propped himself up by his elbow, pulled the comforter up over me, and started to chat.

He asked more compelling questions than anyone had since my adoptive parents in Guadalajara, and his quiet intensity while listening to my—fabricated, of course—answers was intoxicating. He made me want to tell him the truth, and that frightened me to no end.

He made it worth it. We recreated that night every day for the next week. The physical, and then the emotional. We met for breakfast at a diner on Mass Ave, we took long walks by the Charles River. We had *the talk*, when he officially asked me if I wanted to be his girlfriend.

The fear of my secret unearthing lessened as the weeks and months went by. We were still dancing on a cliff's edge, but I learned to trust the steps. Life made sense, and if the day did come when Ben found out about Alessandra, I believed he'd understand what I had run from.

I spent so much time thinking about how he'd appreciate the gravity of my situation—the kidnapping, the betrayal, the hopelessness—that I didn't realize just how much the violence would stick with him.

Not the violence I ran from. The violence I perpetrated. After I came home from the hospital and the reporters finally slunk away, Ben sat me down on the bed one night.

"Veronica, I need you to tell me everything," he said.

"What do you mean?" I folded my legs under me.

"Everything." His eyes were begging me. "As many details, the full story of your childhood. I need to hear it."

So, I told him. I had lied in the hospital after being shot last year—*see, it still comes so easily to me*—about not knowing how many people I killed. That's not a thing you don't know. Anyone who claims to have lost count is lying.

I recounted every bloody conquest of mine. I told him about the time my father asked me to use only a pencil, and how tricky that mission was until I hit my mark and struck the guy's eye. I told him that was when I discovered that a re-engineered handheld pencil sharpener was a great tool for extracting information. I spared no detail.

Did my insistence that I had done it all as a child, not understanding the gravity of my situation, help? That I was a product of violence and had never known normalcy?

Not at all.

That was the crack in the relationship. Although calling it a crack would be an understatement. More like the Grand Canyon. Here's the thing, though. Cracks can heal. It might take a while, it might be an arduous journey, but they do heal.

As long as no one sticks lit dynamite into them.

That I decided to try my hand as a private detective. That was the dynamite. Now one wrong move, and the whole thing will light up in a marriage-destroying blast.

CHAPTER 6
MIKAELA

Morning, March 6

Mikaela scrolled with her fingers as she crouched over her laptop, barely reading the messages that flew by on Tony's memorial page. What was she supposed to do now? No body had been found yet, but she had been assured that it was only a matter of time. Like somehow that was reassuring news. The idea that any hour, any day now, someone would find his waterlogged body, and she'd have to go and identify her dead husband?

Instead, she was sitting in her mismatched sweatsuit, hunched over the little IKEA desk they'd set up in the erstwhile guest bedroom, considered as such before they repurposed it as a study since they weren't close enough to anyone to have overnight guests.

It was a small relief they'd kept the bed in there. Mikaela couldn't bring herself to sleep in her and Tony's shared bed, so she had spent the night tossing and turning on the extra firm twin mattress. It felt like punishment, and she thought she deserved it.

Tony had been her ticket out of the lifelong malaise. The one who could provide her a second chance at the mother-daughter relationship. At a true family.

After graduating from Holy Cross, she moved to the nation's capital, hoping that she'd find some ambitious eligible bachelor. It was either D.C. or Silicon Valley, and, well, tech bros didn't get her motor running.

She knew it wasn't very outwardly feminist of her to think that way, but in her mind, feminism meant getting to choose whatever you wanted to be, and she wanted to be a mom. So, shouldn't feminists support her? Wasn't pursuing your dreams, no matter what they are, exactly what it was all about?

She had been a tech whiz growing up, wowing her foster brothers and sisters with her computer skills. But college, and the subsequent real world, had beaten her back down. An origin story is only good up to a point. After that you're just competing with everyone else. *Look how impressive she is for her upbringing* quickly turns into *she's good, but not good enough.*

She was doing fine, no doubt about it, but just muddling along in a job she didn't fully care about.

Wait a second.

What was that post? Mikaela scrolled back up and gasped as the window stilled. Someone had just posted fifteen minutes ago.

"We all saw it, Tony. You weren't the only one on the bridge."

Mikaela's breathing accelerated. Her heart felt like it had leapt up into her throat. What could that mean? Was there really someone else there? What did they see?

She picked up her phone and ran out the door. She hurdled the four stairs and sprinted through the unkempt grass toward her next-door neighbor's house.

She knocked on the door, gasping for breath. She was someone her foster mother would have called "deceptively unfit." Skinny and attractive, with wide eyes and glowing skin, so everyone assumed she worked out when she'd never elevated her heart rate on purpose in her life.

"Whit, you've got to see this," Mikaela said in a single breath as her friend swung open her screen door.

"Umm, okay." Whitney Bondell stood in her threshold, wearing a matching maroon athleisure set, her bare feet poking out from under the oversized bottoms. "Mikaela, are you good?"

Mikaela paused, taking in Whitney's appearance. She was everything Mikaela wasn't. Her clothes matched, for one.

"Yes, look, sorry. Can I come in? I just need someone else to see this thing I found." She contorted her face into a pained smile.

Whitney considered for a second, before finally saying, "Yeah, of course. Joe is out on a run, and I've got a pot of coffee waiting for him. Come on in."

Mikaela followed her inside and sat down at the kitchen table while Whitney grabbed a Chicago Bulls mug from the cupboard. She poured the coffee right to the brim, leaving no space for milk or creamer. "Just as you like it," she said as she handed Mikaela the mug.

"Thanks." Mikaela put the coffee down, too wired to take a sip. "Look, I'm getting up Tony's memorial page. Tell me this isn't a really weird comment." She put her pointer finger up as she scrolled through, looking for the post she'd seen before.

Her brow furrowed and she cupped her mouth with one hand.

"What is it?" Whitney asked.

"I… it's not here. I can't find the comment."

"Okay…" Whitney nodded expectantly.

"I don't understand. I literally just saw it." Mikaela looked up at Whitney. She saw the pitying look, the patronizing kindness in her eyes. "I swear, I'm not going crazy. You've got to believe me."

Whitney sighed. "What did it say, Mik?"

"Something about Tony not being alone on the bridge. I just…" Mikaela paused. "Hold on, let me just go get my computer, it was on there." She ran out of the house as quickly as she'd come.

A minute later, computer in hand and breathing even more heavily, Mikaela sat back down at Whitney's kitchen table.

She clicked on her Facebook tab and scrolled again. "No, it was just here!" Mikaela put her palm to her forehead and slammed her computer shut.

Whitney leaned over the kitchen island and gently grabbed Mikaela's shoulders. "Look, just take a deep breath. Talk to me."

Mikaela allowed herself to slump forward, letting Whitney take all her weight. "It was just this very accusing tone. Like there was something Tony did or knew."

"Okay, I get that this could mess you up. I understand."

"You don't though, I can tell." Mikaela frowned and pulled away. "I get it, this just seems like I'm looking for answers where there are none. I don't blame you."

Whitney held her hands up. "You believe what you saw, and that's enough for me. I'm here for you, I swear. You're good with computers, do you think you could find out if it was there and then deleted?"

"I'm a computer scientist, not a hacker," Mikaela said bitterly.

Whitney sipped her coffee, watching her friend.

There was one other thing. Mikaela hesitated, knowing that Whitney would definitely now think she was going crazy. But she barreled ahead anyway. "Wait, can I tell you something else about it that was weird to me? The name of the poster. It was Bill Andrews."

Whitney raised her eyebrows. "What does that name mean?"

"I don't know, but doesn't it seem weird that it's basically the reverse of the name of that missing senator?"

CHAPTER 7
EMILIA

Afternoon, March 6

"I appreciate you making time for us, Ben." Emilia offered a gracious smile. "It's good to see you again."

Ben Walsh leaned back in his ergonomically designed desk chair, much plusher and more comfortable than the two wooden, creaky chairs that Emilia and her partner were sitting on. Emilia could tell Fahey was worried his was about to splinter underneath him.

Ben looked much healthier than she'd last seen him. His eyes were bright again, his features less gaunt than they had become when they had first crossed paths. He was wearing a snappy blue suit, complete with Bluey themed dress socks just visible under his desk.

"I'm sure I know what this is about, but what can I do for you?"

"Well, we would *appreciate* speaking to Congresswoman Chamique Moore," Fahey huffed. "But you already know that."

Ben smirked. "Of course. And I *appreciate* that this is your job, but it's part of my job to run interference for her. The Congresswoman is very busy, and anything you want to know I can tell you." He spread his arms wide. "So, talk to me."

Emilia recalled the last time Fahey and Ben had interacted. Fahey had been gruff and rude, while also implying that Ben had killed his missing wife. She could tell Ben was enjoying his position of power here. Fahey silently seethed beside her.

"We want to know why the Congresswoman and Senator Billingsley met two days ago, on the afternoon of March 4th." Emilia cut to the chase before Fahey could turn another conversation into a battle. "We're retracing his steps and his last meeting before he went home was with her."

"And you think that something she said, in an official meeting in the Russell Building, could have led to his disappearance?" He made little attempt to suppress the mirth in his eyes.

"We don't know what we don't know. That's why we're here, Ben," Emilia said, silencing Fahey with a sharp glance as he was about to speak.

"As far as specific content goes, I can't divulge that. But in general, the Congresswoman has been meeting with several high-profile Republicans, attempting to get some co-sponsors on a bill for which we might find some common ground." Ben's tone was maddeningly calm.

"Bullshit politician speak as usual," Fahey said, drumming his knuckles on the arm of his chair.

"Bullshit police tactics, assuming you have a right to know things not meant for you," Ben fired back.

"Boys, will you please?" Emilia had just about had it. Every conversation with another man turned into a pissing contest with Fahey. He was a good detective, and his insights were almost always spot-on, but she was *this* close to requesting a new partner. The email was fully composed, sitting in her drafts folder, just waiting for her to hit send.

It was about time. She was thirty-four years old, and having a senior partner didn't make sense anymore. To his credit, Fahey always treated theirs as a pair of equals. But now she should be taking on someone younger, a new detective to help mold.

A new Emilia.

Her parents had been blindsided by her decision to be a police detective. She was edgy and cool in high school. That kid who could hold their own in any drinking contest at a party, as well as on the next morning's exam, Emilia never liked to color between the lines. She despised the cookie-cutter personalities of most of her classmates, even friends.

So, why did she decide on one of the most regimented and structured professions out there?

The simple answer, that no one in her life really understood, was just that she craved order. She pushed boundaries as a child and found them all to be malleable. She needed to know where the edge was and when it turned out there was none, she just kept pushing. What they perceived as rebellion, edginess, or "teenage behavior" as her mom put it, was just a child searching for order.

So, why not?

She had no interest in the active policing side, walking the beat and all that. In her mind that was too often for people who wanted an excuse to wear a gun and act tough. They and she were as different as lecturers and researchers at a big university. Under the same roof, but two vastly different skill sets—as most college alumni could confirm.

She tuned the men out as they continued to bicker. There was nothing more they'd learn here. Checking in here had just been a CYA —*cover your ass*—exercise. Make sure that there was nothing obviously wrong.

Check the box.

This wasn't how they were going to find the senator.

Her phone buzzed on her lap and she glanced down. *This is how we'll find the senator.*

She jumped up, causing her chair to wobble heavily before correcting. "Sorry, boys. Hate to break up this lovely session we're having, but come on Martin, we've got to move!"

"What's up?" Fahey squeezed out of his chair much more slowly.

"Check your phone. All hands to Roosevelt Island. They found his car."

CHAPTER 8
MIKAELA

Afternoon, March 6

Mikaela sunk lower into her couch. The energy and adrenaline from before had been sapped out of her. Whitney definitely thought she was going crazy. Mikaela knew pitying looks. She'd gotten them for as long as she could remember.

What would Tony do?

No. That wasn't it. Tony didn't know hardship. Tony didn't grow up a close friend of pain and longing. That was what compelled her about him in the first place. He was born in the light and lived his entire life sun kissed. Tony never developed a fight-or-flight response because he never faced true difficulty.

She remembered when they moved in together, deciding the best step in their burgeoning relationship was sharing a one-bedroom apartment in Rosslyn, just across the Key Bridge from Georgetown. They leaned into the classics: bed from Ikea, bookshelves from Craigslist, cutlery from Goodwill. Tony, the classic male stereotype, wanted to prove he could put together the bed by himself. In what Mikaela still felt was the most inevitable event she'd ever seen in her life, she returned from running errands two hours later and found him sitting in the middle of the bedroom, pieces strewn around him, hot tears running down his face.

"Babe, don't worry, we'll get it," she said, dropping the groceries on the kitchen table.

He looked up, ashen-faced, and she crouched down and threw her arms around him. "Is everything okay?" She asked, suddenly concerned that his sadness had nothing to do with Ikea.

"I just..." his voice trailed off and he took a deep breath, as if to steel himself for what he said next. "I've never failed at anything before."

Mikaela's hand flew to her mouth to stifle the laugh. The way he enunciated 'failed' as if it were the worst thing that had ever happened. She knew she needed to validate his feelings, but she just couldn't keep the grin from creeping out beyond her palm.

"Why are you smiling?"

The pain in his voice was too much for her to handle. She started cackling and couldn't contain herself. Poor Tony sat there, dumbfounded, while his girlfriend laughed at his predicament. Eventually he, too, saw the funny side, but that episode took a long time to live down.

So, no. She was the survivor. She was the one who bloomed where she was planted. She would find out what happened. If she wasn't the catalyst, then someone else was. Whoever posted this comment did so for a reason, and she was going to find out why.

But first, she needed to call Tony's parents. She'd put it off for too long now.

CHAPTER 9
VERONICA

Evening, March 6

My husband flung the door open, stumbling into the entryway, the same way he did every workday. He loved his job, I knew, but it sure took a toll. The bags under his eyes at the end of each day were getting bigger and noticeably darker.

"Hi, hun, how was work?" I pecked his cheek as he swept by, offering me the quickest greeting before plopping himself down on the couch between Nico and Maria, disrupting a particularly rousing game of Sleeping Queens.

This was the thing about Ben. No matter what he might be thinking of me at any moment, he was the best dad these kids could ever dream of. He worked hard every day, and I could see the fatigue, but he never let them know. He was attentive, always up for a game, and made them feel like his world revolved around them. That was the easiest part, because I knew it was the truth. I needed him to get through this—us to get through this—because he was the best thing that had ever happened to me.

We'd fallen into this familiar, if not entirely comfortable, routine. He did his best to avoid even thinking about my past, and I tried to determine the best way to move forward with our new normal. So far, I had only gotten so far as creating my little PI hustle and becoming—if

I do say so myself—a MasterChef. That one wasn't surprising to me, though. After all, recipes are just algorithms by another name. Follow a series of instructions and you come up with a finished product. Then decide what needs tweaking to make the algorithm better. Gordon Ramsay, heart your heart out.

I plated the tomato basil risotto, gently slid my hazelnut scallopini (chicken, not veal) alongside, and brought the food over to the dining table. Sadly, the kids did not have sophisticated palates yet, but they were always game to try new foods, which was more than you could expect for six-year-olds.

Ben clomped over to the table with the kids underfoot, each grabbing an ankle and holding on for dear life. "This looks soooo tasty! Didn't mom do a great job?"

I knew what he was doing. Making a big deal of how impressive mom was to Nico and Maria so they wouldn't think I was somehow lesser now that I didn't have a 'real' job. All that did was make it clear what he thought. This is the problem with marrying high-achieving and ambitious people. They're more often than not attracted to that same level of ambition, and then when—for whatever reason—that is taken away, they struggle to separate the person from the career.

But I was nothing if not a shapeshifter. I could fill whatever space necessary. While my plans bubbled along, I could play the tradwife for a bit.

"Tell me about your day," I said.

"I had an interesting visitor today actually," he said, a single eyebrow arched, desperate for me to ask more.

My husband loved nothing more than feeling important. And why shouldn't he? Don't we all, even if some hide it better than others? "Some new lobbyist who doesn't know throwing money at Chamique doesn't get her vote?"

He chuckled. It always tickled him that I knew about his boss. Like he never anticipated having a wife who actually listened to work stories. When I learned about the domestic dynamic of his own parents, the dots all lined up in my head. "About as far from that as you can imagine."

"Okay, go on." Now I was keenly interested.

"Detectives Brown and Fahey came by."

I stilled, my jaw muscles tensing. Nothing good ever came from interactions with the police. Even though things had all been cleared up from a legal standpoint (*who wants to prosecute the woman who exposed Jeremy Wiles?*), I still felt the sword of Damocles hanging over my head. Justice is never final, even in the United States. At any moment they could pull away the safety net, and all the charges would come tumbling down on me. That the two detectives who were the leads on my disappearance last October had shown up at Ben's office couldn't be a good sign. "What… did they want?" I asked cautiously.

"They're trying to find Senator Billingsley."

I let out the carbon dioxide building up in my lungs in one exhale. They weren't there about me. "Why did they need to talk to you?"

"Nothing really, just the boss had a meeting with him the afternoon before he disappeared, so they were recreating his steps. I told them they didn't get to know what was said." He flashed a self-important smile.

Look at my husband go. Standing up to the police like that. He wouldn't have done that in the fall. He would've buckled and spilled his deepest, darkest secrets, safe in the knowledge he was innocent of any wrongdoing so they wouldn't use it against him.

Now he knew better.

He caught me smiling and rolled his eyes but offered a smile in return. "You're proud of me, aren't you?"

"Indeed." For someone who only recently learned my own deepest, darkest secrets, he was always incredible at reading me. Maybe that's part of what blindsided him. He could easily read my book, but it was only the pages I hadn't already torn up and thrown away.

He cocked his head. "I did think it was interesting they didn't even ask the question I was expecting."

"What do you mean?"

"Well, the senator is one of the biggest donors to Georgetown, so I just assumed while they had me, they'd ask if you knew him."

CHAPTER 10
MIKAELA

Evening, March 6

What kind of choice is this? Either break the worst possible news to your husband's parents, or let them find out from someone who doesn't know them? She braced herself as she stood in her front garden.

Isabella and Julio Alonso had been there when she met Tony. She had been with a couple girlfriends, having a casual brunch at her favorite D.C. bagel spot, when a busboy brushed by, leaving a small note fluttering down to the table. Mikaela picked it up and unfolded it. "Call me, Tony," it read, followed by a phone number. Not the most charming pick-up line.

She looked around the restaurant, trying to suss out who he was. Hopefully not the man at the counter, whitefish dribbled down his beard, slurping away at an iced coffee. Her gaze went to the table of frat stars, loudly debating their surely exaggerated golf skills. Figures it would be one of them. Boys who think too highly of themselves, congratulating each other on their moxie as they try to pick up 25-year-olds while hungover.

But then she noticed the man at the table behind them, sitting with an older couple. An easter-egg blue button down hugged his body as if it had been tailor made. A pair of expensive-looking sunglasses hung from the unbuttoned top button. He was engaged in a lively conversation with the couple, who had to be his parents since he was the spitting image of the woman next to him.

But no, it couldn't be. Who tries to pick up a girl when out with their parents?

"If it's him, I'm pretending that note was for me," her friend Bianca said beside her, following her eyeline.

"I say we all march over and let him decide," Morgan quipped, running her hand through her blonde ponytail.

Mikaela held her gaze steady, waiting for him to glance around. If there were any chance it was him, he would look over again. After a few seconds she caught him as he attempted a discreet glance only to look directly into her eyes.

Yep. Definitely him.

His face turned red, and he quickly averted his eyes. Hmm. A strike against. No cowards need apply.

"Wait, are you actually going over there?" Bianca's hissed whisper followed her as she rose from her chair. Mikaela brushed crumbs off her flowy yoga top and smoothed it down. She pushed her chair in, and made her way over, eyeing up the bathroom door on the back wall as a possible last-minute detour if needed.

"Excuse me," she said as she reached the circular table and stood between the man and his mother. "I'm sorry for interrupting, but did you send a note over to my table?"

He looked up at her and his mouth fell open.

"Oh, my goodness. You didn't, did you?" His mother put her fist up against her mouth in a failed attempt to stifle a giggle.

"Well, go on, son. She's gorgeous," his father said, his palm held upward toward her.

He finally held my eye. "I wasn't planning on this in front of my parents," he said after a long pause. "That's why I left that note."

She had never met a man before whose confidence and appearance mismatched in such a way. Any man, even the slightest bit attractive, who had once heard a compliment about a physical feature, walked tall like he was Adonis himself. How did this man not realize what he looked like?

They say confidence is sexy, but she had to admit she was fascinated by his hesitance. She thrust out a hand. "Well, we're doing it here anyway. I'm Mikaela. Nice to meet you."

At least his grip was strong. "Tony," he mumbled.

All right, give him one shot. "What was it about me that made you decide I needed your digits?" I asked, shooting a mischievous glance at his parents, who were clearly having a blast spectating. She could almost feel them willing him to fail so they could rib him for it. If he did, she'd have to get their numbers instead. They seemed like great friends to have.

It was like someone flicked the on/off switch back to on. In an instant he sat up straighter, shoulders back, head up. He looked her in the eye again, but this time his gaze was unwavering. "Your eyes sparkled when you laughed at your friend's joke," he said. "Of course you're pretty, I'm sure you know that, but you looked at her as if she were the most important person in the world, and people who do that are rare."

She turned to his parents, her eyebrows raised, grinning. "Good enough answer, right?"

His mom made an exaggerated thinking face and shrugged. "Maybe for a coffee date. No promises past that."

"Maybe I want to get coffee with you instead." She winked.

"I would welcome that, my dear." She flashed a smile that showed unnaturally white teeth, all perfectly positioned. "But now I think your friends are probably waiting for you, so don't let us take up any more of your time."

Mikaela returned to her table, but not before grabbing a pen and jotting down her own number, telling Tony that if he'd like to, *he* could call *her*.

Seven years later, and after all the ups and downs, it was her turn to make a call that would change everything.

She held her phone in her shaking hand, telling herself she couldn't put it off. They deserved to know.

But did they really? Do any parents deserve to know this? Weren't they better off living their current life, blissfully unaware?

What they did deserve was to hear it from her, not someone else. It would be even more crushing to get this news from a stranger. She could attest to that.

She pressed the call button and placed the phone down on the kitchen table.

"Hi, Mikaela, how are you?" Hearing Isabella's light, buoyant voice through the speaker broke Mikaela's heart all over again. A sob escaped her lips. "Sweetie, are you okay?" Isabella asked.

"Isabella, is Julio there?" Mikaela barely managed the question before she was racked by another sob.

"I'm here," Julio called, his voice distant and muffled, like he was behind a door.

"Mikaela, what's going on?" The buoyancy was gone, replaced with a concern that was about to drag them down into the depths.

She had tried to wordsmith before the call. Figure out exactly how to say it, to strike the right balance of informative but humane. Don't prolong the suffering, don't draw it out. "Tony is missing, he's been gone for days, the police think he may be dead, his car is on a bridge, maybe he jumped, I'm so sorry."

Or just spit it all out in one breath. So much for cushioning the blow.

"No, this can't be," Isabella said. "It can't be."

"Mikaela, tell us everything," said Julio.

She recounted the full story: from her thinking he was just working late up to all the info she had at the present time. She left out her suspicions as to why he might have jumped, though.

"We're coming down immediately," Julio said.

Mikaela nodded without thinking. Then, "Okay, see you when you're here." She hung up the phone.

Now that they were coming, they would expect her to know what to do. That was her role, the proactive one, established in that very first meeting.

The idea popped into her head as if it had been there the whole time. Who could she turn to? There was only one answer.

CHAPTER 11
EMILIA

Evening, March 6

"What do we have?" Emilia asked as she walked up to the chief. They stood in the parking lot for Roosevelt Island, just off the Mount Vernon Memorial Parkway.

Chief Branaman nodded at the Escalade parked in the closest spot to the pedestrian bridge that leads onto the island. "Definitely his. So far, no prints beside his and his wife's. The trail becomes dirt on the other side of the bridge. Hard to follow any footprints with how many people come here daily."

"This is also a great place to drop off a car," Emilia said. "No cameras here in the parking lot and it's easy to get into another one and disappear into traffic."

"Very true. Heading south on the Mount Vernon trail feels unlikely, just because it's paved and well-traveled, but the Potomac Heritage trail going north of here is an option. I've sent a couple guys up there. The rest are on the island already. If he's there, we'll find him soon. God willing, he isn't, because there's no way this ends well if he is out there."

"Why'd you bring us out here then? Sounds like you've got everything you need," Fahey said.

Isn't it obvious?

"I brought you guys out here because I'm not an optimist." Branaman shook his head and looked across the bridge toward the island. "Dollars to donuts, within the next hour we get a call from over there that they've found his body." He turned back to face the pair of detectives. "And that's when you guys get to work. So, stay close."

Emilia watched him trudge onto the bridge and head back toward the island. The K-9 unit had just arrived, two bloodhounds chomping at the bit.

"What are you thinking this is?" Fahey asked. "Murder, suicide, conspiracy? How big are we talking about here?"

Emilia grimaced. "My gut says murder. You never know what's going on inside, but he just doesn't strike me as a guy who would commit suicide. I don't think he's got some grand disappearance scheme planned either. This feels small—personal—to me."

Fahey grunted in agreement. She knew he was hoping she would indulge his larger picture thinking. He was always desperate for a murder to be part of a classic Washington, D.C., espionage and spy thriller. The Jeremy Wiles saga only furthered that. Emilia knew he was disappointed he never got a chance to see Yancey Portillo in the flesh, although whether to arrest him or shake his hand, she was not fully sure.

Senators don't go missing every day, and she would be lying if she didn't acknowledge her own 'step one of overthrowing the government' thoughts. But unless Senator Billingsley wielded huge power over the Republican caucus that no one knew about, Emilia just couldn't imagine him being part of anything of that scale.

"Philandering," Fahey said.

"Sorry?"

"Philandering. That's what this is about. He slept with the wrong guy's wife, and he offed him." Fahey shrugged and nodded his head, like he was proud he'd come up with the theory on his own.

"Okay, but why Roosevelt Island?"

"I don't know. Maybe the lady's name is Eleanor or something."

"You know this is *Theodore* Roosevelt Island, right? And Eleanor was Franklin's wife, not Theodore's."

"Is there anything you don't know?" Fahey scowled at her. "It doesn't make you better than the rest of us that you know that."

"It doesn't, you're right. But it sure makes you feel inadequate!" Emilia shot Fahey a quick smile just to confirm the lightness of her tone.

Every joke holds a little bit of truth. Emilia didn't want to fight, so cloaked her comment with a smile and some charm, but she was tired. Tired of the anti-intellectual mindset from a man who clearly was not uneducated. He was smart and good at his job, so why was it that every time she knew something he didn't it made him feel so small? It had only gotten worse since Jeremy Wiles' spectacular fall from grace —or, more appropriately, Veronica Walsh's unveiling as Alessandra Portillo. Something about the assassin he had borderline revered turning out to be a young teenage girl had broken a part of his brain.

"Fahey, Brown," Branaman called as he approached.

She locked eyes with him as he crossed over the bridge and immediately knew. His distant, unseeing stare conveyed it all.

"You're up."

CHAPTER 12
MIKAELA

Late evening, March 6

"Can I help you?"

Mikaela gasped and jumped back, almost falling off the front stoop. She grasped the iron railing.

Ben Walsh looked at her, his forehead scrunched. "I'm sorry, you knocked. Why did my answering the door startle you?"

"No, I…" Mikaela fumbled her words. Hadn't she planned what she was going to say? She straightened up and looked up at him, dressed in a white polo tucked into chinos, fitted to perfection. "I'm sorry, my name is Mikaela Alonso. Is Veronica in? Can I talk to her?"

"Absolutely not." Ben folded his hands across his chest. "How did you even get our address anyway? We're not listed, and for good reason."

"No, wait," Mikaela pleaded. "Can you just tell her I need her help? I… um, I think my husband is dead."

She saw his eyes soften, even as he said, "I'm very sorry, but what does that have to do with my wife?"

"Nothing," Mikaela said quickly. "I swear, I just need some advice. Just to talk. Can you please let me see her?"

Ben closed his eyes and puffed his cheeks out. "Sure, fine," he said, shaking his head. "Come on in."

He led her into their living room. Boxes of toys were neatly placed at either end of a dark mahogany couch. She looked at the pictures on the mantle above the fireplace. Each a different place, but a version of the same picture. A family of four having fun together.

What she always wanted. She took a deep breath to compose herself.

"Sit here, I'll go get her. She's with the kids," Ben enunciated the final word to make it clear she was a burden in their house.

Mikaela sat on the couch and stared, wondering what it must be like to say the word 'kids' and have it mean more than just that. Have it mean your entire life, your whole heart. Veronica came down a few minutes later. She walked in unassumingly, but Mikaela's breath was still taken away. It felt like seeing a celebrity in person for the first time.

"Hello, I'm Veronica. Ben said you needed me for something?" She stuck out her hand. Mikaela took it, not surprised in the least by the strength of the grip.

"Hi, Veronica. My name is Mikaela Alonso. I want to ask you to hear me out, but I recognize you're going to think I'm crazy."

Veronica hesitated and looked Mikaela up and down. Mikaela immediately felt very underdressed, despite wearing similar athleisure. Somehow Veronica made it look like she could be ready to walk out the door in an instant.

"Go on…" Veronica said, tentatively.

"Will you help me find out what happened to my husband?"

"Excuse me?"

Mikaela clasped her hands together. "Look, my husband's car was found on the Woodrow Wilson bridge, keys and wallet still in it. The police assume he jumped, and they just haven't found his body yet. I saw a comment on his memorial page saying there was someone with him, but it was deleted before I could show anyone else. I don't know where else to go, but I know of you and your… well, your skill set. I found your website and I was just really, really hoping you would help me."

Mikaela left out the most important detail, the reason she'd sought out Veronica in the first place, reasoning that it would scare her away. She almost said it, right there at the end of her practiced soliloquy.

Almost let slip her connection to the Walsh family. But Veronica wouldn't believe her. Now wasn't the time, anyway. Once they got to know each other…

"You say my skill set—what exactly do you mean by that?" Veronica asked, her voice giving nothing away.

Mikaela was ready for this question. "I just want to know if there's a chance my husband didn't jump. At the very least, if someone else was there could they explain why he did. You disappeared during the whole Jeremy Wiles thing, and no one could find you. I thought you'd be the person to ask to help figure out if he did the same."

"Does anything about him or his history suggest he could?"

"No, I don't think so, but I just need to know. I can pay you. We can make it legit and all. I just know I can't do this myself. I don't know how. But you could."

Mikaela could feel Veronica being drawn in. She had no idea whether this would work, or whether Veronica would be able to help even if she wanted to, but it felt good to have a plan. Some sort of action she could take, instead of sitting at home wallowing.

"Tell you what," Veronica said. "Give me his name, let me see what I can find. Leave your phone number too and I'll call you in twenty-four hours. How does that sound?"

"Perfect, thanks so much."

CHAPTER 13
VERONICA

Late Evening, March 6

Well, that was unexpected. I didn't know what I was walking into when Ben told me there was a woman downstairs, but it sure wasn't that. A random woman showing up at our door—*which I was assured shouldn't be possible anymore*—and asking to help find a dead, or maybe not dead, husband.

I was intrigued, though. It was exactly what I envisioned a PI life would be. Helping those in need, for whom the police can only do so much. It also didn't sound too crazy. A husband who killed himself, a wife who wants to know why. She might have thought he walked away and was hiding somewhere, but the odds of that were miniscule.

It wouldn't hurt to just check and see what I could find? I already knew exactly where I would look, and who I would ask for help on my own end.

I needed this. For the first time since coming back home, I had the chance at forward momentum. Despite my baby-steps into the private investigating world, things had stagnated and I needed more. My family was enough, of course, and it always would be. But what was I supposed to do all day, while Ben was at work and the kids at school? Did they really expect me to quit my professional life without a fight? I couldn't teach math anymore, I understood that. I even understood why people would be reluctant to let me tutor the subject that I loved. But if one door closes, you better believe I will make another door.

"What did that woman want?"

I hadn't even noticed Ben entering the room. I looked up from the couch and studied his expression. He was doing his best to be unreadable, but I could always see through that. He thought he was the master mind reader, but he had no idea.

He had been eavesdropping.

"She asked if I could help her find her missing husband." I shrugged, trying to act as if this were a normal enough request.

He shook his head, eyes looking toward the ceiling, the disappointment I knew was there just barely hidden. That confirmed he knew what was coming and had been outside the door.

"Why would you be willing to help? Why get involved in whatever she's doing?" He rubbed his forehead, and I watched a flake of dry skin flutter off and eventually settle on the floor.

"Why not?" I shot back. "Why shouldn't I?"

"Because." His voice raised a few decibels. "Because this is exactly how it starts! One moment you're kindly helping, the next moment you're taking a bullet in the head because you accidentally stumbled upon some big conspiracy!"

"What?!" I couldn't help but chuckle. This man I loved was incredible at catastrophizing.

"Don't laugh about it, I'm serious!"

"And that's seriously funny." I shouldn't antagonize, but this was ridiculous. I had to stand up to this eventually. We weren't going to live the rest of our lives in fear.

"You have no idea what it was like when you were gone. Days and nights of trying to explain to our kids why their mother wasn't here when I couldn't even explain it to myself."

"And now I'm back, and you understand why I had to run to keep you safe. That truth is now out, so no one can use it against me anymore. What do you have to fear?"

"Death!" he said, as if it were the most obvious answer in the world.

"Whose?"

"Any of us! Would it matter?"

"Obviously, but I need to know how specifically to reassure you." My calm tone was only succeeding in riling him up further.

"Okay, look, if you want to put wish fulfillment ahead of our family, then I just want you to understand the consequences."

"Wish fulfillment?" Now my voice did rise to match his. "Do my *wishes* mean anything to you? Does it at all matter what I think, or do you now just want a nice homemaker you can show off at events? A cute little wife with a cute little gig rescuing the neighbors' cats?"

"There's a lot in between putting yourself in danger and being a homemaker. Why can't you pursue some sort of math career elsewhere? Is there really nothing you can do with all those degrees of yours?"

We were back in familiar territory. He looked at me like I was a monster in my past—and maybe my present too—yet couldn't understand that others, especially hiring managers, might feel the same way. Public support didn't extend far enough that anyone felt comfortable hiring me. I was too big a risk, I understood that. "You know the answer to that. Do you think I haven't tried? That I like being unemployed? That my career, which you know was taking off, is over?" I held my hands up to stop him from responding. "No, I have a specific question. What is it you want me to do during the day?"

"I—look, I don't want you putting yourself in danger."

"But you have no actual answer." I shrugged. "So, here we are. I'm not here to engage on this if you have nothing constructive to say. I'm going to help this woman, and then see where that takes us."

"I cannot take this," he said, his voice suddenly low.

"What does that mean?"

"I can't be under the same roof as you while you act this recklessly."

"You... what?" I knew we were on thin ice, but leaving? Never. This was my loyal husband. Through thick and thin. We did it all together.

Well, except when I ran away. But he knew that was to protect the family. *He understood that, right?* There was no way I would ever do anything to put them in danger. "You're not actually telling me to leave," I said, my voice cold as ice. "Tell me that's not what you're saying."

"I…" he trailed off, his face the picture of defeat.

"I'm not going anywhere. This is my home. This is our home, and we've fought hard to keep it that way," I said, my tone measured and deliberate.

"Well, I need to get out then," he said. "I'll take the kids with me. It can be like a vacation for them. Give you a chance to think on your own."

"You'll do no such thing. Are you kidding me right now? The kids are staying here. There's only one person in this house who has a problem right now. If you need to deal with your own head, that's entirely your business."

"No."

I stared at him, disbelieving. "What do you mean, 'no'?"

"You're willing to endanger our family, why should I leave the kids with you?"

"I'm following up on a distraught woman whose husband almost definitely killed himself. What do you think is about to happen here?"

He threw his hands up and huffed loudly.

"I don't hear a response," I said. "This is my house. This is our house. It's not the house we originally chose, but it's what we have right now. We've turned it into a home. This is where our kids live. This is where they are safe, and loved, and protected. You think I'm going to let you take the kids off to what? Some random hotel? Just because you have this irrational fear that I can't protect them. *I* am the one who protects our family. You never knew, but now you know why. I've carried this burden since the day they were born. I didn't ask for any of this. I didn't get to choose my childhood. But if you think I wouldn't use every skill I have before I let anyone harm our kids, or you for that matter, then I'm not sure how much you really know me."

I could tell I struck a nerve. Ben was never any good at arguing. He hated confrontation and would rather apologize to me than stick to his guns if it meant resolution came quicker.

He glanced up the stairs, where Nico and Maria were sleeping soundly. "Tell the kids that dad has a work thing that came up. Tell them I'll video call them each night."

"No."

"Yes."

"You can't." He really was going to go through with this.

"V, I need some space. I can't do this. I can't have my wife be off in life-or-death scenarios, using all her past assassin skills, every day."

"What do you want? If I were a police officer, would it be okay?"

"Yes!" He exploded. "Literally, yes. They have a system, they have backup, they have protections. You're just going to go out there, unarmed, and assume everything is going to be fine just because thirteen-year-old you was a psycho killer."

"Qu'est-ce que c'est?" I muttered under my breath. "Look, do you think I am different from the woman you married?" I asked.

He could see the trap coming. He always was clever. He couldn't say yes because everything he was upset about happened before we met. But if he said no, then he was admitting nothing about me had changed. "The situation we find ourselves in is not something you said could be a possibility," he said in his relentlessly patronizing tone. "I don't understand how you don't see that."

"How can you not understand? This is who I am. It's who I've always been."

"There we go again. You've 'always been'? I thought the whole point was that you put that life behind you!"

"I need you to support this." I barely held back the choking sob that threatened to swallow up my voice.

He clenched his fists and turned his back to me. "I just don't think I can," he said. "I'm sorry, V."

"What are you saying?"

Ben grabbed a duffel bag from the hall closet and marched upstairs. "I'm going to go to the Residence Inn," he called back. "Call me tomorrow when you've decided to start being yourself again and stop trying to be a long-dead version."

CHAPTER 14
MIKAELA

Night, March 6

Tony's parents arrived at a quarter to eleven. Mikaela watched from the front stoop as they dragged their haggard bodies out of their sedan. They looked like they had aged a decade since she saw them last, only a few months previous.

"We're not staying overnight," Isabella announced as they got closer.

"It will be better that way," Julio added, in response to Mikaela's questioning glance.

Mikaela wordlessly ushered them inside, and directed them to the kitchen, where Julio made a beeline for the refrigerator. "This is crap," he said, his face falling. "Do you have any good wine hiding elsewhere?"

"I..." Mikaela faltered, her mind unable to understand how he could care about wine when his son was missing.

"Don't you worry," Isabella said quietly, forcing a smile. "You'll have to forgive us. We're at a loss, and Julio is just trying to control what he can."

After settling for the already opened bottle of Riesling in Mikaela's fridge, Julio settled down onto the couch. Isabella sat next to him, a glass of water in hand, while Mikaela hovered.

"A toast," Julio said, raising his glass. "May our Tony be found, and return to us, where he belongs."

"To Lenny," Mikaela whispered under her breath, without thinking.

"To whom?" Isabella asked.

Mikaela's face turned beet red. "Sorry, just something Tony always says," she said.

"Who is Lenny?" Julio asked.

Mikaela took a deep breath, cringing. "This is going to sound silly, but he always adds a toast to Lenny from *Of Mice & Men* whenever he's drunk," she said. "He says, 'to Lenny, who was a god-damned hero,' every time we toast."

She assumed that this was something from his childhood and had just gone along with it. A beige flag of his, not concerning, and so not worth delving into. But from his parents' expressions she was looking at, it was clear they were as in the dark as she was.

"But, why would he say that?" Isabella finally asked after the silence became uncomfortable.

Mikaela shrugged and shook her head. "He must have seen it in college, and it stuck with him. He's said it for as long as I've known him."

"Look, that's all fine, but what do you know?" Julio asked, waving a hand dismissively. "What are you doing to try to find him?"

Mikaela had arrived home from the Walshes' house only a few minutes before they pulled up. She hesitated, unsure exactly how to mention Veronica. "I reached out to a private citizen, who is going to help me," she said, her tone deliberately measured.

"Like a detective?" Isabella asked.

"Yes. The police think that Tony killed himself, and I just think there's more to it, so I need to find out."

"How much does this PI cost?" Julio asked.

"So far, she's actually willing to help for free."

"Nothing is free, she can't be good then," Julio scoffed. "Maybe we should stay down here," he said to his wife.

Time for a new approach. "Do you remember when Veronica Walsh went missing last year?"

Her in-laws both cocked their heads at the seeming non-sequitur. Isabella nodded, her confused eyebrows scrunched together.

"Now that's a hero of a woman," Julio said. "If she were willing to help find Tony, then maybe I'd feel better. Much better than with whomever you've asked."

Mikaela let the silence answer for her. She watched as they shared a glance before Isabella turned her head back toward Mikaela.

"You didn't? But… how?"

Mikaela filled them in, noting that it was still early, and she didn't know where it was headed.

"I don't know about you, honey, but our Tony married a good one, didn't he?" Julio said, a wide smile filling his face. "She's got a plan, and she's going to find him. I knew everything was going to be okay!"

Mikaela couldn't help but see Tony's features in his father's face. He was so much like him, and they shared a relentless optimism.

Tony was always insistent that blessings would come, that they would eventually have a baby, that good would win out over evil. Born and raised in Miami, he applied to every school he could think of in the Washington, D.C., metro area for college after a middle school trip had him hooked on the city. Like many seventeen-year-olds, he had no idea what he wanted to do with his life yet, but he knew the city he wanted to be in. His final decision came down to Georgetown or the University of Maryland, College Park. One drive down M Street on admitted students weekend sealed the deal. He loved everything about Georgetown and immersed himself in the history of the area. He gave impromptu tours, pointing out each individually famous seat in Martin's Tavern and making sure any walk passed by the Exorcist steps. "This is my happy place," he would say to anyone who would listen. And because it was his happy place it had become her happy place too.

Friends of hers who met him always said the same thing to her after. How did you find a guy so bubbly, so charming, and how can we do the same?

This thought was what now drove her on. How could a man like that take his own life? There had to be more.

Tony's parents stayed for just over two hours, long enough for the conversation to go beyond his disappearance. They asked how she was doing, asked about work, and she was happy to hear about the rest of the extended Alonso family.

But when Julio mentioned that their niece was pregnant with twins, Mikaela's stomach lurched. It was as if the gravity of the entire situation was manifesting itself as waves of nausea, and she had to quickly rush her in-laws out the door. She ran to the bathroom and just barely made it before all the contents of her stomach made an inglorious reappearance.

CHAPTER 15
EMILIA

Night, March 6

No homicide scene is pretty. There's no nice way to die at someone else's hand. All you had to do was look at the government's attempts to 'humanely' kill those on death row to understand this. Each year, some state comes up with a new plan that ends up almost comically horrible.

But some ways are better than others. Or as was the case here, some are worse.

Senator Billingsley died in extreme fear, Emilia could tell. The fetal position was easily recognizable, along with the horrified expression, but the kicker was the bullet wound in his hand. A final, vain, attempt to stop what was inevitable.

But at least the death was quick. A single shot, penetrating his skull just above his left eye. No agonizing minutes twitching or writhing. That's what the government can't get around. The humane part is the speed, not whether there's a big clean-up needed afterward.

Emilia stood on the raised walkway, looking down into the marsh only a few feet below. The body of Senator Andrew Billingsley lay, face-up, in the mud beside a box elder tree. His light blue dress shirt was stained with sweat and swamp. One Ferragamo loafer lay a few feet away.

"Why would he have run this way?" Emilia turned to Fahey. "This seems like the worst place to hide here."

The Swamp Trail on Roosevelt Island was the largest loop, staying right by the edge of the water for most of its path. On the eastern side of the island, a long raised walkway took it through the marshy shallows, populated by swaying reeds and tall trees, their trunks partially submerged.

Fahey nodded. "If you're trying to get away from someone, the last thing you'd want to do is run along a path above water where you've got no lateral move to make."

"Look at the footprints, though." Emilia pointed at the damp ground a few feet away. "He was running through this muck, thinking it would hide him. It's barely better, though. I don't see the play here at all."

Fahey shrugged, a monumental movement that shook the foundations of the walkway. "People do immensely stupid things while scared, so who knows what he was thinking."

"It's got to be that he ran out here, though, right? This wasn't a designated spot he and the killer walked to."

"Yeah, just look at his knees."

Emilia looked at his legs, bent at the knees and splayed out to the side of his body. "Yeah, I see it. He's got grass stains on his knees and this area only has mud."

"Exactly. He fell somewhere else, which must mean he was running away through here. Grass means he went off the path at some point not in the marsh. Still don't know what made him get back on."

Mud and grime caked his face but there was no doubt it was the senator. The scar across his nose—not won on a field of battle, but when an attempted bicycle trick went awry, Emilia had learned—was easily visible.

"Check it out." Emilia crouched down. "That's not a phone in his pocket."

"You're right. Wonder where his phone is, because no way he just happened to show up here by chance." Fahey crouched beside her.

Emilia was barely listening. Her world had shrunk down to the couple meters between her and Senator Billingsley's pocket. She recognized the feeling, the tunnel vision she encountered when investigating. Like a writer saying they just let their characters lead the way, she felt the clues calling to her. She and the answer to the puzzle were two friends on opposite sides of a busy street, waving to each other and trying to find the safest way to meet.

"You, grab whatever is in his pocket," she said, her voice cutting through the still air.

The crime scene tech, whose name she had not yet learned, reached down with a gloved hand, and slowly pulled out a piece of thick construction paper. He lifted an eyebrow at Emilia.

"Go on, what's it say?"

He cleared his throat.

"They All Will Pay For What They Did At The Edge Of The World."

"The edge of the world. What do they mean by that?" Fahey asked.

"There's one obvious answer to me." Emilia looked at Fahey to confirm he really was asking. "You don't know?"

He raised his eyebrows at her tone but didn't comment.

"You know the multi-million-dollar mansion where the Belle family lived? Called *World's Edge*?"

The Belles' McLean, Virginia, mansion was one of the most recognizable houses in the Washington, D.C. area. The property backed up into a cliff several hundred feet above the Potomac River below. With over 30,000 square feet, it had a full indoor basketball court that was the scene of many off-season pickup games and training for NBA players from around the country. The combo of rim-rattling dunks and stunning backdrop meant viral videos were plentiful.

He sighed. "Yes, of course, but why not just write that then? What's the value of changing it around for this note?"

Emilia waved a hand. "A flair for the dramatic? I don't know, but that's an insight into our killer's mind we can file for later."

"Well, that person killed a United States Senator, so low profile is definitely not something they're interested in."

"Agreed," Emilia said. "Okay, partner, let's run with this now. What have we got and where do we go from here?"

Fahey ran his tongue across the front of his top teeth and sucked in air. "We've got to talk to his wife, look through phone records, whatever can tell us why he drove out here two nights ago. Nothing from his work kicked up any leads, and this doesn't feel like some disgruntled colleague. That's not how things play in Congress."

As they each turned, Emilia saw a familiar face coming down the walkway towards the pair of them.

"Zeke!" she exclaimed as he got within earshot. "It's been a while, good to see you, bud."

Dzikamai Jackson was an up-and-coming crime scene tech whose skill was only matched by his ego. Finding the clue after the shooting at Peirce Mill that connected Yancey Portillo had only inflated it further. But Emilia knew the bravado was an act, a role he liked to play, and that behind it was a thoughtful and empathetic young man.

"Hi detectives," he said, shaking each of their hands. "Just got here, sorry about the delay."

"Out on the town, were you?" Emilia raised a playful eyebrow.

Zeke's frown suggested he didn't think this was the place to make jokes.

"Come on, you've got to know this about me by now, Zeke. Our job is too dark to not bring levity as much as we can," Emilia said.

"Fair enough," he replied. "I'm here now. I heard there was a note?"

"Crackpots leave notes, professionals don't," grumbled Fahey.

"You love the idea of professionals so much, Detective, have you ever considered going and playing for the other team, just to show them how it's done?"

Emilia stifled a laugh as Fahey glared at Zeke.

Zeke held his hands up in a faux apology. "I'm saying, you'd make a great criminal. I can just see it. A conspiracy of like-minded individuals, led by a secretly crooked cop—"

"Will you shut the fuck up?" Fahey thundered, raising a clenched fist.

"Woah, Jesus, chill!" Zeke said, retreating several steps. "I'm just messing with you. Detective Brown just said we were supposed to provide levity."

Emilia offered Zeke a reassuring gaze. "Well, don't let us stop you, I'm eager to see what you'll get for us here." She turned to her partner. "Come on, Fahey, let's get moving. The Senator's wife isn't back until tomorrow evening so that gives us plenty of time during the day to check logs, follow up anywhere we need, and keep thinking about this note. Whatever happened that the note is referring to, the key part is 'they all.' This guy is not done."

CHAPTER 16
VERONICA

Evening, March 7

I didn't have many friends anymore. Not true ones, anyway. It wasn't their fault. If Ben could falter after hearing my origin story, what hope did anyone else have? Was my running buddy just supposed to move on as if that information didn't change our entire relationship?

Things had changed before she moved, but I still wished Jennie could have stayed in Washington. I knew she couldn't—such is the nature of international diplomacy. Diplomats only spend a few years in each country. Can't go native, must avoid being clientist. Now, she was off at the Hungarian Embassy in Abuja, Nigeria, no doubt doing something incredibly meaningful. Hell, I probably wasn't even her most interesting friend.

My work colleagues. My wonderful friends whom I'd spent years bonding with over our shared frustrations with eighteen- to twenty-two-year-old students, wondering why getting them to care about mathematics was like pulling teeth. None of them reach out anymore. When Georgetown let me go, there was a flood of messages—well-wishers wanting me to know they had my back and asked for my return. Did they, though? That the flood quickly turned into a stream and then a trickle before drying up completely told its own story.

It felt like being the opposite of an odious political party leader, where everyone speaks ill of you in private but kisses up in public for fear of retribution or—*gasp*—losing voters. Instead, I was stuck hearing colleagues and friends say phrases as out of pocket as "well, look, if it were me, I'd have tried not to kill people" on the local news. Then I'd get a message apologizing, explaining they couldn't say it publicly but that they understood my position and the nuances that led to my decisions.

Like Hell, they did.

My faceless defenders on the internet were a bonus, but it wasn't like I could actually go talk to any of them.

All that is to say that I was left in a situation where I only had one person that I knew I could rely on. My husband had proven it wasn't him, at least ephemerally.

Why wouldn't I go meet with my childhood friend, a man who couldn't be a more perfect secret weapon for a private investigator if he tried?

He sat across from me at the two-person circular high table, his gangly legs dangling down almost to the ground. We didn't always meet here, on the main floor of a two-story Irish bar in Old Town Alexandria, but with its loud music and food neither of us would ever want to touch, it made for the perfect inconspicuous location. Irish trinkets and memorabilia hung on every inch of the wall, and the walnut ceiling darkened the space perfectly for my liking.

"Really appreciate you coming through for me like that, Francisco," I said.

"You ask, I fix. That's how it was always supposed to be" He brushed aside the praise with a faint smile.

He insisted that we only speak in English now that he was permanently in the United States. His English was superb already, but ever the perfectionist, he always sought improvement.

Francisco Orellana spearheaded my father's growing drug business in the Washington, D.C., metro area. As my dad put it to me, "White people and politicians love coke, and you've got loads of both around there so why not expand?" Hard to argue with that logic.

Of course, Yancey Portillo couldn't just waltz into the nation's capital and set up shop (the Feds would be horrified to know how often he visited, though). So, Francisco stayed on after all that messy business last year. A few forged documents, a single well-placed bribe, and David Rodriguez was born. A classic Hispanic-presenting name whose ubiquity made it forgettable.

"How did you find the witness?" I asked, taking a bite of my shepherd's pie, which, despite myself, was growing on me. If I wasn't careful, I'd end up one of those Americans who goes all out for St. Patrick's Day.

"I looked online." He shrugged. "That's where all the answers are now."

"Okay, but seriously, how? If I'm going to actually try out this private investigator thing, I need to know a few tools of the trade on my own, rather than just coming to you for everything."

He smiled, his eyes glinting in the dim bar light. "But if I tell you everything, you will learn it all better than me very fast. I like having something in my life I do better than Alessandra."

I lowered an eyebrow, an unspoken warning. He knew not to mention my real name out loud. The past stayed the past. "Fair enough, but you have to meet me halfway. Give me something."

I knew he would, because who doesn't love to have their ego stroked a little? He was dying to tell me. He spent most of his childhood worshiping me, and then once I disappeared, the rest of it wishing he could see me again.

"All right, I will." He held his hands up in surrender. "But look, Alex, I didn't want to tell you, because it wasn't very hard. You know that there is a public traffic camera at the end of that bridge?"

"I did not, but sure." I decided to let it slide, him calling me Alex.

"Well, there's actually cameras that show the entire bridge, but the one that would show where he was parked is down. Unclear if that's coincidental or not. I can run that down, but that didn't feel as time sensitive. Anyway, I retrieved all the footage from the other camera and made a list of every car that passed by on the correct side of the road within thirty minutes on either side of when they think he jumped. Then I used the DMV to find owner info on each individual one. I found phone numbers, and I called, one by one, until someone finally gave me something."

"Wow, good work." The stamina alone was impressive. "So, you brute-forced the solution?"

"I guess you could describe it like that. I did it all last night. I had to wait until this morning to call because no one was awake."

"Yes, because no one keeps drug kingpin hours," I said, deadpan.

He gave a self-deprecating shrug and handed me a folded-up piece of printer paper. He hopped off his stool, put his hand to the side of his head and gave a two-fingered salute, before disappearing into the crowd.

I unfolded the paper and read it.

Corey McHugh. A man driving his Prius by the Woodrow Wilson Bridge just before noon on March 5th. He saw Tony Alonso standing at the railing, both hands on the top bar, looking over the side. All signs so far point to jumping.

But.

He also saw another man, a 'regular looking white dude.' No second parked car in sight, which could be very interesting unless he, like almost every eyewitness ever, was mistaken and didn't see the full scene. A guy wearing a dark jacket and khaki pants, leaning calmly against the railing with one elbow, around ten to twenty feet away from Tony.

There must be more eyewitnesses. If it was as he described, you don't just drive by and miss this. I knew there were a million reasons to not tell the police what you saw—my rule: *never ever ever talk to the police*—so odds were low that anyone else would come forward.

We could go confront Corey, ask him to tell us more, but what else could he tell? Unless there was some slowdown due to gawking—and as detail-oriented as Francisco was, he surely would have mentioned that—then he only saw the scene for a second.

That was my new task. To find out what happened to Tony, I had to find out who this man was, and how did he get to the bridge?

And, most importantly, what did he say to Tony while they were together?

CHAPTER 17
MIKAELA

Evening, March 7

Mikaela had never before truly felt at home. Nowhere from her adolescence or early adulthood had come close to feeling like the place she truly belonged. She forever stayed a year here, a year there, and then just kept on moving.

No one pulled up roots, left a community behind, and began anew better than her. Rightly so, since this was her sixth new home since reaching adulthood. College had provided some semblance of structure, but even then, she moved often and never settled.

She would settle when she found a man to settle with. Why else would she want to let her roots grow deep in one location? Why tether yourself if you aren't doing it with a family or at least a spouse by your side?

Tony was the one she decided to settle down for. Four years they'd lived in this townhouse in a cute little neighborhood in the nation's capital. The plan was for decades longer.

Woman plans, God laughs, right?

That's what life really was anyway. A big joke. Trying to find some meaning out of a spiteful chaos.

Maybe Idaho next. Flyover and conservative. That could be what she needed. A farm.

I'm spiraling.

She could feel herself losing control. She tried to chase away the cobwebs and creeping nausea as the doorbell rang. When she swung the door open, she was struck again by just how instantly recognizable Veronica was, and not solely from the left hand that hung by her side, missing pinky now shown to the world.

Veronica wore an oversized gray shawl over an eggplant-colored athleisure tank and leggings set, completed by a pair of machine-washable running shoes. A small black bag hung from a long strap over her shoulder. Her inky hair, streaked with blonde highlights, was held back by a white hairband.

Her eyes, though. Equally bright and penetrating, they seemed to be able to look straight into Mikaela's soul.

"Nice to see you again, Mikaela," she said, opening her arms for an embrace.

Mikaela grasped her tightly, maybe a little too tight. "Likewise," she said. "Come on in."

She led Veronica in, steering her past the living room and her no-longer-favorite couch, and into the dining room. This felt like it would be an active conversation, not one designed for sinking further and further into a soporific furniture piece.

"Can I get you anything? Water, tea, something stronger?" She rummaged through her cabinet, trying to find a novelty cup that didn't make her want to burst into tears. She finally settled on the plastic 2013 Boston Red Sox World Champions souvenir cup. From the pre-Tony era of her life.

"Water would be lovely, thank you."

Mikaela and Tony had some nice glass and dinnerware—they did have a wedding complete with a registry after all—but enjoyed using their collection of plastic cups collected from various events down the years. The littlest things, like both collecting souvenir cups, can bring a couple together. Mikaela opened the fridge, pulling out the Brita pitcher that she depended on.

A friend who had lived in a country with non-potable water had once chided Mikaela for her insistence on not drinking tap water, but

Mikaela resisted. To her, it was almost as important as a status symbol as it was a health decision. That's the thing people don't understand about growing up poor. Every inch you fight for, every tiny luxury you snatch, you guard those with your life. No backward steps.

If I hadn't seen such riches, I could live with being poor, as British rock band James put it in their song, "Sit Down."

What the soft, elite, upper crust of society also doesn't know is what it truly takes to be a survivor. And that once you are one, how easy it is to spot other survivors and those just cosplaying.

Veronica was clearly the former. Mikaela used to think as a teenager that she had cultivated a perfect *'fuck with me and I will end you'* vibe, but looking across the table at the extraordinary woman on the other side, she wondered for the first time if maybe she were the one cosplaying true survival.

"I told you I would take a day, and so here I am," Veronica spoke with a soft, even tone.

This was a woman who doesn't fight to be heard. She speaks, and everyone listens.

"I want to start with a question, though," Veronica said. "How did you find our house?"

"What do you mean?" Mikaela responded, her tone guarded.

"Our address is not public anymore, for obvious reasons. I want to know how you found us."

"I..." Mikaela faltered. How to explain what she did without scaring Veronica away? "I followed your husband home one night," she blurted out.

Veronica's eyes narrowed. "Whatever comes out of your mouth next better be perfect, or else I am getting up and leaving right now."

"I'm so sorry, I just... When your story came out, I was fascinated, and knowing where you lived somehow felt like it humanized you more. I knew what your husband looked like, and one day I saw him on the metro. I didn't plan it but just wondered where you were now, so I followed him. I just walked right by, I swear, and I never thought about it again until now."

She watched as the wheels turned in Veronica's mind. She could see her considering and shrunk herself down in her chair to look as meek and unassuming as possible. It wasn't a bad answer for a lie she made up on the spot. She needed Veronica not to ask why she knew what her husband looked like.

"All right, look," Veronica said. "I don't like it, and we can deal with whatever the real reason is later, but right now let's talk about your husband."

"The real reason? I—"

Veronica silenced her with a raised hand. "We found a witness who saw your husband on the bridge. He was with another man."

Streams of thoughts cascaded and crisscrossed through Mikaela's mind. Who was the witness? What did they see? Maybe Tony didn't just go and kill himself. Maybe he was murdered. Maybe he got in the other person's car. If that person saw something, then maybe others did too.

"What does that mean?" was the question she finally asked out loud.

"That means we find that witness, a man who driving by at the time, and we find out what happened. Very simple, straightforward task here. We don't need to speculate wildly, just see where this leads us. I do want to ask you, though, do you think your husband is still alive? Really and truly, what do you think?"

"I—," Mikaela stopped. She didn't have a true answer. One minute he was definitely dead, and she drove him to suicide, and the next minute she absolutely believed he was still alive. Was this all some big setup? Mikaela felt herself swinging from extreme to extreme.

"Yes. I now think that he's alive," she finally said. "That comment on the Facebook page, I just can't get it out of my head."

"Okay. So, we work on that single assumption. We try—together, this has to be you as well—to figure out what could've happened, and we bring your husband home. I'll do the heavy lifting, I'll search high and low, follow the leads, all that stuff, but I need you to rack your brain and tell me every single thing you can think of that's relevant. And when you think of something else later that you had forgotten, you tell me that immediately too."

As Veronica laid out the ground rules, Mikaela paused, a single detail sticking out in her mind.

"Wait. Hold on. You said 'we'." Mikaela looked directly into Veronica's eyes. "You said '*we* found a witness.' Who is we? Who else did you tell?"

CHAPTER 18
EMILIA

Evening, March 7

"What do I do now?"

An unanswerable question. Emilia knew better than to try to respond.

Fahey, with all the confidence of a mediocre man, went for it. "Mrs. Billingsley, our next step is formal identification of the body, which I have to tell you won't be easy because of its condition. Then—"

She burst into tears.

"Fahey!" Emilia hissed, under her breath but deliberately loud enough for the senator's wife to hear. She caught her eye with a conciliatory look. Maybe this should be the last case together. Maybe it was just about time for a fresh start, a new partner.

Mary Billingsley sobbed into her hands, her entire body trembling. Tears dripped down onto the shoulder of her blazer. Despite her missing-now-dead husband, she was dressed immaculately. No sweatpants and old ratty t-shirt. Instead, she was dressed in a navy blue jacket and pants. Emilia figured that must be habit for a prominent politician's wife.

Fahey reached out and awkwardly patted her knee. When that didn't stop her, he looked pleadingly to Emilia, as if he'd run out of ideas.

As Mary cried, Emilia thought back to the last major case she and Fahey had worked together. While there were many—far too many—homicides in the district each year, none since had the priority level of the Jeremy Wiles and Veronica Walsh case from the previous October.

He had been just as useless with the victims' families then. When the parents of Margaret Sundham, one of the students killed at Peirce Mill, arrived in D.C. after hearing the news, he told them that she was killed doing what she loved, and they could take solace in that.

As if parents of a nineteen-year-old gunned down could ever take any solace. He even had the gall to complain later that they seemed very cold toward him.

It had been a tricky period when they discovered that Yancey Portillo wasn't the perpetrator. Fahey seemed to have hyped him so far up in his mind that he was disappointed when they had to arrest Jeremy Wiles.

He was far more upset when he heard that there would be no charges filed against Veronica Walsh. He stormed out of the building, claiming he was going to go give the Department of Justice a piece of his mind. Several times in the weeks that followed, Emilia had to talk him out of driving by the Walsh residence and harassing them. She had breathed a sigh of relief when they moved.

Fahey claimed right and wrong were just like black and white. That the law was absolute and there was no arguing with it.

If only it were implemented that way, Emilia maybe could agree.

Mary gave one final heave, then peeled her hands away from her face. Her skin was red, and she had angry finger marks above her eyelids.

"I'm sorry, Mrs. Billingsley, but we have to ask you some questions," Emilia said, her hand across her chest in apology.

"No, you fucking don't."

The detectives turned to see a young man walking into the room. He wore a black blazer over a garnet shirt, with khaki chinos and bare feet.

"I'm sorry, you are…?" Emilia said.

"I'm Jeff Billingsley, this is my mother." He glared as if he were trying to pierce them with his eyes.

"Jeff, I'm very sorry for your loss."

"Yeah, I'm sure you are. Very sad for you, isn't it? Having something happen that literally keeps your jobs intact?"

"Hold on just a second—" Fahey started, before Emilia cut him off.

"Jeff, we want to find and catch the person who did this to your father. We just need to ask your mother some questions to help us do that, is that all right?"

He snorted. "It fucking isn't."

"We can't help if we're not given information."

"What do you want to do? Ask my distraught mother if she can think of anyone who would want to hurt him? Ask for tips and hints as to who might have done this?" He shook his head. "What good is that going to do? Are you going to bring him back? Does dad come home tonight if mom answers your questions the right way? If she passes your test, is our family whole again?"

"Jeff, I know that you're hurting—"

"No. The answer is no. You'll do your little song and dance about how much this means to you, all the right people will talk about justice and making a statement and all that bullshit, and at the end of the day what happens? Nothing. I don't give a fuck who did this, and you finding out doesn't change anything about our lives from this moment forward." He pointed toward the front door. "So, if you would please —kindly—fuck right off out of here. That would be much appreciated."

CHAPTER 19
VERONICA

Night, March 7

"You know what your father would do if he found out Ben moved out?" Francisco hovered just beyond our back patio's fence, preferring to stay in the alley. *Anyone could be watching your yard,* he always said, which sounded to me a lot like projection. I had made a point to assume he was always watching.

I hadn't called Ben yet. I imagined he was waiting by the phone, desperate for me to give him the green light to come back home. Clever, the way he somehow turned it into my problem that he left last night.

I was torn. I wanted nothing more than for Ben to be back and by my side again. But I didn't want us to go right back to the status quo.

I arched an eyebrow. "You promised, Francisco. You're not supposed to be spying on our life. Keeping us safe, yes, but spying, no." I stood on the other side of the open gate, gardening shears in hand. Ben never understood why I was willing to go near these, when they were the instrument that cost me my finger years ago. To me that was silly—fear of the weapon didn't change anything. If the orchestrators of that ham-fisted kidnap attempt had used a knife instead, should I never let myself into a kitchen just in case?

He held his hands up in apology. "Not spying, just aware."

"You're still giving him regular updates though, aren't you?"

"I—okay, look. I'm not actively bringing him any information from you, and you know you can always reach him directly as needed. But," Francisco offered a conciliatory grimace, "he does ask about you all the time. He knows I see you, so it's not like I can just say nothing."

"What do you tell him, then?"

"Vague life updates. 'She still is unemployed, the kids seem happy,' that sort of thing."

I still hadn't resolved my own feelings about my father. How could I not? It was less than half a year since we reconnected and I learned the truth. Twenty-three years of thinking he abandoned me. You can't just turn that off in a heartbeat.

It's not like we could just meet up for coffee and talk through things. He'd been sending me presents for a while now, though. Classic missing parent trying to buy affection. Just slightly different since the last package contained Cartier watches for the whole family.

There was a moment—well, more like a few weeks—where I truly believed we could reconnect and maybe rebuild what we once had. I convinced myself I could have it all. My normal life here, plus my first father as well.

Ben tried to talk me out of it. He tried to explain that logically it made no sense. That having a relationship with a man like that would bring nothing but trouble.

Not long after the truth about my past came out, I had received a letter that kindly informed me that I was considered a legal resident of the United States, and my visa would remain, as long as there was no contact with known criminals, here or abroad.

Known criminals.

It was clear to me what that meant. Do not interact with your father or else we will deport you.

I knew he visited every now and then. Every so often, one of his unexplained packages would show up at our front door, no return address. Always addressed to 'AP.'

I saw him once, since my old life became my new life. That was all I needed.

Last December, we decided as a family that we needed a vacation.

Once I was assured my immigration status would not change, we decided what the four of us needed was a secluded beach, with a kid friendly all-inclusive resort.

A casual mention to Francisco of our plans had led to a paper bag with stacks of bills inside amounting to twenty-thousand dollars on our front stoop the next morning. I should have known he'd tell my father.

I also should have known my father would find out where we were going. We believed that the Corn Islands, off the east coast of Nicaragua, were the perfect getaway. Secluded, relatively unknown to Americans among Caribbean getaways, stunning beaches. Everything we wanted.

As Ben and I stretched out on loungers, drinks in hand—piña colada for him, rum and coke for me—keeping a weather eye on the kids in the nearby splash pen, I saw him. Leaning against a palm tree, about fifty yards down the beach. His wide-brim sun hat perched jauntily on top of his head, one foot raised, with the sole planted firmly against the tree a couple feet off the ground.

Not looking at us at all and making no scene. Just a single gentleman enjoying the view. Or so it seemed.

It was then that I knew.

He had changed, mellowed, perhaps, but he was still the same man I grew up with. A dangerous man, a man with more power than anyone should wield.

I felt the breath leave my chest as if my lungs had been punctured. I tossed aside my airport paperback—the romance novel with the cheesiest cover, always—and marched over, kicking up a storm of sand behind me.

"What the fuck are you doing?"

He didn't look up, just kept studying the sand and the water. With a final puff of his cigar, he turned and faced me. His bright green eyes glimmered, and his smile told me he knew this conversation would happen.

"I'm spending quality time with my family. Are you not?" He managed to look wistful, his serene smile seemingly permanently etched across his face.

"I'm—how did you even...?" I realized I knew the answer before I even finished the question.

"It's impressive you spotted me. I'm glad to see your skills are still up to par," he said. "I didn't make it easy for you. If you hadn't seen me, I would have gone home knowing you were too far gone to ever fully come back."

"What do you mean 'fully come back'?"

He saw the flash in my eyes, and it only made him smile more. "There she is. There's that anger. I knew you still had it in you. I know you, Alessandra—"

"Veronica."

"Alessandra. Always Alessandra to me." He shook his head, a disappointed parent whose daughter had gone astray. "You convinced yourself that the truth was a lie for twenty-three years. You hid from your true nature. You pursued a life that did not belong to you. Now you know where you belong. Don't worry, I understand it will take some time. You have put down roots, and I don't expect those to be pulled up easily. But just know, I will always be there to facilitate. I will be there to help ease the burden of those roots, and when you come back into the fold, we will all rejoice for our family is whole again."

"You think that's the endgame here? That I just walk away from my chosen family and back into your arms after everything?"

"Of course it is. Just say the word to Francisco, and we'll make it so."

"Make what so? What are you planning?"

"Nothing, my dear. But that is not to say I am... without plans. We will all be reunited, and our business will forever more be ours and ours alone."

I slapped him, and the long-time dormant part of me that enjoyed violence rose up at the speed of light. I savored the split second of his cheek wobbling and his chin quivering, before he shook his head and wiped the sand off his cheek.

"I came on a little too strong." His voice was frustratingly calm. "But don't worry, you've just proven to me that everything I said is true."

I hated that he was even the tiniest bit right. I shouldn't have enjoyed slapping him as much as I did. I spent a long time becoming who I was today, but deep in the recesses of my mind, the animal instinct I grew up with was still there.

He turned and walked down the beach, only looking back once to tip his cap. "See you soon, Alessandra."

Ben saw it all. I could tell from the nervous energy when I returned. I didn't want to discuss it with him. But he was not a dumb man. He knew what he was seeing, and he too finally understood that there would never be a true split between our life and my childhood. That anywhere we would go outside the United States, he would be there.

So, yes, Francisco, I did know what would happen if my father found out that Ben moved out. My autonomy be damned, he'd sweep me and the twins right up and whisk us back to San Salvador and that would be that. I wouldn't even put it past him to kill or maim Ben first out of some patriarchal fatherly rage over someone hurting his poor precious baby.

Do fathers of daughters ever grow out of that? I'm sure someone could rattle off lists of things that particular generation of fathers has done for the world, but to me it's just full of parents who never understood that their kids grew up.

I allowed Francisco to stay in our lives, but as far as I was concerned, my ties to my past had never been this irreparably severed. My feelings for my father were still complicated. But that's not what mattered. Only my chosen family, my *true* family, mattered anymore.

My adoptive mother was on the way up to D.C. Unlike Yancey, she wouldn't dismember Ben for this, although her own anger at him would not abate anytime soon. Ever since my parents met me and I told them the truth of my background, they had been afraid of what would happen if it all came out. They watched every new relationship I had with hesitancy and fear, wondering if this was the one that caused the house of cards to fall apart.

As it turned out, I ended up bringing it on myself. I still was upset at myself for not realizing my water bottle had ripped off when I jumped into Rock Creek to escape Jeremy Wiles after he'd shot the runners. There was nothing I could have done, and I knew that logically, but a small voice in my brain kept telling me I should've done better. Should've somehow snagged it as the rushing water carried me downstream, away from danger.

I knew that if I was to continue pursuing this case for Mikaela, then there was a chance I'd have to run out at a moment's notice. The twins were in school most of the time, but what if I was home alone with them? What if Ben stayed away for weeks, even months?

Of course, my mother agreed to come up, even though my father had to stay behind because he couldn't just leave his high school students. My mother could more easily have someone cover her college classes or just make them online for a bit. She liked to say his job was of more importance, since by the time students got to her class in college, they'd already solidified their personalities. He at least still had a chance to mold them. I understood the half-truth of it, when a college educator meets a student and wishes she could have taught them earlier in life.

"You haven't asked for my take, but I'm going to say it anyway," Francisco said, peering past me to make sure we were alone. "Ben is a good guy and he's going through something he never thought he would. Give him time, he'll come around."

CHAPTER 20
EMILIA

Morning, March 8

Emilia drove alone, her notepad for company in the passenger seat of her personal vehicle, a hardy old Honda Civic.

Fahey stayed back at the station, having muttered something about this idea being a fool's errand.

She drove west on the Georgetown Pike, heading away from the Beltway. Away from civilization, as Fahey liked to grumble.

Emilia loved the simplicity of a country road. One lane either way, one little painted yellow line—two sometimes, dotted other places—imbued with full power to control traffic. Trees on either side, blocking out all but a sliver of sunlight. A minute later a field of cows. Farmland whizzing by. A picture of bucolic innocence.

This was how she grew up. A small-town girl, raised in aptly named Farmville, Virginia, halfway between Richmond and Lynchburg.

She loved the family cows, up until her parents showed her the Disney classic, Beauty & the Beast, thinking she'd be a fan of Belle. Instead, she thought the Beast was a cow, and for the rest of her childhood was scared to go out into the fields. Even as an adult, she carried a healthy respect for them and an unwillingness to get too close.

But the rest of farm life still had a stronghold on a piece of her heart.

Simple directions. Waypoints and landmarks.

Pass both Bullneck Run and its little spur, then you'll make a right. Follow the road until you see the mansion. As precise as needed, and not any more.

World's Edge.

The aptly named behemoth that sat at the end of an unnamed street off Georgetown Pike. The only hint of life from the larger road was the existence of two mailboxes just before the turn. Emilia bumped along the dirt road for almost a mile. Pavement returned as the road widened into the cul-de-sac, and the driveway gates loomed. Imposing wrought iron, heavy and strong. Gates designed to keep the riffraff out.

The riffraff being anyone who isn't a billionaire, Emilia thought, as she pulled to a stop next to a row of wreaths. She got out of the car, intentionally slamming the door just a little too loud, announcing her arrival to anyone who might be listening. This wasn't a place you just knocked on, even as a police detective.

She looked down at the immaculately preserved memorial, wreaths of red and black roses lined up precisely so, each equidistant from the next. A framed portrait of the Belle family stood on an easel, just before the gates, where the road became paved again. All four of them were beautiful. A sort of beauty that only extreme wealth can achieve.

Ulrich Belle, the father. Son of an American tycoon father and a German heiress. He took over his father's business—Emilia couldn't remember what it was, one of those boring ways millionaires made their money—and quintupled the value of the company. When he sold it and bought Washington's basketball team, he had said it was the most important thing he had ever done. He reigned over an era of prosperity previously unheard of along the Potomac.

He stood proudly in the portrait above his seated wife, with a daughter to each side.

Yvonne Belle, née Fourier. A striking woman, her own independent wealth the result of a lengthy and high-profile modeling career, hot on the heels of an Olympic Bronze medal in gymnastics at the age of 17. She was supposed to be the great new French Olympic hope, an all-arounder with a combination of power and poise rarely seen before. A nagging back injury forced an early retirement, but her passion for sport led her to couple her modeling with a side hustle as a reputable sports agent, focusing on rising stars in tennis and gymnastics.

The two girls, standing on either side of their seated parents. Tracy and Miranda. Emilia couldn't hold back a tear as she looked at their smiling faces. That neither of them would live to age thirty was unfathomable. Children of local—if not national—celebrity, they had spent most of their teens in the public eye. They had handled it better than just about anyone Emilia could think of.

Emilia hadn't worked the accident scene—it hadn't been considered a homicide and wasn't in D.C. anyway. She remembered reading the report when it happened and had pulled it back up to refresh her memory before visiting the house.

The Belle parents had been in the front seats of their Aston Martin, Ulrich driving. Tracy was sitting behind him, with Miranda behind Yvonne. The crash reconstruction team had concluded they were likely driving just slightly over the 25 mile per hour limit, but nothing egregious. It was a dark and cloudy night, but unseasonably warm, which explained why the top of their car was down.

They were in the right lane when a dark SUV cruised by. The one witness to the accident was driving a car ahead of them. He said that he was in front of the truck at a stop light, and that the Belles pulled up to his side. He remembered them, not only for their expensive car, but because of how they all were singing loudly along to Toto. The two sisters were sharing a fake microphone and belting out "Hold the Line." The witness had helpfully reported that it was his favorite Toto song.

When the light turned green, he sped off. He didn't notice that the SUV and convertible were next to each other until he heard a loud screech of metal. He looked back and saw the truck attempting to switch lanes, and he saw the Belles' car go off the side of the road.

Of course, he didn't stop. No one stops unless they have to. But when he read online the next day that three of the four had died, he called in and told what he saw.

How they didn't find the SUV driver, Emilia could not understand.

Someone didn't look hard enough, and there was no reason why they shouldn't have. A prominent member of the city, along with two members of his family, dies, and the driver who caused the accident isn't found by the police? It did not make sense.

Then, poor Miranda.

Haunted by the death of her family, she finally seemed to be doing okay. Someone else might say 'moving on,' but Emilia always thought that was a callous phrase. No one moves on from death. Accepting the new normal? Sure. But moving on? That's not what happens.

Finally turning a corner, only to be in the wrong place at the wrong time. She didn't even know the connection she had made. Just an inkling that she recognized Jacob Jordan. Emilia knew why Jeremy Wiles thought he had to get rid of her—she might have eventually pieced together that Jacob was the one in the SUV. But how he thought that would ever come back to him was beyond her.

Emilia was tough. She understood death, suffering, and all the pain that life had to offer. But seeing Miranda's lifeless body, waves pushing it up against the craggy rocks and logs, had touched her core. No one deserves to die, but some people deserve the best out of life, and it's all the more sad when their lives are brutally taken away.

The saving grace, that Emilia kept coming back to, was that Miranda had been happy at the end. Ben Walsh had told her about Yancey Portillo's henchman, Francisco, and how Miranda had been genuinely happy spending time with him that night.

She had gone out on a date with Francisco, who initially just wanted to use her for more information about the Walshes. But he had enjoyed spending time with her, and she was not wrong for thinking there could have been some future there. But at the end of the night, after Francisco had dropped her off at home, Jeremy Wiles slipped over the wall into her garden and shot her in the back as she gazed into the night sky. Her only crime was that she told Ben she recognized Jacob Jordan. He passed that on to Jeremy, not realizing the danger he was putting her in. Jeremy thought there was a chance she could piece together his entire plan with that tiny bit of information and decided he couldn't take the risk.

The gates were only meant to keep cars out, so Emilia walked around the marble pillar to the right of the driveway and continued toward the house. The paved driveway stretched out for almost a quarter mile before curving in a semicircle just in front of the main house, where another road led into the property. Emilia wondered where the other driveway went, since she had seen no sign of any other possible egress. She jotted down a note to check a map of the surrounding area.

When she arrived at the semicircular portion, she stopped to look up and admire the house.

She gazed at the French Colonial exterior with symmetrical limestone stucco walls surrounding large French doors. There were two identical wings, with three stories of large arched windows.

The curtains were all pulled shut, and no lights were on. Emilia hadn't expected anything less. With no one currently living in it, there was no reason to think she'd find anyone here. That was why Fahey hadn't made the half-hour drive out with her.

But Emilia wanted to get a feel for the place. She was sure she was right, that this was the place referenced in the note found on the senator.

The perfect state of the lawn told her someone had been here. The trees and bushes in front of the house were trimmed to military precision. Not a single leaf or stick was visible in the grass.

Miranda had been in the process of selling the house when she died, preferring to live in her own comparatively modest four-million-dollar townhouse in Alexandria. There must be a realtor with continued payments from the estate to maintain the property. She made a mental note to check into them later.

What happened here?

Emilia jotted down anything that stuck out to her as she walked around the grounds. She tried the front doors just in case but knew they would be locked.

The second story balcony was larger than her entire house and cast a shade over the infinity pool below. The backyard, cut so short that the U.S. Open could have been played on it, extended all the way to a sheer cliff. Emilia walked along the edge of the yard, realizing that even one step into it in her muddy boots would leave a clear mark in the grass.

She peered over the side, and saw it wasn't as dead a drop as she originally thought. A steep gradient, but several small trees stuck out of the side, obstructing much of the water view. The placement reminded her of a pinball machine.

She looked back toward the house. Almost the entire facade was glass. This was a house from which you were meant to enjoy the outdoors. Every room had a view. Which also meant it was unlikely anything could have happened out here in the back without someone inside seeing.

After almost a full hour, she reached the front entrance again. Now she knew the layout, could have a picture in her mind, but only of the exterior. She needed to talk to that realtor, get a look inside as well.

As she walked back up the driveway toward the road, she saw a man next to her car, his arms crossed and a stern expression on his round face. A pink collar peaked out from underneath a pastel blue V-neck sweater. She could already guess the wheels turning in his brain. An unidentified car in front of World's Edge, and a mohawked woman walking around the grounds.

"Young lady, excuse me, you are not allowed here," he said as soon as she got within earshot.

Young lady.

At least he'd set out his stall early. She liked to know immediately where she stood.

She smiled and waved. "Good morning." She reached him and extended a hand. "Are you a neighbor?"

"No one is allowed on the grounds without permission," he said, avoiding her hand.

She offered a wry smile. "Yes, that's normally how permission works."

"I'm asking you kindly to leave. I don't have to be kind."

"Wow, then I would like to thank you from the bottom of my heart for your graciousness. In today's cruel world it's so heartening to see such unsolicited kindness. You, sir, are a beacon of goodness and light." Emilia couldn't help herself.

His features hardened. "Tell me what you're doing here, or I'm calling the police."

"All right, crazy coincidence here," Emilia said, flashing her badge. "I am the police. My name is Detective Emilia Brown. I'm with D.C. Homicide. Thank you kindly for reaching out to us. Can you please tell me your name?"

He blanched, his complexion turning ruddy. He looked her up and down twice, his eyes lingering each time on her hair. "You're a... cop?" he finally asked.

Emilia stayed silent.

"But, why?"

She decided to answer the question she wanted him to ask. "Why am I here? I can't tell you, especially since you haven't even given me your name."

"Oh. Um, I'm Travis McDowell III. I live just over there." He pointed to what appeared to Emilia to be an unremarkable group of trees.

That explains the second mailbox.

"Nice to meet you, Travis. Mind if I ask you a couple questions?"

"Go right ahead." He over-enunciated the long 'i', like now that he'd told his name there was no point hiding the strong Southern accent.

"Did you know the Belle family well?"

"Why, yes, of course. Us types need to stick together."

Emilia thought of a handful of follow-ups to that line but decided to stick to the target. "Okay, do you know of any connection between them and Senator Andrew Billingsley?"

He stroked his chin, despite looking like he'd never had to shave in his life. "Well, of course, they were friends, but I don't know what else you mean. Surely Ulrich didn't come back from the grave to kill Andrew, did he?" He forced a smile that came out looking pained.

They were friends. Something to go on.

"That's good to know, thank you. Tell me more about their relationship, please." Men like Travis were the easiest to talk to as a detective. All they wanted was to seem smart and helpful, so all it took was massaging their ego, asking polite questions, and they'd tell anything they knew. These men began as boys who had never had a run-in with the police that their parents couldn't smooth over. As adults they didn't have that battle worn fear that so many others exhibited.

"Well, you know how busy Andy is—excuse me, *was*." He actually placed his hand over his heart. *Lord have mercy*. "So, they didn't see each other too often, I'm sure. I can't imagine Andy and Mary came over much when I wasn't around, either." He pointed again at the grove of trees that must be hiding another mansion behind them. "That's just me now, no one else after the missus decided she'd had enough of the good life years back. She took the kids and that was that."

Surely it was the good life she had grown tired of. "The Senator has been to World's Edge?"

"Oh, don't make me laugh, of course he has!" The patronizing tone was back in full flow. "Why, he spent many a night there, sipping whisky and shooting the breeze." He paused and blinked, his mouth falling open. "Now, wait, you don't think I'm in danger, am I?"

"Is there a reason you would be?"

"Well, two people I've been in a room with have been killed now, so it'd stand to reason that maybe I'm connected too, wouldn't it?"

He wanted to be in danger. His eyes were practically begging her to answer yes. Something to tell the rest of his waspy friends, to ooh and ahh over, and for them to slap him on the back and compliment his bravery in the face of such hard times.

"Well, did you, the Senator, and Mr. Belle meet together just the three of you?"

"I wouldn't say that." He offered up a 'gee, shucks' shrug that made her think that's exactly what he wanted to say, the truth be damned.

"Then I think you have nothing to worry about, Mr. McDowell. Thanks for taking the time to talk."

"I… wait." He searched for the words, eyes flitting about, trying to hold on to the fleeting sense of importance. "It probably is curious, at least, that Andy just stopped coming around ten years ago, right?"

CHAPTER 21
MIKAELA

Morning, March 8

Someone had been on the bridge with Tony.

The same eight words kept repeating through Mikaela's head, a playlist heading straight to the top of her Spotify Wrapped. *Someone had been on the bridge with Tony.*

There was a person out there who knew. Knew what happened, had spoken to her husband. Hundreds of cars must have driven by while he and this mystery man were out there. Only one witness had spoken up, but surely she could find more.

She couldn't get the bridge out of her mind. The image of Tony, standing there, peering over the edge into the abyss below. In her mind the water was replaced by a dark pit, the blackness descending down all the way to Hell.

She couldn't take it anymore. She jumped up, grabbed her keys, and marched out the front door.

Since she wanted to be on the south side of the bridge, heading east on the Beltway, like he had been, she drove down to Route 395 and merged onto the highway, heading west toward Virginia. She crossed the river and took the exit for Route 1, passing through Arlington and Alexandria before getting to the Beltway, and the Woodrow Wilson Bridge.

She pulled over into the breakdown lane just before the sign announcing that you were now entering Maryland. She turned on her hazard lights and swung the door open, a quick glance confirming it was safe to do so.

She immediately noticed something she had never seen before. There was a pedestrian walkway along the bridge. How many times had she driven on this bridge? *You only see what you know*. Some teacher had said that to her class once, and even though she could think of a million counterexamples, the line had still stuck in her brain all these years.

She should have parked at the end of the bridge and just walked up, that would have been the safer plan, but it felt like too much effort to turn around now. Cars whizzed by and the wind forced her to clutch her purse tightly to her side. What was she even doing out here? What could she find here? What good would it do?

It had been three days since Tony stood here, right on this bridge. Someone stood alongside him, and then what?

She leaned over the railing, noticing how much it rattled and shook as every car went by. Again, the same intrusive thought popped into her head. What did she think she would see? Some clue down in the water that she would somehow spot from hundreds of yards away?

She tried not to think about what Tony must have been thinking if he did go over the side. What were his thoughts on the way down?

The first time they went on a trip together, a quick weekend bop to New York City, she'd suggested an observation deck for scenic views. They were eating breakfast at a cute cafe on the upper east side, and she thought he would think it was a romantic idea, maybe they'd snap a picture of themselves kissing to put up on the mantle someday. Future kids would groan at it but learn to appreciate that their mother and father never hid their affection.

She hadn't expected him to physically recoil when she said it.

"No view is worth the danger," he had said.

When she pressed him about why, he responded with his own question. "What's scarier than death?"

"Death of someone you love?" she had guessed.

"Sure, maybe," he conceded. "But for me the one thing scarier than death is knowing you're about to die and there being nothing you can do about it. And I don't mean dying from old age, or even long-drawn-out diseases. I mean when you make a mistake, or someone else decides to end your life, and you have a few seconds knowing what is going to happen. There is no way out, no last card you can play."

"What does this have to do with a scenic view?"

"Falling. An unsuspecting tourist takes a wrong step, tries something maybe they shouldn't have, and gets five to ten seconds of sheer terror before their life ends." He had grabbed her hands and looked her in the eyes. "Victims jumping out of the twin towers, people slipping at the Grand Canyon, plane crashes, why do those horrors captivate us? Because we all share the same wiring. Fear of certain impending death compels us all."

Mikaela had sat there, dumbfounded. "How… often do you think about this?" she finally asked.

"Every single day," was the reply.

A voice brought her back to the present. She whipped her head around and saw a man in a gray Carhartt trucker hat and aviator sunglasses, stepping out of a jet-black pickup truck. His bushy beard swayed, caught in the wind as he called out to her, forcing him to turn his face away.

She couldn't discern any of the words, so reluctantly pulled herself away from the railing and walked toward him. A tiny voice in her head suggested that this might be exactly what Tony had done—accepted an interaction with someone who could wish her harm—but the man's wild and worried eyes convinced her it was safe. He seemed more concerned about her.

She realized her own eyes probably told their own tale. Their sunken appearance, with deep bags below each, made her appear a likely candidate to jump off the bridge.

"Ma'am, are you okay?"

As he approached, she was struck by just how attractive he was. The beard barely hid a strong jawline, and defined muscles rippled under a skin-tight t-shirt.

"Yes, I'm sorry. I'm fine," she said, stepping away from the edge.

"Were you…" he looked out over the water.

"No, but thank you for thinking I was and jumping to my rescue."

He cocked his head, trying to figure her out. "But then, what are you doing?"

Before she knew what she was doing, Mikaela said, "my husband. He was here three days ago, and the police believe he jumped. I guess I just…" she glanced downward. "I just wanted to come up here and see what he saw. Try to think whatever he was thinking."

"Have they found…?"

She shook her head. He offered a sympathetic grimace in return.

"But isn't that weird? Wouldn't you find a body by now?"

Mikaela had no idea. What would be the reasons a body didn't resurface? She didn't know anything about the Potomac's riverbed but assumed there were probably plenty of logs and branches that a body could be stuck on? Or maybe it had surfaced but somewhere remote downriver? That sort of knowledge was just not part of her life up until now.

Of course, the other option was that he was still out there. The possibility that she could not rid her brain of. She looked at the man in front of her and imagined getting in his car and riding away. The only evidence that she was here would be her parked car, left on the side of the road. The police would hear about an abandoned car on the Woodrow Wilson Bridge. There would likely be some witness who saw her standing looking over the edge. They would put two and two together.

This is it. This is what happened.

She felt her heart soar. That man who saw Tony one step from the abyss didn't just talk to him. He *saved* him. Tony left with the mystery man.

But… why? And why wouldn't he have contacted her?

The thought formed in her mind as soon as she asked the question. She waved a quick thanks to the handsome man and jumped back into her car.

She had to call Veronica immediately.

CHAPTER 22
VERONICA

Morning, March 8

"He was kidnapped! You know, like you were once!"

Mikaela's voice came through my phone so loudly I had to check if I was on speaker. I closed my eyes and rubbed the bridge of my nose.

I was kidnapped—firstly, as an actual kid—in San Salvador by a bloodthirsty rival gang who then cut off my pinky with a gardening shear. I escaped, ran away from them, my own father, and everything I ever knew, in the first of a series of deliberate choices that led me to my present-day life. Tony was seen *near someone else* on a bridge just south of the nation's capital. I could point out a few more differences too, but to what end? She may not have realized it, but she was doing me the favor here. A chance to investigate. To see if this was really a path to pursue.

I took a deep breath. "Slow down, Mikaela. Talk to me."

"I'm driving away from the bridge right now. I was out there looking for clues, and then this nice man came and wanted to help, and I realized, that's what must have happened to Tony!"

"You think the mystery man at the scene was there to help, and also kidnapped him?"

"No, I think he was pretending to help but now is holding him somewhere."

Her voice held so much hope. I hated to do this to her. But I couldn't let her go too far down this path. "Okay, Mikaela, let's talk this through," I said. "There was a man seen with Tony on the bridge just before he *possibly* jumped. We're hoping that this man can help tell us what caused Tony to be up there, and what happened. But now you think this man, who just happened to drive by and wanted to help, actually then decided to kidnap him? Why?"

"You're supposed to be the one who understands criminals," she said weakly.

I could hear the hurt in her voice. I understood it. She felt like she had a breakthrough, and an answer to where Tony was that didn't end in heartbreak. Being held hostage, where there was a chance of escape, was the best-case scenario.

It was a nice theory. I didn't buy it, though.

Firstly, that happens much more rarely than you'd think. If you read a steady diet of mysteries and thrillers you could imagine that adult kidnappings are much more ubiquitous than in reality.

More importantly, though, was that she was hiding something. Mikaela knew what he was doing on the bridge, or at the very least had an idea of why he went there. That much I knew for certain. Concocting wild ideas of what might have happened made sense to a point. But what was she hiding? Guilt?

"But the person who posted that comment about seeing someone with Tony," Mikaela said.

"But what?"

"His name was Bill Andrews. Isn't that really close to Andrew Billingsley, the senator that was killed?"

Oh boy. Now she really was grasping at straws. "What do you think that means, Mikaela?"

"I don't know! But couldn't it be something? What if it's connected?"

Everyone has done this. You want something to have more meaning. You need there to be a bigger picture.

Bill Andrews, though? That seemed so shoddy, so… lame, even. A schoolboy level prank.

I heard a sharp intake of breath.

"Veronica!" she whispered, her voice shaky

"What is it?"

"The guy in the truck. He's following me."

CHAPTER 23
EMILIA

Midday, March 8

"Fahey, come here!" Emilia barked as soon as she re-entered the police station. A few heads spun around, but she paid them no mind. She didn't have time to worry about what others might consider an inappropriate tone for a junior partner to use toward her senior. Especially not that immature new detective, Iverson, who looked like she could pass for a pre-teen.

Fahey ambled over to Emilia, deliberately taking his time. His way of poking at her used to be a source of enjoyment, a back-and-forth bit of banter, but she was growing weary of it. "Did you find the killer in the big old, abandoned house?" He asked, his grin showing off two rows of gleaming white teeth that could moonlight as tombstones.

"If you'd get your head out of your ass, you'd maybe learn something now and again, you know?" Emilia didn't bother pretending that one was a joke. "Look, the Senator used to go to the Belles' house—World's Edge—all the time, until ten years ago when he was never invited back." Emilia filled Fahey in on the rest of her conversation with the neighbor.

"We trust this uppity guy who clearly just wanted to show off how important he was?"

"I was under the impression we were the people who *follow* leads, not throw them away because we're annoyed at where they came from."

Fahey grunted.

"It's thin, I'll grant you that," Emilia conceded. "But I'm still running with the note referring to that house. There are plenty of other edges of the world—an art exhibit at the National Nordic Museum a few years back, a similarly named HBO series about extreme athletes, a movie about Borneo—but those all seem too peripheral. This feels like a D.C. case. And now, we have an insinuation that the Senator was a regular, and then for some reason wasn't. To me that sounds like someone did something *at the edge of the world*."

"So, we really think that this connection between Billingsley and Belle is the one to follow the hardest?" Fahey shook his head. "I'll go with it, but I just think we're stumbling down a blind alley at this point."

What happened to the gruff but fun partner I first joined up with? Emilia looked at Fahey and wondered whether he'd always been like this and was she really just noticing for the first time. What kind of detective doesn't want to investigate? Blind alleys were the lifeblood of investigations, and surely, he knew that.

One more tick in the 'ask for a new partner' tally.

"Detectives, come with me."

Emilia looked up to see Chief Branaman walking by, tilting his head for them to follow. "What's up?" she asked.

"Going to see what Charles Wills and the crime scene team have to say. They should be done with the scene by now, and I'm tired of waiting. What have you got? Fill me in while we're walking."

Emilia explained her thinking about World's Edge and the Belle family.

"Thanks, good work," Branaman said, a smile appearing at the corners of his mouth. "I think you're right to chase down that angle."

Fahey grumbled behind them.

"What was that?" Branaman turned his head back, raising an eyebrow.

"Nothing, sir."

"Thought so. Fahey, if you would, we don't need all of us so let's divide and conquer. Run down anything you can find on the Senator's son. I need to know if he's going to be a loose cannon. Brown can come with me."

Fahey turned around and stalked off without a response.

"Charming guy, isn't he?" Branaman smirked.

"He has his moments," Emilia said, as diplomatically as possible. They walked on in silence, their shoes clacking along the tile floor, until Branaman pulled the lab door open for Emilia.

"Oh, shit, Chief." Zeke turned around and saluted as they entered the crime scene tech lab. "Wills just ran out, do you want me to call him?"

Branaman waved him off. "No need, as long as you can tell us what we need to know."

Zeke's eyes sparkled. "And what do you need to know?" He asked, a grin covering his entire face.

If he weren't so damn likable, his self-importance would be grating. But Emilia couldn't help herself. She enjoyed every interaction she had with the young whiz.

"We need to know what we don't know," Branaman said. "Tell me something from the crime scene I couldn't have picked out myself."

"All right, well mostly it is what you would expect. But I do have one thing." He beckoned for them to follow him over to a table at the back of the room. "Check this out."

Emilia looked down at a reproduction of a footprint, a large sneaker. "How many people go running in there, though? This could be anyone."

"Ah ah ah," Zeke said in a sing-song voice while wagging his finger. "You must know we would have considered that. This footprint comes from just a few feet from the body. So, if you remember where the body was, that's a print off the raised walkway where no one would be unless they had a very good reason."

"Good work, then," Branaman said. "What can it tell us?"

"The obvious one first: if you find a suspect we can hopefully match soles. They're a size twelve Asics running shoe, and we can see some wear on the bottom right. The subtle second one. Trace evidence of lavender and potatoes in the footprint. Now that's an odd combination if you ask me, so we're left to wonder where you might find both of those."

"I imagine you're about to tell us?" Emilia said.

"Almost," Zeke held up his pointer finger. "Since each is ubiquitous enough on its own, the idea that they were in close proximity isn't conclusive, but I think you'll find that the Georgetown University Community Garden is growing both of them right now. I'd put down a strong wager that your killer has spent recent time on Georgetown's campus."

CHAPTER 24
MIKAELA

Midday, March 8

"Do something, Veronica!"

Mikaela steeled herself and chanced another glance in the rear-view mirror.

Yep. The black truck was still there.

"Okay, Mikaela, listen to me." Veronica's voice was maddeningly calm. "Tell me exactly where you are right now."

"I'm driving on 295, north towards D.C. I just passed Joint Base Anacostia-Bolling." The steering wheel was getting slippery under the grip of her clammy palms.

"JBAB, got it. That's good, a highway is what we want. Now, first, we need to confirm he is following you. Tell me what you saw."

"I got in my car and drove north from the Woodrow Wilson Bridge, and then got off the exit and onto 295. When I was merging, I noticed the truck behind me, and then it slowed down and just stayed there."

"How slow are you going?"

"Well, I'm not going slow anymore!"

"Okay, but you were going unreasonably slow, there's no way he'd have just normally been cruising behind you?"

"No! And now he's still keeping up, and I'm going fifteen over the speed limit now."

"All right. Keep calm. You're going to drive into the city, and you're going to take several turns before ending up at one of the police stations, okay? You could call the police and try to have them cut him off on the road, but trust me, I think this is best."

"Why is that best?"

"He's following, he's not instigating. You need to get to where you have lots of witnesses—in the city proper—and then the police station part speaks for itself. He won't try anything in front of one unless he's an idiot, and we can handle idiots, right?"

"Right," Mikaela said, not fully believing. *Why would he be following me?* She couldn't understand. They had just talked out on the bridge. What could make him decide to follow her?

"Did you get his license plate number?"

"YVE 5009." Mikaela had seen enough cop shows where the victim doesn't get the bad guy's license plate, so she didn't need Veronica telling her. Memorizing the plate was the first thing she had done.

"Good, good," Veronica said. "Now, what I want you to do is get to the National Mall."

"Why there?"

"You'll get to the Mall, and you'll do several laps around it. Don't go further west than the Washington Monument. 4th and 14th streets. Constitution and Independence Avenues. Got it?"

How could her voice be that relaxed? Mikaela realized just as quickly as the thought formed. Of course she's calm, this sort of thing wouldn't phase her. She's probably done it before, maybe from either side. Mikaela took a deep breath, glancing back and confirming he was still behind her. She felt better knowing that Veronica had a plan. He wouldn't confront her in front of thousands of tourists.

She listened as Veronica explained where the nearest police station would be, and that under no circumstances should she go into a parking garage. Just pull in right in front of the station, as close as possible, parking tickets be damned.

"What can I do for you ma'am?" The police officer asked after Mikaela rushed into the police station and over to the front desk.

"There's a man following me," she blurted out. "Please, you have to help me."

"May I have your ID, please?"

I'd be that calm if I were behind bulletproof glass too. Mikaela wrestled her ID out of her wallet and placed it down on the counter. "He could walk through this door any minute! Can we go into some room, or something?" She knew how hysterical she sounded, but that was how she felt.

The officer, whose name tag read Travers, sighed, as he copied down her information. "Okay, come on around, let's go sit."

Mikaela glanced over her shoulders, watching carefully as she walked through the doorway. When she was satisfied no one was following her, she finally allowed herself a deep breath.

Travers led her down a hallway and into a small, windowless room. Mikaela looked at the oval table and swivel chairs and tried to imagine detectives huddled over it, trying to decipher clues.

"Okay, please tell me about this man."

Mikaela described her interaction on the bridge, and then how he tailed her after. When she was about to say who gave her the advice to drive in circles, she paused and tried to play it off. Veronica didn't need any more hassle. That family deserved to be left alone.

"I'm sorry, who told you to drive in circles?"

Guess that didn't work.

"I'm sorry, it wasn't a person. It was from one of those cop TV shows, I can't remember which. Maybe a British one?" Mikaela felt herself floundering trying to hold the lie, but somehow her answer appeased him.

"Okay, stay here. We'll run a check on that license plate and see if it's anyone known to us or possibly you." He circled something in his notebook and walked out of the room. It looked to Mikaela like he had done that solely for show.

As she waited, Mikaela allowed herself to take a deep breath, and take stock. She was safe from that man. She was here, sitting inside what looked unsettlingly like a potential interrogation room, but she was safe.

He returned five minutes later. "All right, the registration came back to an Alex Diophantus, resident of Alexandria, Virginia. Do you know him?"

"No, and I already told you, I met him today on the bridge, so I don't know why you think I'd know him." Mikaela said, allowing her frustration to seep into her tone.

"I understand, ma'am. We'll log this in, but there's no crime here. But please let us know if you see him again and call us immediately."

"I don't understand why they can't do anything," Mikaela said into the phone, standing along the street outside the police station.

"Because the police don't actually stop crimes," Veronica said flatly.

Mikaela could hear the cynicism in Veronica's voice over the cacophonous city sounds around her. "I can't stop thinking that this means something, though. Why would this guy follow me if there wasn't more going on with Tony?"

"It's possible there's some reason, we can't discount it. Did they give you his name? I can check him out and I'll be much more helpful than the police, I can promise you that."

Mikaela thought about what she knew about Veronica, and how little that must scratch the surface of what her childhood truly was like. All she cared about was that talking to Veronica made her feel safer, and she was thankful for that. "Yeah, they gave me a name, and said he lived in Arlington. They said his name is Alex, with some Greek sounding last name."

"A Greek last name?"

"Started with a D, I think. Alex... umm, wait, I remember because his name reminded me of an elephant. Alex Diophantus."

Veronica let out a sharp gasp. "What?"

"Alex Diophantus," Mikaela repeated.

"No way."

CHAPTER 25
VERONICA

Afternoon, March 8

I must have misheard her. The mind makes connections where there are none. It fills in the blanks in the most logical way, based on its own experiences and knowledge. We spend all our time trying to make order out of an unordered world. Our mind is always playing tricks on us.

But I didn't mishear her. I had Mikaela repeat the name back to me. *Alex Diophantus*. The man who stopped to talk to Mikaela on the bridge, appearing for all the world just to be a Good Samaritan. The same man who then chased her up into D.C.

What did she say? He had a big bushy beard. A bearded man driving a pickup truck. No one is going to ask any questions. No lingering stares to check exactly who that man might be. To ask whether he might have an infamous face, hiding just below the protruding hairs.

Alex Diophantus. Diophantus of Alexandria. He was always so clever. A name that almost no one would think twice about, other than remarking on its uniqueness. A perfect fake name for a man who knew so much about the original Diophantus. The ancient Greek man often called the "father of algebra" in the Western world, even if the rest of the world would argue it was actually al-Khwarizmi, of modern-day Uzbekistan.

Diophantus' *Arithmetica* was a text I used to pull from every semester. The elegance and intrigue of Diophantine Equations drove several of my research projects. Everyone who had ever taken a class from me had heard me drone on about that book. And everyone had also heard about the curious little anecdote relating to *Arithmetica.*

That it was within that book's margins where Pierre de Fermat scribbled his famous boast. *I have discovered a truly marvelous proof of this, which this margin is too narrow to contain.* Fermat's Last Theorem.

What were the odds? Could there really be someone else out there who felt that strongly?

Or was my former protégé, the best student I had ever taught, back free?

There was so much to be upset about when Jeremy Wiles tried to kill me, and made his murderous push towards the presidency, but one fact that had uplifted me in the aftermath was that Jacob wasn't this rash attempted assassin like everyone had thought.

I was heartbroken after learning that the assassination attempt on President Leishear had been committed by my favorite former student, Jacob Jordan. He never spoke after he was arrested or during his trial, and when he was sent away, I was desperate to just get one more chance to talk to him. To understand why. I managed to get him to allow me to talk with him once a week, but he rarely said anything. What kept me going back was that there was an inflection in his voice, a tone that made me think there was a story to be told, right there on the tip of his tongue.

When he mentioned Pierre de Fermat, and his eponymous theorem, I knew he was trying to direct me somewhere. When I puzzled it out and realized what he was saying, I immediately understood why he had stayed silent all that time.

He wasn't just getting blackmailed; he was getting blackmailed by the man who everyone believed was going to be the next President of the United States, Jeremy Wiles. What hope did he have against that? But he knew and trusted that I would work it out.

My confrontation with Jeremy at Pierce Mill was the inciting event for my life being flipped on its head. But Jacob's story began when Jeremy Wiles saw him cause the car accident that killed three-fourths of the Belle family and decided to use that knowledge to his own advantage. Jacob followed along with his plan to have Jacob *attempt* an assassination, that conveniently was heroically thwarted by Jeremy Wiles, catapulting him into the national spotlight, just as intended.

When Jeremy was caught, thanks in no small part to my husband, his former best friend, I wondered what would happen to Jacob. His conviction got thrown out, and he pled guilty to vehicular manslaughter instead, and I felt such a relief.

But this couldn't have been him. He was still in jail. Right?

I held the phone in my hand, the keypad staring back up at me. I hated what I had to do next, but I needed to be certain. I took a deep breath and dialed.

"This is Detective Brown," her clipped voice answered after a single ring.

"Detective, this is Veronica Walsh." I could just about hear her scrambling to attention at the sound of my voice. It's a strange sensation that I haven't fully come to terms with yet. As a child, I was notorious, but, because I was anonymous, most of life had continued like normal.

I hadn't actually anticipated that. I assumed after I took down Maynor Mejia that everyone inside our organization would learn immediately, including all the children. I didn't know that my father swore his lieutenants to silence. It was only a few days later when all the boogeyman talk started on the playground that I realized no one really knew. I almost gave my secret away before I even knew it was a secret. The other kids had several details of the story wrong, and I came close to correcting them.

That night, my father came into my room just before bedtime. He closed the door and sat down on the corner of my bed, folding his legs underneath him. "Alex," he said, his voice much lower than it needed to be. "I need you to never tell anyone what you did the other day."

He silenced my retorts with a stare. "I mean it, Alex. No one. Not even Francisco."

"Why?"

"Because I need you to do it again."

Detective Brown's voice came through the phone louder than she intended, I'm sure. Or maybe she wanted others nearby to hear. "Veronica Walsh? What can I do for you?"

As if the police do things for callers.

I wanted to ask why no one told me that Jacob Jordan was out of jail, but I'd made it clear I didn't want anything to do with the police. So, as annoyed as I was, I could hardly blame them. "Did Jacob Jordan escape?"

She gasped. "Jacob? Why would you think that?"

She didn't know. Interesting. I wondered who dropped the ball there. Probably the jail. It never is a good look to spread the word a prisoner escaped. And he had to be out, it was far too coincidental otherwise.

"Look it up. Then, when you have information for me, you know my number."

CHAPTER 26
MIKAELA

Evening, March 8

A petite woman wearing a black jacket, dark wash jeans, and riding boots stood at Mikaela's front door when she arrived home. For a brief second, Mikaela worried that it was someone else following her, before she recognized her friend's shock of bleached blonde hair. She got out of the car and hurried up the walkway, kicking a couple small fallen branches out of the way.

Billie Brenton offered her elbow, and Mikaela gently bumped it with her own. She asked the question with her eyes.

"Yep, still no skin contact," Billie said, nodding her head slightly. "Therapy has helped, but we ain't there yet."

Mikaela gave a sympathetic grimace. "What are you doing here?" She asked as she punched in her keycode and opened the door.

Billie marched in and kicked off her boots. "I'm here to find your husband. What, did you become some sort of dummy? Relax," she added as she saw Mikaela's stricken look. "I'm here for moral support. I saw it on Facebook and drove up. Figured you could use the company."

"But… is Cade okay with that?"

"That good-for-nothing husband of mine? Hell, even disappeared, your husband does more around the house than that slob. He'll be fine, he's got beer in the fridge and delivery apps on his phone. He won't even notice I'm gone."

Despite the circumstances, Mikaela couldn't help but smile.

She and Billie grew close during foster care, the two of them forced into bonding by the harsh world in which they grew up. Billie had it much worse than Mikaela.

The first time she met Billie was when Mikaela moved into the Mortons' house at age thirteen. Billie was the only girl among four foster children already placed with Caitlyn Morton and her husband, Patrick. Billie was a year younger than Mikaela. That first night, as they lay in adjacent twin beds, Billie told Mikaela in a quiet voice that her parents had died in a fishing accident three years previous and she had no other family to take her in.

Billie also told Mikaela that she was lucky, possibly the luckiest girl that ever lived, for showing up when she did.

"Why is that?" Mikaela had asked. Billie didn't answer, just shivered and burrowed further under the covers.

The next day, Caitlyn and Patrick got everyone out of bed early, demanding they dress in their best clothes and not embarrass them. They drove wordlessly to a cemetery and joined a procession of cars. When the cars finally stopped, Caitlyn ushered them all out, and Mikaela tip-toed over the dirt at the side of the road and into the grass. "Come on, we have to say our goodbyes to my brother," she said. She looked past Mikaela and saw Billie hovering behind, unwilling to move away from the car. "You too, Billie. You're the one he liked the most."

The three boys snickered in unison. Mikaela looked into Billie's eyes, and her jaw dropped as she understood. Her hands clenched into fists until she saw Billie's expression turn to stone and make a barely perceptible shaking motion of her head.

Mikaela was Billie's protector from then on out. She never asked what happened, she never pressured Billie to tell her. To this day, she didn't know.

She was there when Mikaela met Cade, a farm boy from Buchanan, Virginia, and saw a spark in her friend's eyes that she'd never seen before. She had been the one to tell Cade if he ever hurt Billie, she would hunt him to the ends of the earth.

Instead, he married her and worshiped the ground she walked on, and Mikaela was able to breathe a sigh of relief. Her friend was going to be okay.

Billie took on her husband's deep country affectations and loved to play the role, but Mikaela always thought that Cade was a thoroughly decent man, and more than did his share in their partnership. He was probably the one who told Billie she should make the drive up from their rambling farmhouse in the Blue Ridge Mountains.

Mikaela waved her arm toward the living room. "Come on, make yourself at home. I assume you haven't gotten a hotel room and are planning on staying here?"

"You know it, girl." Billie grinned and plopped down onto the couch, snatching a pillow and clutching it in her lap. "All right, talk to me."

Mikaela marveled at just how well Billie put her at ease. No one else could have shown up unannounced, making light of the situation, and made her feel *better*. She recapped everything that had happened, watching as Billie's eyes widened when she told her about Veronica. When she finished, she slumped down onto the couch.

"Okay, then. What we need is alcohol. What you got?" Billie hopped up and walked into the kitchen.

Mikaela watched as she rummaged through their liquor cabinet. The inevitable big sigh came when Billie realized just how bare it was. She returned with a bottle of Bacardi.

"This is embarrassing, but it will have to do. Drink."

They spent the afternoon drinking and reminiscing. As they got progressively more drunk, the stories got more riotous, the laughter more raucous. Mikaela allowed herself to breathe, to enjoy her friend's company. To relax. To realize that no matter what happened, her life would go on.

She had told Tony that she didn't want to be with him if they couldn't have kids. He knew she wanted them but had no idea how much. She wasn't sure she could ever have put it into words. When it just wasn't happening naturally, he told her that he would support any treatments necessary to help.

A lifelong Catholic, she had a fraught relationship with IVF, believing that leaving unused embryos behind was immoral.

So, when month after month they came up disappointed, and fertility tests showed no obvious problems, she knew it was only a matter of time before Tony asked about IVF. She rebuffed it at each attempt and could tell he couldn't quite reconcile her desire for children with what he perceived as stubbornness over IVF.

Just before he disappeared, they had a brutal fight. Each of them was mentally drained. Tony asked if maybe they should give up, if being together was enough.

She shouldn't have yelled at him that the two of them on their own would never make a family. She shouldn't have said that if she couldn't have a child with him, she'd find someone else. If only she could talk to him now, she would tell him they could make it all right. They would persevere, they would do whatever it takes. And in the end, if it didn't happen, they'd accept God's will. Maybe even look into adopting or fostering. Be the kind of foster parents Mikaela would have given anything for as a little girl.

Mikaela wiped a tear from her eye. Billie noticed but mercifully didn't say anything. She understood better than most when sadness should be met with silence. She tossed back her final Cuba Libre, gave Mikaela a kiss on the cheek, and carried her bag upstairs to the guest bedroom.

Billie was asleep and Mikaela had finally dragged herself off the couch and up to bed. Her eyelids felt like boulders. She plopped down onto the bed, not bothering to take off her clothes. They were soft enough to be pajamas, anyway. But just as sleep was about to take her, Mikaela's phone buzzed. She groaned, and clumsily reached for it, charging behind the lamp on her nightstand. She didn't recognize the number. "Hello?" she croaked.

She bolted upright as the voice on the other end told her she needed to come now, because they had found Tony's body.

CHAPTER 27
BEN

Evening, March 8

Ben walked toward the exit out of Brooks Brothers, three new dress shirts in hand. It was getting hard to hide at work that he was living out of a suitcase. He'd only packed a couple shirts as he hastily threw together his bag. A little post-work bop over to his favorite clothing supplier would at least hold the questions at bay a bit longer.

Almost 48 hours, and she hadn't yet called him telling him to come home. He realized he'd deluded himself into thinking she wasn't just as stubborn as he was.

He didn't know how much more he could take. He knew he'd acted in anger, and before he knew it, he was making a much bigger gesture than he planned. All he knew was that he had to get out of the house immediately. He could feel his anger taking over.

Not that he was worried about hurting his wife. If it ever came to that, she'd destroy him, and, to Ben, that was part of the problem.

What she didn't understand was that he could see her point perfectly well. He knew what she was trying to get across.

But she didn't see what it was like when she was missing. No number of discussions—and they had had plenty—could make her truly understand. *Shawshank Redemption* popularized this idea that fear holds you prisoner while hope sets you free. But when your mind is overflowing with both hope and fear, all you get is paralysis. You can't think, you can't eat, you can't sleep. Fear makes you spiral but that inkling of hope can serve to just make that spiral even worse.

Ben turned down Rhode Island Avenue as he began his walk toward the Farragut West metro stop. Farragut North was closer to him, but going on the Red Line was of no use to him tonight. He would rather walk a little further than have to take multiple lines.

As he descended the stairs into the Metro, he caught a glimpse in a mirror of a man behind him, wearing a large gold cross over a bright red tee shirt.

The same clothes he had seen this morning on the way to work.

He took a deep breath. Nothing inherently scary here. Lots of people do the same commute, and, anyway, who would wear something that ostentatious if they were following someone? Still, he watched as the man got to the bottom of the stairs, glanced in his direction one time, and then walked over to the same platform as Ben.

He didn't panic when he watched the man get onto the same train, one car down. Nothing to see here.

But then why couldn't he shake the feeling in his head? He turned away, hoping out of sight truly would be out of mind. This man couldn't do anything from the other car, anyway.

As the blue line veered south out of Washington, D.C., and across the Potomac, Ben allowed himself another glance. The man was still there. He couldn't see much of him through the crowd and the glass. He was light-skinned and thin, but that was all he could tell.

Who would be following him, though?

He felt the now familiar pang in his heart as he stayed on the metro past the Old Town Alexandria stops, before finally disembarking at Eisenhower Avenue.

A quick 360, pretending he'd forgotten something on the train, and there was no sign of the man in red. Just another commuter. Not some possibly foreign-born former or future assassin wanting to strike another blow at his family.

This is exactly what Veronica couldn't understand. How could he live his life being this paranoid all the time? He really thought after she got out of the hospital that she would want to put the past as far behind her as possible. Francisco showing up after her recovery party was not part of the plan, but what was Ben supposed to do when her eyes lit up at the sight of her childhood friend?

He trudged back to his hotel, the loneliness in his heart threatening to envelop him fully. It had always been Veronica. She was the one he could talk to about anything, and she would listen intently before invariably giving sage advice when requested.

Veronica was the one who had pushed him to apply for a position with Chamique Moore's campaign back when they were still just dating. She saw the shooting star that was the now Congresswoman before even Ben, with all his political acumen and education, could.

"What if I'm not picking a winner?" he had asked her one night, dribbling chow mein down his chin as he spoke.

She wiped the trail of liquid off his chin with her thumb. "Then you lose." She shrugged. "That's life. Not everyone wins."

"I was sort of hoping for some reassurance there." Ben gave a nervous chuckle.

"You want reassurance? All right then." She pushed herself forward in her chair and leaned her elbows on the dining room table. "Chamique Moore has gravitas, an ability to explain her positions, and is on the side of the angels. You happen to have those exact three qualities as well. So, you're going to elevate all of what she already has, and her campaign is going to be unstoppable. Most of all," she said, holding her index finger up. "You'll be working for someone you'll be proud of, and you'll feel fulfilled in what you're doing. And that's all you can ask for."

As had happened more times than Ben could count, she had turned out to be exactly right. That's what happens when you marry the woman who is exactly right for you. And she still was that woman, Ben knew that. As long as this dormant piece of her from her childhood didn't rise too far, displacing all the good in her that he cherished.

Ben stepped into the elevator, careful to keep his new shirts from getting caught in the closing doors. As they pulled shut, he looked back into the hotel's foyer and his breath caught in his throat. The man in red was standing there, his phone out, snapping pictures of Ben as the elevator doors closed and he disappeared from Ben's sight.

CHAPTER 28
MIKAELA

Morning, March 9

Tears streamed down Mikaela's face. *Still haven't turned into dancing,* said a little voice inside her head. She shivered violently inside this cold, sterile, room and turned to face the police detective next to her. Her mouth opened but the words wouldn't come out. All she could manage was a short nod between sobs that had already answered his question.

He really was gone. Tony was dead. All that was left of him was lying on a slab in front of her.

The man who had danced with her once a week at salsa classes early on in their relationship, desperate to get her to enjoy the music he loved. Who had smiled patiently as she stumbled over and over, ungainly and off-balance right from the start.

He was the first man who had ever forced her to really, truly, think about the future. Not the next day, or next year even, but the long-term. What did she want? Where did she see herself in five years? A decade? He had been so good about always having long-term goals. Lighthouses far in the distance, directing him—and them—to safety and prosperity.

This wasn't part of the plan.

She wasn't supposed to be called to a morgue, since the terrain on the bank of the Maryland side of the Potomac where they found him was too treacherous and dark. She wasn't supposed to sit there, waiting with a single police officer as an escort, while they prepared his body for her. She wasn't supposed to see that face, looking so serene and unharmed he could have just been asleep if it weren't for the bloating.

"We don't need to linger," the officer said in a tender voice.

Mikaela couldn't make her legs work. It was as if her brain had just turned off. She somehow made her way back out of the morgue, her legs eventually moving on autopilot as her brain descended deeper into a fog. Billie rushed forward and Mikaela collapsed in her arms.

"Sweet baby, I got you," Billie murmured as she stroked Mikaela's hair. "We're going to get you through this."

"How? How do I get through?" Mikaela choked out the words.

Billie grabbed Mikaela's shoulders and extended her arms, so their eyes were locking. "First, we're going to make sure whoever did this goes to jail. And then once we do, we are going to rebuild your life, okay? You can come stay with me on the farm. We'll make everything work. You're not alone."

Mikaela squeezed her eyes shut. This had to be a mistake. People went missing and ended up dead all the time, but that was in books and on television, not here. Not in her life. He was supposed to be off with a buddy blowing off steam, complaining about his nagging wife. He'd come home in a couple of days, tail between his legs, and promise to never do that again.

But of course, that's not what he did. Instead, he pulled his car over on the side of a major bridge. Someone saw him alive there, but then no one ever saw him again, until some poor soul found him, half submerged, tangled in tree roots on the bank of the Potomac. Mikaela shuddered to try to rid her head of the intrusive image.

The police confirmed his injuries were 'consistent with a high fall into water' and she had frozen in the moment, torn between desperately needing to know more detail, and being horrified at knowing it. Her horror won out, but now she wished she knew more. Her own imagination was going to drive her crazy.

She allowed Billie to lead her out to her car, which Billie had mercifully driven. They rode home in silence, only punctuated by sobs Mikaela couldn't keep in.

When they arrived, Billie made a beeline for the dining room table, and shoved the placemats and assorted loose papers off.

"What are you doing?" Mikaela asked, her eye catching on a bill with her and Tony's names together. She would need to do a major cull. She couldn't stay in a house where everything reminded her of him.

Billie put her hands on her hips. "What do you think? You say someone killed him. I said we're going to find who did this, so that's what's happening. This table is going to be our base camp. You don't have a whiteboard, do you? That's what everyone in the movies has."

"I…" Mikaela's voice faltered.

"Look," Billie said, her tone calm and empathetic. "We need to do something. You get to be sad; I'm not arguing with that. But that needs to be channeled somewhere or else it will overwhelm you and drag you right down."

"No, I know that." Mikaela said. "Just… I need you to meet someone."

CHAPTER 29
VERONICA

Morning, March 9

"So, is he out, or not?"

I didn't bother with formalities when I saw who was calling. There's no other reason she would be calling me back. I heard a deep sigh.

"He is."

"How?" I nodded over to Francisco, seated beside me on a bench at the Old Town Alexandria waterfront, black raspberry ice cream dripping down his hand. The sun had set, and the brisk spring air meant we were the only ones lingering. A small shrug was all I got in return from him.

Whenever I needed to think, I always did my best by the water. My mother used to say that going for a swim changed your disposition. Healing waters, as good as any therapist. Since the Potomac wasn't fit for swimming, at least not in Old Town, I made do with the gentle sound of water lapping against the concrete.

"I don't know," Detective Brown said. "And I don't understand how I wasn't immediately informed. It seems like after he was transferred, his new arrangements meant much less security, and he was able to escape. That was a few months ago."

Months.

My protege, my favorite ever student, blackmailed into causing a shooting because he, in fact, had caused death previously.

Now out on the street and doing what? Stalking some woman who showed up at the place her husband disappeared? "What do you know?"

"Nothing. He escaped and disappeared." The detective paused. "Come on now, spill it. What do *you* know?"

I rolled my eyes. "You were supposed to be giving info to me."

Detective Brown barked out a mirthless laugh. "That's not how this works, no matter who you are."

"All right, check the name Alex Diophantus. I think that's the name he's using now. Resident of Alexandria." I recounted what I learned of the man who had chased Mikaela Alonso.

"Wait, Mikaela Alonso, as in Antonio Alonso's wife?"

I did not like the foreboding tone of that question. "Yes, I'm working with her to try to find her husband."

"Ah, shit. Give me a second, I just saw that name pop up."

I listened to the loud clacking of computer keys.

"Yeah, here it is. Antonio Alonso's body was found in the Potomac last night."

I gasped. *Fuck.*

That poor woman.

"Okay, look," I said. "I don't know what Jacob is doing and why he's using a fake name that I can easily identify, but can you look into it for me? I've got to go call Mikaela."

I hung up before she had the chance to tell me no.

"Mikaela's husband is dead, isn't he?" Francisco asked.

I'd given up asking how he intuited so well. "I wonder where that leaves us now."

"Your first PI case, already over, it looks like." He went back to licking his ice cream cone. Nothing phased him.

"Looks like it, but I need to talk to Mikaela." My phone buzzed and I looked down. "Speak of the devil. Mikaela, hi, I'm so sorry to hear about your husband," I said.

"I... wait, how do you know?"

I recapped my conversation with the detective, but only telling her it was a follow-up about her mystery man from the bridge. She didn't have to know about Jacob Jordan just yet. Not when she'd just had the worst few hours of her life. That could come later.

To me, death was always like a good long-distance friend. There in the periphery, it checked in on me every so often, and the specter of it loomed large during my childhood. Even though I'd had a stable end to my teenage years, and a smooth, calm, and loving adulthood up until recently, the friendship never wavered. I imagined death wherever I went, whether it was my own, or in the last years, my husband's or children's.

I thought about what it would be like to walk down a cold, empty corridor, knowing that nothing but your worst nightmare awaited you beyond the doors. Someone you loved laying there, forevermore unmoving. No more talking, no more laughter, no more love. Just one last footnote: your formal identification that yes, this is who we all know it is. A feeling of helplessness I could not begin to fathom, and yet permeated my thoughts regularly.

Unless they had Mikaela come to the bank of the river, then that's exactly what she must have done today. Nothing can bring you back from that abyss.

"Uh... listen, Veronica." Mikaela paused, like she was trying to extract the correct words. "If it's okay with you. I think, no I know, that I need to find out what happened. I need to know that Tony didn't jump, and I need to find out who killed—" a sob escaped her lips before she could finish.

"I will help you, Mikaela."

"Oh, thank you, Veronica. Um, okay, call me if you learn more?"

Veronica let her hang up. No one would want to be talking in her position.

"Ben won't be happy." Francisco offered me a wry smile after I got off the phone.

Ben. This was an out, I could've stepped back. Offered the olive branch, as it were. But then we'd be right back to our uneasy truce.

This wasn't going to be a marriage ender. That wasn't the man I married. It's not like I didn't understand where he was coming from, but I married a resilient man, even if he didn't know it yet.

"No, he won't, but we'll cross that bridge when we come to it."

"Just hope you haven't burned down that bridge first," Francisco chuckled at his own joke. "But since you're back up, I have a thought."

"Hit me."

"I was doing a little more digging and found a person who was close to Tony in college who might be helpful. Bridget Lowe. She lives in Burke now, only about thirty minutes from here."

CHAPTER 30
EMILIA

Morning, March 9

Emilia couldn't articulate to herself exactly why she needed to do this herself. She could have easily sent someone. It was just a routine check. But she still felt like some part of her owed it to Jacob Jordan. She needed to be the one to find him, because she was the officer who best understood what he'd been through. Iverson was running down whatever she could find on the Georgetown community gardens, so this was Emilia's task.

But more than that, there was a subtle itch that she just couldn't scratch. Veronica told her about Mikaela's encounter and his subsequent pursuit of her. Why would he chase after Mikaela Alonso's car? She had been stopped on the bridge where her husband jumped. Did he just happen to be driving by?

Emilia didn't like not having answers. She didn't know much about Antonio Alonso's case, she had enough on her plate as it was, but any connection between Jacob and another death made her spidey senses tingle. Of course, he wasn't going by Jacob Jordan anymore. Occupational hazard of breaking out of prison. You can't just go on living your life—you have to become an entirely new person. And even then, the historical odds were not on your side. No matter how perfect you were, one single slip up and you'd be headed right back to prison.

No longer Jacob, now Alex. Alex Diophantus, resident of Carlyle Place, an aptly named apartment complex in the Carlyle neighborhood of Alexandria. Just west of Old Town, and north of the Beltway, its selection of high rises set it in stark contrast with its neighbor.

Emilia drove by the National Science Foundation headquarters and made a U-turn before pulling her car up against the curb. She flashed her badge after she was buzzed into the building. "I need some information on one of your tenants," she barked at the young man, lounging behind a counter drinking a Pepsi Max.

"I'm sorry, miss. We can't enter any apartment without a warrant," he said with a confident air.

Emilia looked down at him. He could not have been shaped more like a pear than if he had been trying to. "Sir, I am not asking for access, I just have two questions. You'll let me ask you two questions to help stop a killer going free, won't you?" Technically he had killed people, even if the charges had been lowered. As far as this case was concerned, Emilia didn't know at all if he was involved.

"Just two questions?" He raised a single eyebrow.

Appealing to common decency was Emilia's best tool in her arsenal. With mistrust of police at an all-time high—at least on a national level—her best bet was always de-escalation. She came in looking tough and no-nonsense but now would give him a chance to prove helpful. She'd get what she needed, and he would feel good about his interaction. "Just two," she repeated. "In and out, and we can each keep doing our jobs. And just to be clear, I do have a warrant." She pulled a thin envelope out of her back pocket. "

His eyes widened "Okay."

"Is Alex Diophantus a current resident here?"

"Umm, how do you spell that last name?" he asked as he peered at the desktop computer in front of him.

She spelled it out loud as he typed.

"Okay, yeah, Alex. He rented a studio here, but…" he paused, his voice trailing off. "Huh."

"What does 'huh' mean?"

"There's a note here that says he paid six months' rent up front."

"How common is that?"

"Here? At these prices? Not very." He shook his head as he spoke.

"Was there a background check? What does the application entail?"

"I'm sorry, this is way more than two questions now." He pushed his chair away from the computer. "What is this about? Who is he?"

"Well, his name is not Alex Diophantus, I can assure you of that. I'm going to need to see inside that apartment."

"Sure thing. Just one second." He looked around, searching for a pen. "I need to write a note for anyone who might come by."

"Fine. But if you write 'helping serve a warrant' I am leaving you here," Emilia said.

She followed him as he waddled to the elevators, pushed his key card for access, and stepped in.

"We have lots of important people living here," he boasted, filling up the silence. "People that work for senators, and that sort of thing."

"Wow."

He watched her, waiting for her to say more. When he realized she wasn't, he sighed and turned toward the elevator door. When the elevator reached the floor, he stalked off without looking back.

Emilia walked several yards behind him, mentally preparing herself. From everything she knew about him, it seemed unlikely he'd be quick on the draw, but anything was possible. She tensed as he knocked on the door, her fingers caressing her gun.

When there was no answer, she pointed at the keyhole. As soon as he turned the key, she jumped in front of him. "This is the police!" she yelled, throwing the door open.

To an entirely empty apartment.

"There's… no furniture?" the concierge said, creeping in behind Emilia.

"Unfurnished and empty." Emilia crouched down, looking in each corner. "Not even any fuzz. I don't think he was ever here."

Why, then, did he rent this place at all?

Of course, because he needed a legal address. A fake name, now on a legal document with a proof of residence. He could do anything now. And as of yet, there was nothing she could do to stop him.

She had all his info: his name, his car, his address. And yet, she was nowhere. He was out there, somewhere nearby, and Emilia had absolutely no idea what his next move would be.

CHAPTER 31

Afternoon, March 9

He watched from a safe distance as she went up and down the aisles, filling up her cart haphazardly. This was not someone who came to the grocery store with a meticulously curated list. Tonight, she was going to cook whatever assortment of ingredients caught her eye.

Well, that was her idea, anyway.

He knew he'd have to be fast. The parking lot would be easiest. No security cameras, enough hustle and bustle that if he moved swiftly, he could be in and out before anyone noticed.

Her short hair was covered up by a worn navy baseball cap, and she wore a t-shirt from a recreational 5k running race at a nearby park. Her slow and deliberate steps suggested she was in no hurry.

A box of pop tarts caught her eye, and she reached for them—her long, delicate fingers almost making contact before she pulled them away. Having thought better of it, she gave one final glance before moving on down the aisle.

She stopped and chatted with the man behind the meat counter. He said something funny, and she offered a polite laugh in return as she reached over the glass to grab the package of sliced turkey he handed her.

She moved on, picking up several varieties of Annie's Mac &

Cheese, studying each box, all the while still oblivious to the man following her.

Grocery stores made for great targets. People let their guard down, focused far too much on the food, and disregarded their own personal safety. There was always a surety of purpose inside grocery stores. Everyone was there for the same reason, and the social contract implicitly signed upon entering was taken for granted.

He put a bag of avocados into his cart. Why not kill two birds with one stone? He decided to hover near the fruit and veggies in the front of the store. There was no other exit, and he needed to be ready to leave when she did. Plus, who is going to think twice about a handsome young man stocking up on veggies?

She wandered off, and he allowed himself to lose sight. She wouldn't duck out the employee exit. And if she did, well he'd come up with a new plan. Plans were made to be changed.

A burly man grunted at him, and he looked around, realizing he was standing in front of the tomatoes. He held up a hand in apology and moved along.

She reappeared, her cart full. She was efficient—he had to hand it to her. He watched as she got in line, eschewing the self-checkouts for a personal interaction. The friendly smile and query about how your day is going that the machines did not replicate.

The cold calculation with which he watched her was replaced with white hot rage. How dare she go about her day exchanging pleasantries? How dare she get to live this normal life?

He slid his own groceries through the self-checkout—no need for any interaction—keeping his eyes on her the entire time. He was glad to see her put the bags back into the cart. She would have to return it after the transfer to the car. If her manners in the store were any indication, she was not one of those people who ditched their cart.

Now he had the perfect opportunity to get in position.

She pushed her cart out the door, patiently waiting as a dark sedan ignored the crosswalk and drove right by.

No angry gesture, no huff of disappointment. That response, coupled with her willingness to make polite, friendly, conversation, and he had to admit she seemed like a decent human being.

But he knew. People are not what they seem.

The parking lot was almost full, and his view was obscured as he snuck toward the driver side of her mid-range SUV. She finished putting the groceries in the trunk and turned away to return the cart. He watched as she made sure she placed it correctly, in line with the others of the same size.

She didn't see him until she rounded her car. She stopped, suddenly, next to the driver side door, her eyes growing wide under her cap.

"Hi, I'm so sorry, do you have a second?" He put on his most charming smile as he positioned himself between her and the door, swinging his grocery bag of avocados. Deliberately obfuscating her view of his other hand.

"No, and please move away from my car." She fumbled around in her purse.

"Do you recognize me?" He cocked his head, showing his face in profile. That was normally how people knew.

"No, I—"

He watched as recognition spread across her face. Her eyes narrowed, and her mouth hung open. This was what he was here for.

"Yes, Bridget. It is me. I'm glad you can still easily pick out these features." A happy smile spread across his face.

She saw the flash by his hand. "Wait—"

But he did not wait. He dropped his bag and grabbed her shoulder with his left hand. With his right he slipped the four-inch blade between her ribs, in and out, in and out.

In.

And out.

CHAPTER 32
EMILIA

Afternoon, March 9

"Brown!" Chief Branaman's voice boomed through the police station.

Emilia locked her computer and hustled over to his office. Normally soft-spoken, he only raised his voice when he was upset.

"Someone's in troooouble!" She heard a voice whisper as she walked past. She made a point not to turn and look. Probably that new detective, Iverson. She looked like a teenage girl. Adulthood was just like childhood, Emilia had found, except kids at least didn't pretend not to give in to their worst impulses.

The chief stood in the open threshold, leaning against his door. His white hair was getting thinner every year, and the whole station wondered when he was just going to give up the fight and shave it all off. "Come on in," he said, ushering her inside and closing the door.

"All good, sir?" Emilia asked as she sat down, adjusting her position to try to look the most at ease.

He looked her up and down, lingering on the hair just as everyone did. Today's style was a scarlet red pompadour. A sucker for subversive history, she'd grown attached to it ever since she'd learned that the hairstyle was named for a mistress of King Louis XV.

"I take it you want a new partner," he finally said.

Emilia's jaw dropped. "I—I do. How do you know?"

Branaman chuckled and readjusted his glasses. "I was a detective. Just because I'm now a figurehead doesn't mean I've forgotten those skills."

Emilia sat, silent. This was not what she was expecting, and she had no idea what was coming next.

"I called your name loudly," Branaman continued. "Because I don't want anyone thinking this is anything more than my annoyance at the Billingsley murder remaining unsolved. That's what you'll tell anyone who asks what this was. Pressure from above, me passing it down to you, yada yada yada." He waved his hand dismissively.

Emilia still didn't know what to say.

"You look like you have a few questions. Let me help clear some things up for you. Fahey and yourself will each receive new partners, effective immediately. You will continue to head the Billingsley investigation, Fahey will cover others."

A million thoughts swam through Emilia's head. She was finally about to get what she wanted. A new younger partner, a senior role. Leadership and the ability to mentor. But who? There weren't that many other candidates in the station. And what would Fahey think? Wouldn't he be hurt he's been taken off the most high-profile case?

She looked at the chief, trying to discern his expression. She had never seen this side of him before. She'd never really seen any side of him besides his no-nonsense self.

"I'm sorry, can I ask why you're doing this?"

The corners of his mouth flitted upward for just a second. "Why don't you tell me why you wanted this?" he asked.

"I think I could be a useful asset in training younger members to see their full potential," she said.

He snorted. "Good one. Now tell me the truth."

Emilia scanned his face, trying to decipher if he had an angle. When she realized she couldn't tell, she decided to barrel ahead. "Detective Fahey is a bore, and has gotten lazy and, frankly, clueless, recently. I don't know that there's any more that I can learn from him, and I might even go so far as to say I feel hindered."

She searched for any hint of approval that she was desperately craving, but his only response was to steeple his fingers. "Very well," he said.

Emilia wished it didn't have to end like this. She had been thrilled when she was assigned to work with Detective Fahey seven years ago. He was the big man on campus. The detective everyone respected. He worked the hardest and he worked the smartest.

They solved the Gates murders, when three Kalorama neighbors were all killed in quick succession and the fanciest people in the district were up in arms. They'd put away Ian Oswald, the murderer of the Howard University couple. And to top it off, they'd taken down Jeremy Wiles.

But all good things must end.

So, here it was. A new lease on life. A new, junior, partner. As long as it wasn't—

"Detective." Branaman waved his hand in front of her face. "You zoned out there for a second. I was saying, your new partner will be Detective Iverson. I will bring her in and tell her in one second. Wait just outside and bring her up to speed on Billingsley immediately. That will be all."

CHAPTER 33
VERONICA

Night, March 9

Ben was still off at his hotel. Well, he was pulling long days working in his office, but he wasn't coming home when he was done. He called the kids each night, telling them that he loved them, and he was just away temporarily. He must have realized the bind he put me in, having to be a single parent, but I assumed that was part of the deal. I got to see the kids, but I also *had* to see the kids. He knew that my mother was here, and I guess that made him think it was okay to take longer before coming back home. I tried to think of what must be going through his head. We always jokingly argued about which of us was more stubborn. I didn't think he realized just how much I understood his feeling. Not the "maybe my wife is a monster" underlying thought I knew he couldn't rid from his head, but the fear. Sometimes you just have to live with fear. A life without it is a luxury that does not belong to everyone.

Nico and Maria were reserved at dinner. The initial high of abuela being here had worn off and I could tell they were having flashbacks of when I was gone, the last time grandparents had come to visit. They were sharp, keen in the way that children are. They knew something was wrong. Dad doesn't just announce one day he has a work trip. Those trips are planned well in advance.

I sat with them both, reading before bed. My priority was them, even with my mother here. She could easily become an excuse to spend my time investigating, but that would be playing into part of Ben's fears. I was here, present as a parent, while also able to work with Mikaela. That's what he still didn't understand. I could be a parent and help solve crimes. This wasn't a zero-sum game.

"Men have been kicked to the curb for a lot less," mom said when I came down the stairs. She was sitting in the living room, nursing an old fashioned, watching the news on television like only people of her generation did anymore.

"Mom, we don't need to get into it again," I said.

"Your father agrees."

"Of course he does. That's what parents are there for. You guys get to remember all the tiniest slights and hold grudges forever, that's your role."

"I'd say this is a bit more than a slight," mom said, her tone turning more serious.

"And don't I know it? Look, mom, I love how much you're in my corner, and I promise you'll be the first to know if I do 'kick him to the curb,' okay? But right now, I need to do some work on this investigation." I didn't need to right that second, but I wasn't in the mood for further conversation. I took my laptop, kissed her goodnight, and headed up to our bedroom, flinging myself down onto the bed.

I wasn't able to follow up on Francisco's info about Tony's friend Bridget and had to let him take the lead out in Burke. Instead, I learned everything I could about her, typed it all up nicely, and sent it off to him. He probably knew it already—I still wasn't exactly sure how he acquired information in America.

Bridget Lowe graduated from Georgetown University, with a degree in international relations. She moved on and got a master's degree at the prestigious Johns Hopkins School of Advanced International Studies and wanted to become a diplomat. She took the foreign service exam three times and failed all of them—no real concern for a test with a miniscule success rate. But then she began to notice a rash on her nose that always flared up after she was in direct sunlight. After hours spent frantically Googling, a doctor's visit confirmed her fear. She had developed lupus. With the crushing realization that even if she made it into the diplomatic ranks, she would have limited options due to the lack of a full medical clearance, she made the difficult decision to change her career ambitions.

She got a Master of Education and for the last several years was a successful and well-liked civics and government teacher at South County High School.

Nothing I could find referenced anything that would connect her to Tony, besides that they both were students at Georgetown. Time to talk to Francisco again.

"Alex," he responded after barely a ring.

"I just sent you a file on Bridget Lowe. It's pretty extensive, but I couldn't find what connected her to Tony. I'm hoping she'll have plenty to say because otherwise this feels a bit like a dead end. What did you find that made you so confident?"

He swore under his breath. "You didn't hear?"

"Didn't hear what?"

"Fuck, V. Bridget Lowe is dead. Someone killed her in the Burke Centre Shopping Center this afternoon. Stabbed her a bunch of times with a short blade after she came out of the grocery store. I'm here now, watching the police work."

I sat back, leaning my head against the headboard, snuggled deeper under my duvet. I felt slightly ashamed that my first thought wasn't grief about a life violently taken away, but a spark that this meant that, to shamelessly steal from the world's most famous PI, the game was afoot. Tony and Bridget both being killed within a couple days of each other? That was too coincidental.

"Francisco, what was the connection you found between the two of them?"

"They had three classes together, more than he had with any other former classmate whom he still follows on social media."

Damn, he was good. Cross-referencing class lists and social media was a smart idea. "Okay, so they definitely knew each other."

"Yes, but they have no interaction online anywhere, which struck me as a little odd—oh, shit, something's happening."

"What do you mean?"

"Lots of running and yelling all of a sudden. Looks like something by the car. Got to go. I'll text you."

Forty-five minutes later, I slipped my shoes off as I slid past Mikaela, who was holding her front door for me. This wasn't news to tell her over the phone. I left a short note on the kitchen counter, telling my mom where I'd ducked out to, just in case she woke up.

"What is it you wanted to talk about?" Mikaela perched on the edge of her couch, while her friend Billie stood across from me, as if unwilling to sit because it gave me the upper hand. I was still used to sizing everyone up as a possible threat, but it was clear that Billie's presence was a comfort to Mikaela.

"Did you know someone named Bridget Lowe?" I watched closely for her reaction. But she wasn't a suspect, or a professional, so I needn't have anyway.

Her mouth gaped open. "I… yeah. A friend of Tony's from college. But why is she important?"

"Can you tell me about their relationship?"

"Now, hold on a minute there," Billie said. "Wasn't no stuck-up college type out there trying to steal Tony back from Mikaela."

"Back?"

Billie's mouth opened and then abruptly closed.

"I think they might have had a thing in college," Mikaela said quietly. "She's gorgeous, so I always wondered what changed. He never talks—talked—about her except one time he got drunk. I asked him what the prettiest thing in the whole world was, assuming he'd say it was me. He called it a tie between us."

Billie rolled her eyes. "Tony was a good man, but he had absolutely no tact. Dumb as rocks, sometimes, when it came to relationships."

"So, they had a strong connection in college?" I asked, my eyes staring directly at Mikaela, silently willing Billie to stay quiet.

"Yes." She played with her wedding ring. I couldn't tell if she was doing so consciously or not.

"What does this matter?" Billie asked.

I needed to be less subtle, clearly. I looked at Billie, then pivoted my body away from her so I was only facing Mikaela.

"That's why I'm here. Mikaela," I sat down on the couch beside her. "Someone killed Bridget Lowe earlier today."

"What the fuck?" Billie exclaimed, putting her hands on her head as Mikaela slumped down into the couch. "Jesus fucking Christ. That guy from the bridge killed her *and* Tony?"

I glanced sharply at Billie. "No one said anything about that guy being the killer."

"Well, sure," Billie said. "But it has to be him. Why else would he have followed Mikaela after?"

"I don't know, but we have to widen our search before we narrow it. We can't focus too hard on one person and miss the real killer if it isn't him." I didn't tell them that I did not want Jacob involved. I hoped he was simply exhibiting some repressed male behavior, seeing a pretty woman and then following her without thinking.

"Hold on," I said, picking up my phone. "My friend is calling. I'll put him on speaker."

"This is some weird shit, Alex," Francisco said.

Alex? Veronica saw Mikaela mouth.

"Francisco you're on speaker with Mikaela and her friend…" I looked over. "Bobbie."

Billie intensified her glare at me.

"Okay, hi, Mikaela nice to meet you, and you probably would want to know this too. The police just found a note here, and it caused quite a commotion."

"Does that mean something to us?" I asked.

"Not sure yet, but you know who just arrived?"

"Who?" I could feel Mikaela and Billie's breaths pause in anticipation.

"The D.C. detectives," Francisco said. "Brown and a young one. I think they've found something."

CHAPTER 34
MIKAELA

Night, March 10

"What the actual fuck is going on?" Mikaela gripped the remote, the closest thing to her she could squeeze, her hand turning red.

Billie put her hands to her temple in reply. "This is fucked up," she finally said.

"I mean it, like is this some fucking joke? A fucking serial killer?" Mikaela seethed. "Maybe if the police actually took my husband's disappearance seriously, they could've helped stop a fucking madman."

She realized she had had enough. Enough of the *woe is me*, enough of the sadness. What she needed was rage.

The denial stage was over. Tony's body was lying in a morgue. He was gone. Forever.

She didn't know if it was because she knew anger was next on the list, but that was all she could feel.

"They still think he killed himself, but this changes everything," Billie said. "Don't you agree?"

"This is way too much. How could Tony and Bridget both die within days of each other?"

She knew Tony and Bridget still followed each other on various social media platforms, but, as she had told Veronica before she went back home, Tony rarely mentioned her at all.

The wave of nausea doubled her over. Mikaela steadied herself, her clammy hands gripping the arm of the couch. "Sorry, I think it's all just catching up to me," she said, bolting upright and racing to the bathroom.

She barely made it to the sink before her insides erupted, a violent burst that seared her throat as it came out. Steadying herself with several deep breaths, she grabbed her mouthwash and gargled aggressively. She noticed that the splatter had gotten on her white tee shirt, so pulled it off and tossed it in a heap in the bathroom corner before walking back out into the living room.

"You good?" Billie asked, giving her an exaggerated up-down look.

"Yeah, sorry about that. That came on so fast." Mikaela looked down at her exposed stomach. "And come on, don't give me that look, you've seen me way more naked than this."

Billie cracked a grin, but it quickly disappeared. "It's not that," she said.

"What is it?"

"You've been nauseous multiple times now, you realize that?"

"So what?" Mikaela said. "I should be, it's a totally natural reaction."

Billie took a deep breath. "Um, I don't mean to pry here, and I realize this could be a hugely insensitive question considering the circumstances."

Mikaela looked warily at Billie as she trailed off. "That wasn't a question."

"You don't need a pregnancy test, do you?"

CHAPTER 35
EMILIA

Night, March 10

Emilia stood under the grocery store's awning, watching the rain pour down, trying not to think about just how much evidence it was destroying. She was already upset that the homicide had happened six hours ago, and she was only just now getting a chance to take in the scene.

The local detectives were perfectly adept at their jobs. She couldn't blame them. But why did the killer go through such a fuss to hide the note at this scene? If it hadn't been for the gust of wind that shook it loose, who knows how long it would have taken for them to notice the flimsy piece of paper, tucked up under the wheel well?

Iverson breathed loudly beside her. She closed her eyes and took in a breath, willing herself to not get annoyed by every little thing her now junior partner did.

"I tell you this is my first murder?"

Yes, a thousand times already.

In the station, in the car, five minutes ago.

Droplets of rain from Iverson's pigtails were pooling in dueling puddles on the concrete either side of her feet. She claimed she 'didn't like umbrellas' so had simply run from the car to their shelter.

What was Emilia supposed to do with someone like her? She

wanted young and malleable, yes, but she needed intelligence. There had to be some clay there to mold. A young woman with her background could have chosen so many other options, but was here, so shouldn't she be showing more interest in learning?

"So, like, what's the first thing you do? What's your vibe with these?"

Emilia rolled her eyes. "My 'vibe,'" she did air quotes with her hands, "is that we inspect every single inch, and we take meticulous notes, and we learn everything we possibly can here. *Then,* we go over it all again, follow up leads, gather new evidence, and eventually catch whoever did this. I'm sorry, what part of that is a surprise to you?" She asked, taking in Iverson's bewildered face.

"I just thought maybe you had a secret." She shrugged. "You seemed like someone who could do it all. That's why I asked so many times to be partnered with you."

Interesting. Despite herself, Emilia felt a slight softening of her resolve to dislike Iverson. At least this kid wanted to be here.

"Okay, first—or tenth, whatever—lesson for you, Iverson. Become the enemy of certainty. No fact you discover, ascertain, or unearth, is to be taken as gospel truth. You question everything, you don't just look at a piece of evidence, you ask why it was there, who had a motive to leave it, could it possibly have been put in a specific location just to trip us up. You do all of that, for every single thought that goes through your mind while you work, until the case is down. Then, you pick up the next one and start over. That's the job. We are professional thinkers and problem solvers, and we owe it to these poor people whose bodies we stand over far too often to be one hundred percent on at all times. That's the secret. We're homicide, so we come in after the murder has been committed. Our job can be dangerous, sure, but what we mostly are doing are puzzles. Are you good at that connections game in the *New York Times*?"

Iverson screwed up her face. "What game?"

"It doesn't matter. What you need to do is make the connection no one else can. I read about you; I know your background. I know you can ace tests but you're inexperienced in terms of real police work. You look like a tiny puppy dog who wouldn't know how to tie her shoes without asking for help, so I'd like to know where we stand. Are you ready to put in the work?"

A meek nod was the only response.

"Okay, go inside and interview anyone working inside the grocery store. Take down all their contact info. Write down every detail, no matter how inconsequential it sounds."

She watched Iverson take a small, scared breath, and stalked off. This wasn't what she had in mind. She needed her partner to have some moxie, or, at the very least, the good sense to stay out of the way and let Emilia do it on her own.

The rain pooled by the cart return as Emilia stood in the parking lot, stooped down to inspect the spot where Bridget Lowe was found. No working cameras in the area. It would have been a long shot to see the stabbing between two SUVs, but she would've appreciated a look at the killer's getaway, at least. The medical examiner would have details for her, but it sounded like she was found only a few minutes after the attack.

The witness, an octogenarian named Malcolm Bonner, said he had been returning his cart, and happened to glance to his right and see her, half of her body underneath her SUV. He said he thought she'd gotten run over. She was already dead when he got to her, but he noted that the pool of blood around her was still growing. He must have only been minutes late. Emilia had his information on hand as needed, but they'd already let the poor, frail man go home and try to get some sleep. She didn't think he'd have anything more to add, but she would tell Iverson to do a follow-up just in case.

"Do you think she was having an affair with him?"

Emilia whirled around, startled, only to see Iverson, her feet braced on the concrete as if she was worried the next sheet of rain might sweep her away.

"Iverson, what are you doing? Go back inside, keep talking to the store employees."

Iverson's eyes grew wide, and Emilia could have sworn she saw her chin start to quiver. "Providing a second set of eyes, like the Chief's handbook says I'm supposed to do."

Emilia put her hands on her hips. "Isn't rule one of that stupid little junior detective cheat sheet to always listen to your senior partner?"

"Nope!" Iverson said brightly, regaining her composure. "Rule one is to always maintain your timesheet."

Emilia stared at her. Every time she looked at Iverson, the word "pipsqueak" popped into her head. Her mother used to use that term to describe only the people with the smallest presence. "Are you asking me if I think that Bridget Lowe was having an affair with Senator Billingsley?"

Iverson answered with a single nod, her pleading eyes begging Emilia to tell her she'd done a good job.

I wanted a partner and now I'm stuck with a child. "Enemy of certainty, remember? We have no evidence to suggest that, and even if we did, hypothesizing gets us nowhere."

"But it's safe to say they are connected, or at least were to this killer? As far as I know we haven't released the contents of the previous note to the public, and with how swiftly we moved to get over here, that's what you believe, isn't it?"

Damn kid. Emilia sighed. "Yes, we can obviously use evidence to guide our investigation, I'm not saying otherwise. But right now, it's just as likely they each ate at a random pizza place called World's Edge in the middle of Podunk Nowheresville as any other theory, and that's how we'll treat this. We *discover* the connection—we don't guess."

Iverson squinted up as the moon peeked out from behind the clouds. She cocked her head and pursed her lips. "Well, then isn't it curious that the suicide from the Wilson bridge graduated in the same class as Bridget Lowe?"

"Excuse me?" Emilia had to work to rein in her shocked expression.

"That guy that they pulled out of the water a couple of nights ago. I read about him just in case."

Emilia arched an eyebrow. "You know, Iverson, maybe there's hope for you yet."

CHAPTER 36
MIKAELA

Night, March 10

O*h, fuck.* The first thought that popped into Mikaela's head. As soon as the words came out, she knew it must be true. It made too much sense. The nausea, the aching boobs, needing to pee all the time. All those symptoms she'd spent so much time agonizing over. Wishing and praying that somehow her devotion and obsession with pregnancy would manifest itself into one for her. Willing each stomachache, every cramp, to be the first sign.

But month after month of seeing a single line, of tracking cycles, of using ovulation strips, had worn her down. It was supposed to be easy and natural. After all, it was the reason humanity existed, how could it be so hard?

Knowing that others went through the same, and even much worse, hadn't helped. Sure, misery loves company, but nowhere does it say the company balances out the misery. Sometimes you just end up with misery and company.

Now the symptoms she prayed for were all present, and she hadn't even noticed.

Billie had walked with her to the drug store on the corner to get a new pregnancy test. If this was happening, she needed to be sure, and she only had one test left that was ever so slightly expired.

Two lines. And then two lines again.

Clear and definitive.

She grew up devoutly attending mass far more often than was necessitated by the church. It provided a stability that foster care couldn't, and she liked the idea that there was something larger at play, someone else in charge.

But the God she believed in would not create a situation this cruel. First, she told her husband she didn't want him if they couldn't have kids. Second, if there wasn't some foul play, he possibly killed himself in part because of her. Then third, as soon as he's gone, she's pregnant?

She had spent her entire life thinking about mothers. At some point it switched from wishing to have a mother to wishing to be a mother. She imagined the moment when she saw the test, the first tangible proof. She would cry the happiest tears. The type of tears that could be turned into dancing.

Not like this.

Not crying into her best friend's arms. Not wondering how she was going to handle it. Not thinking of just how much she had drunk recently. She would keep the child, of course, there was no question there. But was she cut out to be a single mom? And what about her job? Daycare?

The thoughts swirled in her head until she had to excuse herself. She slipped into a pajama set, did a quick check to look for a bump she knew couldn't be there, and then climbed into bed and pulled the covers up tight. She needed to close the world away.

She squirmed around in bed, tossing her down comforter off and then hugging it close minutes later. Hot, then cold. A single thought kept rising to the surface. This baby was going to need a father figure.

And she knew just who to talk to. The certainty lit a fire inside her. She had to go, right now. She pushed her comforter off her one last time and hopped out of bed.

Mikaela gave a single hard rap on the door and took a step back. A concierge wheeled an overloaded luggage trolley by as she did her best to act like she belonged here. Not like he would care anyway. She studied the red and blue speckled carpet. A bland, boring thing that made all the sense in the world here, in a mid-range hotel hallway.

Maybe he wasn't here. There was no guarantee he would be at ten on a weeknight. She was sure this was his room. The bored girl behind the check-in counter, who barely even looked up from her phone, had not been nearly as discreet as Mikaela had expected. She was ready for a fight, to make her case she needed to see him, maybe even lie and claim to be bringing delivery food. As it turned out, all she had to ask for was his name. Some higher-ups would be upset if they knew the check-in girl was being so cavalier.

But if he wasn't here, where would he be? Or, even worse, could there be someone else in the room with him? What was he even doing here in the first place? How dare he...

She felt her thoughts careening out of control when finally, the latch popped, and the door swung open.

He looked at her, confusion and annoyance etched on his face in equal measure. "What's going on?" he asked.

She steeled herself and tried to give him a reassuring smile.

"We need to talk, Ben."

CHAPTER 37
BEN

Night, March 10

It had been two days since he saw the man in red with the big gold cross. He couldn't get him out of his head, though. Why had he followed him, and why was he taking pictures? He had asked the concierge if he could see security footage, but his request was met with a resounding no.

Ben sat in the small desk chair, the novel he had planned to read lying untouched next to him. He didn't want to use the bed for anything but sleeping, and that was not forthcoming.

He began to doubt himself. With two days passing without incident, maybe he was just being paranoid. Could he be sure that the man had taken his photo? Was there something else he could have been taking a picture of? Or maybe he was just holding his phone up looking at something? The elevator had closed, so Ben didn't have any idea where the man went next. Maybe he was just heading to his room, a regular guest in a long-term stay hotel.

If this man was taking photos, then to what end? Why had nothing come of it yet?

Ben had attempted to read and relax, but each night since, he hadn't been able to turn his brain off. He mindlessly scrolled on his phone, the Instagram pictures flying by and barely registering. He couldn't cut his mind loose.

He remembered the first time he had seen Veronica. She had been in a group of women in an Instagram photo a mutual friend posted. They were all posing, celebrating what looked like the end of a semester, seated on one side of a long wooden table with more empty beer glasses than people present.

He didn't have that storybook, googly eyes, I-can't-breathe-because-of-her-beauty feeling in his chest. But he kept coming back to the picture, hour after hour, day after day. Drawn back to this woman in the yellow tank top that accentuated her olive skin.

He couldn't believe his eyes when he saw her the very next weekend, dancing away in his favorite club. It was as if he'd manifested their eventual meeting. Little did he know that they'd meet eyes on the dance floor and then never look away.

There was a sharp knock on the door.

Ben felt the back of his neck get sweaty and he could feel his pulse racing. Is that the guy? Who else would be coming for him?

What would V do? He looked around for a weapon and settled on the butter knife in the small kitchenette.

What would V do?

A thought flitted through his mind and then left as quickly as it came. In a time of crisis and fear he wanted his wife next to him. His mind went to her.

He tip-toed toward the door, remembering the now seemingly ubiquitous advice to put an object over the peephole first, just in case an assailant was waiting to shoot through it. Had that ever actually happened? Wouldn't he have heard if that was a real threat? Were there people walking around without fingers or palms because they took that advice and succeeded?

This is stupid, he thought, as he raised his hand to the peephole. He pulled it back down and brought his eye up close, peering outside.

Fear morphed into confusion as he saw her. *Why would she be here?*

CHAPTER 38
MIKAELA

Night, March 10

"I'm sorry, I have no idea what you're doing here, and you need to leave." Ben pushed the door closed, but it came to an abrupt stop against Mikaela's outstretched foot.

"Don't you?" Mikaela looked at Ben's ocean-blue eyes.

"I literally have no idea, I told you. I don't know how you found me, and it's weird that you did."

"Do you think it was a coincidence I came to Veronica for help?"

She saw the flash in his eyes, the tiniest hint of curiosity, barely creeping out from behind the anger.

"Why?"

"Not for her. For you."

"Me?" He pointed a bewildered finger at his own chest.

"You."

He kicked at her foot, trying to slam the door as she withdrew it. She leaned her knee in to keep it open, and her one-size-too-big black camisole slipped off her left shoulder. She quickly pulled it back up, noticing a movement at the end of the hall as she did so. "Do you want me to make a scene?" she hissed. "Let me in."

"Fuck's sake." He sighed and allowed her to enter. She looked around, expecting to see a bachelor pad-style dump of a room.

"It's so... neat," she stammered. Besides a Megan Miranda novel on the top of the immaculately made bed and a computer on the desk, there was no sign that anyone was staying there. "Is this even your room?"

"Of course it is," he said, standing next to the still open door. "Was I supposed to have clothes flopped all over and beer stains on the counters? Would that make what you're doing here make more sense?"

"I need you," Mikaela said.

"This is wildly inappropriate."

She affixed a piercing gaze directly at him. "As if you don't already know why I'm here."

"I still don't even know how you showed up at my house!"

"Ben, look." She put her hand to her stomach.

She followed his eyes as they made a ponderous journey down toward her stomach. His eyes widened with understanding. "You're pregnant?"

"Yes, and I'm going to need your help."

"My... help?" His beautiful blue eyes clouded again.

How does he not get this? Does he really not know?

"This child needs you."

"Look, you must have confused me with someone else. I don't know what you think I did here, but I am not the father to your child."

Mikaela blanched, unable to hide her reaction. "The father?"

He really didn't know.

He had lived this protected, sheltered, life for decades. Silver spoon, everything he wanted. Powerful job in D.C., a beautiful wife—okay, admittedly, he bit off more than he could chew with that one. He didn't have to scrap and fight for everything. He didn't know what it was like to be cast aside. He just lived his carefree, elite life.

Never knowing the consequences of one man's actions.

But not his.

"Not you, you dumbass. Not *you*. I'm talking about your father." She locked eyes with him. "*Our* father."

He took a step back, as his mouth opened and closed. She watched him blink several times, his brain trying to process what he had just heard. "Our father. I just... how?" He aggressively shook his head.

Mikaela pursed her lips. "My mother was Diana Peterson, the COO at Dickson Wharton."

"Diana Peterson," he repeated. "She worked with him. She was the one who forced my parents' divorce."

"Forced?" Mikaela scoffed.

"Wait, sorry, not forced." Ben held out his hands in apology. "That was the wrong word. My father was the cause, he was a horrible philandering husband, and, if you can believe it, an even worse dad. I just meant your mom was the one who my mom caught my—our—dad with."

"He told my mom he loved her." Mikaela felt a familiar lump rise into her throat, the same one that always appeared when she talked about her mother. "And then he threw her to the curb. Diana Peterson was a successful woman, with a strong community, and he destroyed it all. He claimed she tried to force herself on him, that she was hysterical, that she couldn't be trusted. He cooked the books, making it look like she was embezzling money. She lost everything. Everything except me. Everyone else, even her own family, turned their backs. They didn't want to be stained by association. Cowards, all of them. But none more than our father, who couldn't handle the consequences of thinking with his dick so had to ruin someone's life. Do you know what happened to her? Did your parents ever tell that side of the story?"

"No," Ben said, his voice barely above a whisper.

"Drugs. Because that's what happens when you hit rock-bottom. She didn't even know she was pregnant until she was too far gone. Isn't that some crazy shit? She didn't try to get your dad to leave your mom because of the baby. He just kicked her out because he got tired of her."

Ben leaned his head back against the door frame and closed his eyes. Mikaela didn't know the nature of his relationship with his father, so watched closely, trying to judge his reaction. He seemed to be accepting the truth faster than she expected he would. Maybe it didn't come as too much of a surprise.

"I knew he had broken that off. One last-ditch attempt to get my mom to forgive him." He opened his eyes again and fixed them directly upon hers. "I'm so sorry."

"She died in a gutter two weeks after I was born," Mikaela said flatly. "There are no sorries that can ever make up for that."

Ben was silent, his fingers anxiously worrying a nail.

"You're looking at my eyes. Don't you recognize them?" She didn't mean for her voice to sound so pleading, so desperate.

His mouth curved into a bitter smile. "My dad's eyes. You're right. I don't know how I didn't see that before."

"I've been staring at your eyes ever since you opened the door, trying to get you to notice for yourself." When Mikaela had discovered her birth father's identity and found the photo online, she couldn't believe what she was seeing. Her deep blue irises that shimmered and sparkled in the light were the first feature anyone commented on. There they were looking right back at her, on the face of the CEO of her mother's company.

"Does Veronica know?"

Mikaela shook her head with a sad smile. "No. She tried to help me find my husband purely out of the goodness of her heart."

"Oh my God, your husband." Ben's face was panic-stricken. "I didn't even realize. They found his body…" his voice trailed off.

Mikaela gave a somber nod and recounted her story, including how she initially believed she pushed him out onto that bridge, but now thought there could be something else at play.

"Which brings us back to the start, and why I'm here." Mikaela exhaled through her nostrils. "I first had just thought asking Veronica for help seemed like a good way of finding him and also getting to see what my half-brother was like. But now, I'm sorry if this is so forward, but I think I need to be part of your life."

Ben grimaced and gestured around the room. "Well, I'm willing to talk and listen, and I'll do what I can, but I think *lives*, plural, might be the optimal word at the moment."

So, he really had moved out. With some minimal amount of clothes, he was spending his nights here at a long-term stay hotel.

"Is this about Veronica?"

"It's about you! You pushed her deeper into this stupid PI shit, and it's going to get someone killed."

"You mean, like my husband?"

He grimaced, his face red and chagrined. "You don't understand. We almost lost her last year. We can't go through that again. That can't become a normal thing in our lives."

"Let me ask you a question." Mikaela put her hands on her hips. "How many people would you kill to keep your family safe?"

"That's not the same, and you don't know what I have learned."

"No, answer the question. To make sure your wife and children were safe, how many people would you be willing to kill?" She held up her right hand. "Wait. Actually, let me clarify it further. How many people who are an active threat to your family's health would you kill to keep them safe?"

"I would actively protect my family from immediate harm, yes. Anyone would."

"And if your kids grew a few years older and believed that was what they were doing? That doing their father's bidding and killing rivals was keeping the family safe? If their not-yet-fully-developed brains couldn't process all the nuances, and just knew they had a job to do?"

"That's not it."

"Okay, then what is it?"

"It's not that she did all those... things"—he shuddered— "as a teenager. It's that I can't tell if she doesn't wish she still could now. I can't trust that she wouldn't still be that person."

Mikaela gaped at her brother. "I'm sorry? That's the whiniest bullshit I've ever heard in my life. Look, I know that I'm here asking to be a part of your life, so I need to tread carefully, but what the fuck, man? You think she wants to be out murdering people and wondering every day if it's going to be her last? You think she wants to be under the thumb of her terrifying father again? You've got some massive fucking issues of your own, Jesus Christ. She literally *ran away* from that life."

"But now part of it is back," he said defensively.

"You need a therapist. Are you that fragile that you think the woman who chose to marry you and have kids with you is going to uproot it all?" Mikaela softened her tone. "Look, I'm sure you're scared, and you get to have your feelings, and no one can invalidate them. But whatever it is you're doing here, this shit is not healthy, and neither of you deserve it. Call her, for goodness' sake."

CHAPTER 39
VERONICA

Night, March 10

"Hi Ben, how are you?" I picked up the phone and tried to keep the wariness out of my voice. I shooed away my nosy mom, who'd appeared out of nowhere and was peeking into our bedroom. She was either the lightest sleeper ever or had been prepared for this.

The last thing I was expecting was an all-out assault on my eardrums, as he word-vomited through the phone. I listened, scarcely believing what I was hearing, as he told me I've been helping his half-sister locate her husband, and that soon he and I will be aunt and uncle to her unborn child.

"I don't understand, why did she not tell me?" I asked.

"She said she just wanted to know about me and my family, so she didn't want to affect us, I guess?"

"You seem pretty sanguine about it, I have to say."

He sighed. "You know my father. It doesn't exactly require a big stretch in imagination to realize he could be capable of this."

I knew his father was loathsome, that wasn't a surprise. But that he actually had a kid who he ignored, even after her mother's death?

I met him once. Ben never knew, but I wanted to see him for myself.

He didn't know who I was, even though Ben and I were already married. I assumed he was not involved in Ben's social media life, so the only way he'd know what I looked like was if he saw a wedding announcement picture in the local paper, which wasn't high on our to-do list.

I walked right up to him in the cafeteria of his workplace, a Fortune 500 company called Dickson Wharton. One of those places that has inspirational sayings like "Aspirational Leadership" and "Together We Can" up all over the walls, but even the people working there can't actually articulate what it is they do. Security at places like that looks imposing but always tends to be laughable. Sure, it'll stop a random, spontaneous attempt at entry, but any bit of time and planning can easily bypass the front entry point.

He looked me up and down, taking in my robin's egg blue power suit. His eyes stopped on my badge, conveniently resting on my chest. He studied it closely, a spectacularly amateur attempt at feigned innocence.

"Good afternoon, Mr. Walsh." I reached across him and loaded two cinnamon rolls onto my plate.

"Why hello there, Alex, how are you? I don't believe we've met." His eyes went to my plate. "A good eater—I like that. Although looking at you, you'd never know," he said, giving me the most obvious of up-downs.

It's always nice to have your priors confirmed immediately.

"Alex Hayes, new in HR. Nice to meet you." No one wants more details about HR work, especially those who spend time skirting the rules by doing things like, say, cheating on your wife in your office after hours.

"Well, I've got to say, you're someone I wouldn't mind getting in trouble with."

It was all I could do to not plant an elbow in his stomach as he smiled with the ease of a man who had never known consequences.

There was so much of Ben I could see in his face. It was unfathomable, though, just how Ben grew up to be the sweet, loving man I knew when he had a father like this. His blatantly racist mother wasn't any better.

Ben didn't talk too much about it, and, not wanting to open up lengthy discussions about our respective childhoods when everything he had known about mine was a lie, I didn't press much. I gathered that his parents hadn't always been so far gone, and that their descent into hatred and madness happened just after Ben's formative years, so he managed to get away relatively scot-free.

"Look, V—" Ben's tone changed, and his voice got softer. "She also gave me some harsh advice, but I think she was right."

I waited, but he clearly wanted me to say something. "Go on," I finally replied.

"She knocked some sense into me, told me I need to straighten up, and recognize who you are as an adult. Basically, she told me to stop treating you like shit." He chuckled wistfully.

The words I'd been waiting to hear. I felt the pain that had found lodging in my chest start to slip away. But right before the words came out, telling him to come home, I realized I needed to be sure. I needed know this was real. "I'm glad to hear it. But look, the ball is in my court now, okay? You agree you treated me like shit, so you need to understand that I'm going to decide when to forgive you."

"How are the kids?"

Oh, come on. "Don't use the kids to try to make me sound like I need to allow you back for their sake. You're the one who went to a hotel because you couldn't handle your imagination. *You* left *us* because you had an idea in your mind of me, I don't know, stabbing the mailman through the heart with a sharpened stick just because he doesn't always throw our paper close enough to the front door."

"I didn't—"

"Ben, stop. We don't have to rehash it all. The kids do need you, it's true." I took a deep breath and brushed away the single tear from my eye. "But give me time. You live your work life, and then we'll see."

CHAPTER 40
EMILIA

Morning, March 11

"Three bodies. One—" Emilia pointed to the senator's photo on her white board, "—Senator Andrew Billingsley. Shot at close range after a chase through Roosevelt Island at night. Seemingly knew his assailant, or at least had what he believed to be a legitimate reason to be there. Two—" she pointed to Bridget Lowe, "—schoolteacher Bridget Lowe. Stabbed thirteen times in a grocery store parking lot in Burke, where witnesses say they saw her buying groceries within the hour of her estimated time of death. And now, three—" she gave a nod toward Iverson "—thanks to my partner here for the catch. Antonio Alonso, fished out of the Potomac River after his car was spotted parked in the breakdown lane of the Woodrow Wilson Bridge. Three dead, very likely all connected. Why, how, and are there others? Those are our questions. Find me answers."

Emilia watched as the two other detectives and handful of patrol officers assigned to assist on the case scurried away, each with their individual assignment in hand. When she approached the chief after realizing there might be other bodies associated—can't assume it's not linked just because there's no note—she asked for more manpower, some extra hands to go through other recent cases, to canvas witnesses, and all the things she would do but didn't have enough time for herself.

She hated the cliché of the detective who liked it when the bad guy was smart. Fictional private investigators like Sherlock Holmes could spend their days waiting for the "fun" criminal, but she was out here trying to solve murders every day. Every second counted when you never knew if the murderer was done. There was no time for enjoying the hunt. She wanted the first lead to pan out, the suspect to do something stupid, and to stop them. Using her brain to try to bring down the most clever, now that was interesting, of course. But she would never be so crass as to think her enjoyment of the job should take precedence over public safety.

She didn't like the feeling in her stomach that this guy was one of the smart ones. She would have to be meticulous. Follow each lead as quickly as possible, but with no room for error. *Festina lente*. Make haste, slowly.

The most obvious lead she would follow up with first: Tony Alonso's wife.

"You know, I'd almost have wondered if he was the connection, and our main suspect, if he were just missing right now," Iverson said, appearing at Emilia's elbow and following her gaze up to the picture of Alonso. "Faking a death with a car on the bridge is a decent idea."

"Not bad, Ivy," Emilia said, enjoying Iverson's wince as she tried out her new nickname.

"Iverson," her partner muttered under her breath, enunciating each syllable, as she turned around and stalked off.

They pulled into an empty parking spot, on the narrow street a couple blocks down from the Alonsos' house.

"Why are we parking so far away?" Iverson asked.

Emilia raised an eyebrow and looked at her partner, fidgeting with the seatbelt in the passenger seat. "How often have you driven in this city?"

"Barely ever, why?"

"This is as close as we could reasonably hope for. Parallel parking spots don't grow on trees."

"But… we're police, we could just park right in front of her house."

"And then what? Illegally park and block traffic just because we can? To what end?"

"Fine, I get it, you win, let's go," Iverson huffed, pushing the door open and climbing out of the car.

"All right, the widow is named Mikaela," Emilia said, as they walked down the sidewalk. "Thirty-two years old, data scientist at Leidos. They married five years ago, no children, nothing else jumps out. I'm not considering her a suspect right now, but as always, keep an open mind, and listen to your gut as she talks."

"All due respect, but how many lectures are you planning on giving?" Iverson held her gaze steady. "I've been in this job for more than a day."

My, hadn't she grown a spine overnight? One compliment and Miss "I've never worked a homicide before" thought she was hot shit. Emilia didn't mind the change, though. This was what she had wanted. A young, brash detective with the raw tools she could mold. And now she'd at least shown she did have some tools. "Not with me you haven't," Emilia said. "Prove to me you don't need the lectures, and the lectures will end, simple as that."

Emilia opened the small wooden gate at the edge of the property, and they walked through the small yard, sidestepping an overgrown magnolia jutting out into the path. Emilia eschewed the doorbell and rapped hard at the door. She took a step back, held up her badge, and waited.

A lean woman with amber skin cracked the door open and leaned her head out. "Can I help you? I've already talked to loads of cops. I don't know what else I can say."

"Mikaela Alonso, correct?"

"Yes." Her voice was emotionless, the energy and life seemingly drained out of it.

"Detective Emilia Brown." Emilia held up her badge, noticing in her peripheral vision that Iverson followed suit with a flip and a flourish. "We have reason to believe your husband's death was connected to two other deaths, and we'd like to ask you some more questions. May we come in?"

With a defeated huff, she opened the door and led them inside.

Emilia introduced herself and her partner as they settled down in the living room, her eyes catching on a large portrait of the Virgin Mary next to a slender bookshelf. "Mrs. Alonso—"

"Mikaela, please," she said, as she set down glasses of water for each of them.

"Mikaela. We are looking into the connection between your husband and Bridget Lowe. Can you tell us more about them?"

She grimaced. "Well, they were friends from Georgetown, part of this small tight-knit crew apparently. Tony didn't talk too much about them but every once in a while, he'd say something. He always sounded a little sad, like he wished they would have remained close. It seemed like one of those short-fuse hot burning friendships that happen in college."

"What about Tony and Bridget, specifically?"

"Well, I think they might've had a fling, or started out as an item. There was one picture of them at some Greek life party. I think it was on Facebook, some album that's long gone now that we're all adults. It was a group of people, but the two of them looked much more than platonic. He was behind her and his arms were draped over and across her chest, each hand holding one of hers." She paused, biting her lip. "I think they met in some class or other. Tony didn't talk much about Georgetown. I always got the feeling it was because I went to a much smaller, lesser-known school, and he was being kind by not talking about a school I could have never afforded."

"Okay, thanks, that is all very helpful, Mikaela," Iverson said. "I want to ask you about the other victim who we know is connected to Bridget Lowe. Do you know of any connection between Tony and Senator Andrew Billingsley?"

"The… Senator?" Mikaela screwed up her face. "Wait, what?"

"We cannot discuss specifics, but there is a clear connection between the deaths of Bridget Lowe and Andrew Billingsley. So, we want to know if we're looking at three deaths that have two coincidental connections, or three interconnected deaths."

Mikaela leaned forward, engaged. "Okay, so like network theory. Is this a line with three nodes or a triangle? Two edges or three? Each edge a connection. That's what you're getting at."

"Exactly," Iverson said.

Emilia glanced sharply over at her partner. *Exactly?*

"And what you need to know is whether the edges are directed or not, right?"

"Yes, again," Iverson said. She met Emilia's gaze. "Come on, boss, you never learned any graph theory? I thought you knew everything."

"I can't say that I did."

"It's surprisingly accessible." Iverson's tone morphed into that of a lecturer. "Nodes, edges, vertices, it's not difficult and it can be really useful for understanding the dynamics of all sorts of networks, like cartels or terrorist cells."

Mikaela helpfully nodded. "It's true, Detective."

"When were you ever involved with cartels or terrorists?" Emilia asked.

"Never, but why not equip yourself with the tools you might one day need?"

Why does she sound like a young version of me?

Mikaela scratched at her eyebrow. "I really don't know about the three of them, though, I'm sorry. Can I ask if you think there's a connection?"

"We think—" Iverson began.

"We're pursuing all possibilities," Emilia cut in.

Iverson wilted back into her chair. Emilia would deal with that later. She couldn't be sure what was about to come out of her junior partner's mouth. Trust takes time.

Mikaela took a fast, shallow breath, followed by several more in a row. Her face turned red, and she jumped up and ran into the kitchen.

"What was that?" Iverson asked, her jaw slack.

Emilia shrugged, taking a sip of water. "Ivy, we need to be careful with what we tell and to whom," she said.

"I wasn't going to say anything! I was just going to tell her we think it's possible."

Emilia could hear the hurt in her partner's voice. She was about to address it, but Mikaela returned before she could speak again.

"Sorry about that," Mikaela said, her voice garbled by multiple hard candies in her mouth.

The picture came into focus in Emilia's mind. She had all she needed, no need to push and prod a pregnant woman about the death of her husband any more than absolutely necessary.

"We'll show ourselves out. Thank you for your time, and we're very sorry for your loss." She began to rise and nodded to Iverson to follow.

"Wait." Mikaela furrowed her brow. "Aren't you going to ask about the other death that could be connected? I thought that was what you meant originally when you said two deaths connected to Tony."

Emilia could feel the sense of foreboding spread between her and Iverson. They shared a nervous glance. "What other death?"

"Tracy Belle. Well, her and her whole family."

"Why would she be connected?" Emilia asked.

"She was another one from their group in college, of course."

CHAPTER 41
BEN

Morning, March 11

"What were you doing at the Residence Inn?" Congresswoman Moore's steely voice cut through the air.

Ben felt everyone pause, their eyes all focused away, pretending they weren't listening. "How do you know that?" He hurried over to her office.

"Because of this." Moore waved her phone at him before placing it down on her desk and sliding it over.

Ben looked down at the screen. The Instagram app was open and there was a picture of him standing at his hotel room door, looking out. Most of his frame was blocked by the back of an unidentified woman, the shot focused in on her curves, with her tank top strap sliding off her shoulder as if on purpose. The caption read *Is D.C.'s most violent couple on the outs? Ben Walsh spotted in hotel room with voluptuous vixen. What will vindictive Veronica's vendetta be this time?*

"They really leaned in on the 'V' thing, didn't they?" Ben grumbled.

"Spill. You get your own life, and I don't give a damn what you do with it, but this shit being public is not going to fly. We've already spent far too much of my time and effort on PR after your wife's identity came out. Convince me you're not a liability, that this isn't the final straw."

Ben shook his head and shrugged. "That's my half-sister."

She raised a single eyebrow. "You do realize that makes it worse, right?"

"How so?"

"Ben don't be blind. No one is going to hear 'that was my half-sister I met late at night in a hotel' and think anything other than you're banging your sister. I need details, now."

"Well, these details absolutely should not be out in public, and they're not all mine to tell. But"—Ben sighed and shook his head—"she's pregnant and her husband died recently, and Veronica and I are currently on the rocks so I've been staying in that hotel for a little while. Mikaela—that's my half-sister—found me there."

"You know what, that's a lot going on there." Moore waved her hand dismissively. "I don't have the time to unpack that all, but get your shit together for me, okay?"

Ben grimaced as he pulled out his phone. He hated dealing with reporters. But he needed to do this. He found the number he needed and dialed.

"Gary Tiller, speaking!"

God, he was far too chipper. And pompous. Can you be those at the same time? No one who runs a half-rate attempt at a Beltway insider blog and social media account should be that sure of themselves.

"Gary, this is Benjamin Walsh, I work with Congresswoman Chamique Moore. Everything from here on out is off the record. Repeat that for me."

"Ben Walsh! As I watched those retweets pour in, I wondered if I might be hearing from you." He paused. "Re-X's? What do we call them now? Anyway, what can I do for you?"

"Repeat what I said."

Ben heard a pronounced *harrumph* through the phone. "Off. The. Record," Gary finally said.

He was enjoying this far too much. "I know your whole charade, and I don't particularly care about your little viral moment. Enjoy it, give the people what they want. Drain the swamp, yada yada yada."

"Okay…" Gary's voice trailed off.

"What I need from you is one piece of information. In return, you get to keep your little moment in the sun."

"You couldn't stop it even if you wanted to," Gary blustered.

"Legally? I could make life miserable for you, but you're right I'd probably end up on the losing end. But you know how you insinuated that Veronica might still be dangerous?" Ben paused for dramatic effect. "You were spot on about vindictive. And *she* has her own ways of getting payback that I truly don't think you're up for. So let me do you a favor. I tell Veronica not to enact whatever type of revenge she's planning for you airing our *completely false* dirty laundry in public. All I need is a name."

Gary was silent, and Ben could tell he was mulling over just how serious a threat this was.

"To be clear, Gary, I have not talked to my wife about this photo. So, I am merely speculating as to what her—what did you call it? — *vendetta* might be, and whether or not you'll be in the firing line."

"Fine, what name?"

Obtuse to the end. "I think you know. Who took that photo? I know it wasn't you."

"I, well, it was given anonymously."

"Gary…"

"Okay, okay, it wasn't anonymous. It was some guy named Jamie Simon. He just reached out and asked to meet, saying he had some photos I might be interested in."

"What did he look like?"

"Hm, Hispanic I think? But pretty light-skinned. He had a giant cross necklace on, if that helps."

CHAPTER 42
VERONICA

Morning, March 11

I did not enjoy the feeling one bit.

I've been called a lot of things in my life, many of them hitting that elusive sweet spot of hurtful and true, but never have I been publicly "exposed" as a jilted lover.

I was not someone who got embarrassed. I was definitely not someone who was in any way humiliated. The idea that I would be the butt of a joke was anathema to my very core.

And yet I couldn't stop myself from scrolling. Joke after joke, laugh after laugh, on all my socials. *Ben Walsh finally found a woman who won't go all praying mantis and kill him after mating.*

Fuel to the fire if I did anything, so I knew the only option was to grin and bear it. Especially since I knew that was Mikaela in the picture, and the idea of Ben doing anything untoward, especially in her current state, was laughable. Let them think what they want. None of them knew the true me anyway.

Everyone's got an opinion, though, right?

My phone rang, and I looked down to see which of the two obvious candidates was calling me first. Mikaela, of course. Ben was likely too nervous now that this was public.

"Hi, Mikaela." I put on my most pleasant, devil-may-care voice.

"Veronica, you've got to know that was entirely not what it looks like." Mikaela's words raced out of her mouth as if the green flag at the Indy 500 had just been waved.

"Mikaela, relax, it's okay. Ben already told me who you are. He told me quite a bit, actually."

"Oh my gosh, I'm so relieved." I could hear the tension drain from her voice.

"So, sister-in-law, huh? Didn't realize we had a family affair going on." Friendly voice, hint of humor in the tone. I'm the unflappable one, I'm always cool and collected. I don't get to fly off the handle and say *what the fuck, how did you not say anything?!* no matter how much I might want to. I guess that's how it goes when everything thinks you might just start murdering people at the drop of a hat.

"I, uh, I'm sorry about that, Veronica." Her voice did sound genuinely sorry. "I didn't even know if I was going to tell Ben when I showed up at your door that first time. I just wanted to see what it was all like, the life you could end up with if our father actually cared about you."

"I get it. I really do." I didn't. But I always tried to empathize. Growing up the way I did meant there was a lot I didn't understand about normal childhoods.

"Look, Veronica, that's not actually why I called, though."

Oh, really? "Go on."

"I just felt like you should know, since it sort of affected you when it happened..."

"What happened?" So much for that green flag waving. Speed it up.

"Well, I just talked to the police, and they were saying how these deaths might all be connected, and that seemed to make sense since Tony and Bridget were friends in college. But I swear to gosh I didn't think this at all until today."

"Think what, Mikaela?"

"Well, Tracy Belle was in the same friend group with Tony and Bridget. Doesn't that seem suspicious?"

I could feel the color drain from my face. Good thing this was a phone conversation, because even I wasn't good enough to hide that reaction. "Tracy Belle, as in the Belle family who died in the car crash?"

"Yeah, that's her."

What. The fuck.

"Three people from a close group of friends at Georgetown, all dead now, of course we're going to look into it, Veronica."

Here I was again, talking to the police. I spent decades of my life avoiding all law enforcement, and my life was the better for it. And yet now it was like we were on speed dial. "Okay, Detective, I get that. But listen to what you're saying. If this is actually true, if there is some connection here, then you're accusing Jacob Jordan of being a… what? A serial killer? What would the term even be?"

"I thought you'd know, Veronica, considering what we might call you," Detective Brown said.

Rude. Not necessarily untrue, though. I liked it more when people just spoke their feelings straight to my face. None of the cowardly whispers.

"Anyway, Veronica," the detective continued. "I'm following clues. That's the fucking job. People end up dead, and I try to find out who did it."

I'd never heard Emilia raise her voice, and I couldn't think of how to respond.

"Look, I get that you think you have some sort of stake in this, but I'm going to keep doing my job, so would you please let me get back to it?"

I muttered an assent, and she hung up the phone.

Could I be wrong? Was Jacob actually a murderer?

I was so rarely wrong. I didn't recognize the feeling. Regret? Embarrassment?

My mind carried me back to our first meeting. I was standing in front of the chalkboard at the end of the first day of introductory linear algebra. I had my back to the class as I erased the lesson's notes. Hours of prep work, knowledge passed along to students via multicolored chalk, then immediately wiped away, a clean slate for the next class.

"Excuse me, Dr. Walsh?"

I turned around to see a shy, handsome boy dressed in a black polo shirt and khaki shorts standing below the raised stage. His blonde hair flopped over his right ear, and he had a crisp line shaved through the opposite side. Clearly a fresh, first-day-of-the-semester, I-have-to-make-a-good-impression-on-my-peers haircut.

I smiled down at him, brushing the chalk off my white pants—*pro tip, don't ever wear black when teaching with a chalkboard*. "How can I help you?"

He extended his hand and offered a solid, hearty handshake. Not the type I usually got from cautious students, working up the courage to introduce themselves after day one. "My name is Jacob. I'm a freshman, and I wanted to say I'm thankful to be in this class. I'm excited for the semester."

"Jacob, my lone freshman in the class of almost entirely sophomores. I thought you might say hi." I had studied my class roster as always, the week before classes. It wasn't unheard of for a freshman to be in a linear algebra class, but it was rare enough that I'd made a mental note to keep an eye out.

I always gave an early quiz, exhaustive but for very few points overall. Just a diagnostic so I could get a sense of the level of the class. Several matrix manipulations, some theoretical true/false (plus explanations!) questions, designed to really test them. Most students got between 60% and 80% correct.

Jacob absolutely nailed it. Calculations all perfect, and brilliant reasoning for the true/falses. I'd seen perfect scores before, but never one with such depth.

I pulled him aside after handing back the graded quizzes. "Look," I said in a quiet voice, doing my best to make it seem like just a casual chat to the other students walking out. "That score. You know what you're doing, and you've got the ability to go far in this field. When you're making any decision about your future, come talk to me first."

I watched as his eyebrows shot up and his eyes sparkled.

"Thank you, professor," he said, pushing his hair out of his eyes. "I will, I promise."

He kept that promise.

I mentored him through cyclic groups, finite fields, the Chinese Remainder Theorem, Galois theory, and more. He gobbled it all up. When it was time to think about post-grad life, I pushed hard for him to continue in academia. I was thrilled when he said he was headed to the University of Michigan for graduate school. When he left after his master's degree and started working outside academia, I was saddened but understood. He was the type to make immediate impacts, not take years on our more esoteric research projects.

I knew that sweet boy had made a huge mistake when he caused the car accident that killed the Belle family. I was the only one who believed that he wasn't the mastermind behind the President Leishear assassination attempt before that whole messy truth unfurled itself.

But now? I didn't know what to believe about Jacob Jordan anymore.

CHAPTER 43
EMILIA

Midday, March 11

Emilia was about to lose it. She hadn't meant to jump down Veronica Walsh's throat, but she had just about had it with people—*Iverson*—questioning her. If she heard one more *'wait, so why are we doing this?'* she was going to lose her shit.

Why are we looking into Jacob Jordan? Because when you find a lead, you chase it.

Would it be better if it weren't Jacob going on a multi-year killing spree? Yeah, she'd sure say so. But you don't get into homicide if you're into happy endings. Best case scenario was catching a perp who planned to kill again, because at least you could consider it a life saved. All the rest was simply punishing someone for a heinous deed after the fact.

That's what this job is, Iverson. She looked over at her partner, suspiciously quiet, her head hidden behind her computer. Emilia didn't know if Iverson had it in her. She was too bubbly, took things too personally. This job was going to crush her.

Emilia pulled up the file on Jacob Jordan. She was surprised by how sparse it was. For months, everyone wanted to know what made him tick. Both talk news radio and the unwashed masses online speculated wildly, and it drove ratings like mad. But no one was able to find anything noteworthy.

Jacob Jordan, twenty-six years old, born in Valley Forge, Pennsylvania, to Betsy and Mitch Jordan. One older sister, Janet. Emilia remembered that his family shut out reporters completely. She couldn't really blame them. No one wanted to hear their story, they just wanted blood.

Jacob graduated as valedictorian from Great Valley High School, reportedly well-liked by jocks and nerds alike. His calculus teacher, Mrs. Sandworthy, sang his praises to the heavens and it was her influence that led him to be a math major at Georgetown. He double majored in Mathematics and International Politics, mentored by none other than Dr. Veronica Walsh.

After graduation, he was accepted into the University of Michigan's Applied and Interdisciplinary Mathematics program. He got a master's degree in two years and then moved back to the D.C. area, where he began working at the Johns Hopkins University Applied Physics Lab. From then on there was nothing interesting; coworkers said he was friendly but not outgoing, he paid all his taxes, nothing out of the ordinary.

Until the night he crashed his car into the Belle family's convertible, knocking it off the road and into a pond, where three of them lost their lives.

That no one ever caught him for that still boggled Emilia's mind. No one except Jeremy Wiles, who just happened to have been nearby and seen the incident.

That Wiles filed that information away for use later was a perfect encapsulation of him as a person, Emilia thought.

It never made sense to Emilia, even with Wiles' full confession, why Jacob went through with Wiles' blackmail plan. Any number of things could have gone wrong, and he could have easily been shot and killed by the Secret Service before Wiles got to 'heroically' save the day.

After a year in prison, the truth of Wiles' plan finally came out, and Jacob's role as the patsy was revealed. Emilia wondered now if Jacob's silence the entire time was a ploy, a trick intentionally done so as to garner sympathy when it was decided what to do with him. A low-security facility that he could easily escape from.

Risky, but maybe his only move.

Now she had to go back to the start. The inciting event that put Jacob on the map, if only to Wiles in that moment. Did Jacob cause the car accident on purpose, and, if so, why?

She stood up with more force than she meant, knocking her chair backwards. Iverson's head whipped around.

"Grab that and come with me," she said to her partner, indicating the file on the Belle car accident. "We can read the full report, but I think it'll be better to go see it with our own eyes."

"What are we looking at here?"

Emilia had to admit, this time Iverson's question was a good one. She'd forgotten that they'd redeveloped the area for the new Potomac Yard metro stop. She didn't get down into Virginia much and hadn't thought anything of the news about the additional stop on the blue line.

The pair stood on the eastside curb of Atlantic Avenue. The pond was gone, the slope down toward it sodded over. If you didn't know a pond used to be there, you'd have no way of knowing.

"Well, nothing useful." Emilia shook her head and rubbed her eyes. "We can't recreate shit looking at it like this. What do you think, Iverson? Any snap judgments?"

"I don't get it." Iverson shrugged. "I know it was at night so it was dark, and accidents can happen anywhere, but it just doesn't look like a spot where a deadly accident should happen. This is a fender-bender place."

Emilia nodded slowly. "I'm with you. Follow that thread, then."

Iverson extended a long, slender finger. "Well, if the pond were here, I'd be looking at literally only one way this could turn deadly. They'd have to have been hit with considerable force at exactly the right moment to make them careen off the road and toward the pond.

There's a full sidewalk here—a simple missed blind spot should not have forced them all the way down."

"I agree, good observations," Emilia said and watched Iverson's cheeks flush. "Two things. Force of the impact, and location. Both have to be precise to turn this from an annoying hit and run to a multiple-casualty accident."

"I…" Iverson hesitated.

Emilia made a 'keep going' motion with her hand. "Voice the thought," she said.

"This is no accident. This is vehicular homicide."

CHAPTER 44
VERONICA

Afternoon, March 11

Mikaela sat on her couch, while I paced, full of nervous energy. I didn't think that I had the capacity to be surprised anymore. Nothing could shock someone who'd seen more as a child than most adults could stomach. "Why didn't you say anything before?"

"About Tracy? Well, it wasn't exactly important, was it?"

She was right, although I didn't want to admit it. She came to me for help finding her missing husband and hoping to learn a bit more about her long-lost stepbrother in the process. Nowhere in there was there room for a discussion of one of her husband's college friends who happened to be killed by someone I once taught. "I need to tell you something, that I didn't think you needed to hear before now."

She looked at me with wary eyes. "What is it?"

"There's a much clearer connection than you already know. Detective Brown found out who was following you, the man from the bridge."

Mikaela gaped and then narrowed her eyes. "Wait, how could you not tell me this before?"

I sighed. I knew she would be upset, and that my answer would likely not placate her. "You had just found out your husband was dead. I didn't think you needed any more surprises in that moment."

"Tell me."

"Jacob Jordan. My former student, and the man who caused the car crash that killed Tracy Belle."

Mikaela put her hand to her mouth. "Holy shit."

I nodded grimly. "So, help me out with Tracy's connection to Tony. Tell me everything."

"Well, I don't know *that* much. Like I said, he was always guarded about college and his friends from then. But I remember when he heard that she and her parents died, his face turned white. We were just mindlessly trolling on our phones and had the news on the TV, and he dropped his phone. It landed on the floor with a loud bang, and I got mad at him because I was worried that he'd broken the screen. It was a new phone," she added, as if that was important info to me. "Their names didn't mean anything to me—I'm not a big sports fan—but clearly, they did to him. I assumed it must have been the sports connection, but he explained to me that Tracy had been his friend."

I perched myself on the corner of the couch. "How did he meet her?"

"I probably would've never known, but he talked a bit more about her after that. Each time he drank, it was like there was a battle waging inside him as to whether to talk about her or not. He said they met through Lindsey. I don't think it was a sorority thing, but some organization that the two of them were in? Anyway, then Lindsey introduced Tony and Tracy at some party, and they hit it off."

"But what doesn't make sense to me is that if this has something to do with Jacob, how does he know them? He's several years younger. I don't get it." Like any good mathematician, I understood probabilities well. I also understood how the innumerate frequently thought they understood them but would use them horribly.

The Monty Hall problem is the classic example. Given three doors, with a car behind one, you choose a door. The game show host opens a different door, with no car. He asks you: do you want to change your pick now?

Very few people have the intuitive understanding that changing your pick doubles your odds. You *absolutely* want to change your pick.

The probability question that snuck into my head and wouldn't leave was this: what are the odds these current murders happened—with a clear reference to the Belle family estate—and weren't connected to the car accident? Jacob escaping from prison, three close friends from Georgetown all dead, how astronomically coincidental would it be if Jacob weren't involved?

One of the proudest moments of my academic career was watching Jacob accept our department's highest honors award. He asked me if I would be the one to present it, and I had never known a student more fitting of the honor.

After the presentation, I stood alongside my friend Dan—Dr. Flint to the students—who leaned over to me, and said, "It's incredible, you know."

"He really is." I beamed.

"Yes, that, of course." he chuckled. "But I meant that I can't believe I haven't gotten the chance to teach him once. I kept waiting to see his name on a roster of mine, and yet somehow it never worked out."

"Well, I am sorry for your loss." I didn't know what else to say.

I thought about what my life would be like if I hadn't met Jacob. Not decidedly different, I recognized, but lacking a certain spark.

That's the thing that every teacher understands. Students give you energy. You're in charge of the class, but they drive it. They are the heart and soul of the classroom, and they make just as much an impression on you as you do on them.

Jacob was the brightest light. Not just the smartest kid—every class has one of them. But the intellectual curiosity, the creativity of thought, even the humility. I'd never seen anything like it. He was eager and engaged, charismatic to classmates and professors alike.

For how charming he was, I always wondered why he entered class alone. He never had friends or a partner with him. He arrived alone, he left alone. I assumed he must have trouble connecting outside the classroom with people not as smart as him, which included just about everyone else on campus.

Everyone else on campus.

I couldn't believe the question hadn't jumped into my mind immediately. "Mikaela, who else was in this friend group? Who else is in danger?"

Mikaela's eyes widened and she opened and then closed her mouth. "I—he only talked about Bridget and Tracy."

"It was just a group of three?" That didn't sit right with me.

"I don't think so," Mikaela said, running her hand through her hair and sighing. "But I can't think of any others."

"Did he have any memorabilia or anything from college? Keepsakes, items he couldn't get rid of? Does Georgetown have yearbooks?" I was a little embarrassed that after all my years there I couldn't actually remember if they did or not.

"Wait." Mikaela's head shot up. "Of course. That yearbook with the dumb name that Georgetown does. It's called 'Doomsday something' I think? We definitely have that somewhere here."

She jumped up to her feet and ran upstairs. I imagined her heading into some dusty attic, blowing off cobwebs until she found the book she was looking for. She'd likely be up there for a while, searching around. Flipping through old boxes until she finally uncovered the right one, memories flooding back as she looked at each item. I let my mind wander. Maybe today would be the day Ben came back home. After the shock of finding out he had a half-sister, maybe he'd realize the importance of family—

"I found it!"

Okay, that was faster than expected. She thudded back down the stairs—*why is it always the lightest people who are heaviest on their feet?* —and plopped a book onto the coffee table with a large clunk.

"Ye Domesday Booke," I read. "You're right, that's not great."

I flipped open the pages, quickly realizing the futility of the venture. This wasn't a high school yearbook that cataloged every student. It was a volunteer exercise. Only seniors who made a point to sit for a picture were included. I could feel my frustration rising. I looked over at Mikaela, sitting uncharacteristically quiet next to me, hiding something small inside her hand.

"What is that?"

She hesitated for a second, then unfolded the piece of paper and held it up. "A picture. It slipped out from between a couple pages when I picked the book up."

I pulled her hand toward me to get a better look. It was a print of a digital picture, probably from Facebook. It should have been a full-sized piece of printer paper but it had been ripped down the middle. What was left showed three people in swimsuits posing at the edge of a backyard pool. Bridget was on the left, with Tony next to her, and Tracy to his right. They had their arms around each other's waists and their mouths were open with laughter.

"It's only the three of them," Mikaela said. "Maybe it was some event, but he just wanted to keep the picture of his friends?"

"That doesn't make sense, ripping it is such a violent act. Cropping has been around for a while now, he could've just done that. Who is this person, then?" I pointed to the jagged edge, where about half of another woman was visible. Tracy's arm extended behind her back. She was shorter than the other three, with a dark tan, providing a stark contrast to her white bathing suit.

Mikaela snatched the picture back and held it up close to her face. "I can't tell, but you're right, she was definitely part of the picture."

"You don't recognize her, do you?"

"How can I?" Mikaela shook her head. "You can barely see any of her face."

"She looks like a friend, though, doesn't she?" I couldn't remember a time I had ever stood, arm in arm, with someone who wasn't a close friend.

"That means whoever this woman is, she's in serious danger."

CHAPTER 45
EMILIA

Afternoon, March 11

"I think you're ready."

Emilia glanced at Iverson, knowing what she was implying. She didn't like that Iverson waited until they were seated in the chief's office to mention it, though. This young woman was growing more backbone by the day.

Maybe Emilia had misjudged her. She didn't think she was a snob—she just saw a timid young detective who asked too many questions, and she decided she already knew the path laid out for her, just because that wasn't the way Emilia had been when she first started out.

Imposter syndrome was anathema to her. You get hired for the job, so you can do the job. If you don't think you can do the job, then don't apply in the first place.

All right, maybe she was a snob.

"Ready for what, Detective?" Chief Branaman asked.

Emilia took a deep breath. "Ready to go public. Jacob Jordan is the suspect in these homicides, and no one even knows he's out of prison."

Branaman raised an eyebrow. "You want to tell the public he's out?"

Emilia nodded resolutely.

"Even though we aren't sure he is our guy? What makes you confident enough to say to the press he is the main suspect?"

"We won't say *that*." Iverson's voice lingered on the last word.

"Oh?" A questioning stare from Branaman. "And pray tell, what are we going to say?"

"Just a simple person of interest, potentially armed and dangerous," Emilia answered for her. "An implication of the top suspect, sure, because we're not bringing out the press for anyone else, but subtle enough to walk back just in case."

"Okay, what is our case against him?" Branaman asked.

Emilia recapped what they knew about him.

"That's all circumstantial at this point," came the expected reply.

Emilia shrugged. "It is. But this isn't just a homicide investigation. This is the most high-profile homicide we've had in a while, committed by someone who isn't stopping. We have to be more proactive here. We can't wait."

Iverson nodded enthusiastically, a bit too golden retriever, with her pigtails bouncing up and down, but Emilia appreciated the support.

Branaman sat, silent. He puffed his cheeks in and out. He bit at his bottom lip. Finally, he gave a resigned shake of his head. "I don't like going too strong too fast, but you're right."

Emilia was so exhausted she almost missed her recliner and collapsed on the tiled floor when she returned to her apartment in Takoma Park. Branaman had insisted she run the press conference. It made sense, of course, but that didn't mean she had to enjoy it. Public speaking wasn't her forte. At least the sharp back and forth with reporters was fun—well, as fun as the circumstances could make it. They threw out their 'gotcha' questions, and she swatted them aside.

Yes, the public should be wary of all *people, not solely this guy, thank you uppity news reporter.*

They had gone ahead and plastered Jacob's face all over the city. Every electronic billboard now also showed his prison picture, along with a mockup based on the beard and trucker cap description from

Tony's widow. If someone knew him, they'd see it. Whether they acted upon that, that was a different story entirely.

Emilia had left Iverson at the office, telling her that it was important at least one of them was available at all times. She'd get a few hours of sleep and then go spell Iverson for the wee hours of the morning.

She felt hopeful, cautiously optimistic. She was chagrined that they even had to be chasing Jacob when he should've stayed in jail—who agreed he should have been moved to such a low security facility anyway? —but she felt confident that they were on the right track.

She took a quick shot of vodka, a vice learned from a semester-long study abroad in St. Petersburg and reclined back fully. This wasn't a night for the bed. It would be too hard to wake up from. But at least in her recliner she'd get a couple hours of blessed sleep.

Bzzz.

Her eyes were closed for mere seconds before the godforsaken cell phone rang. She heaved herself up and said an irate hello.

"Wow, you okay Brown?"

"What is it, Iverson?" Emilia grumbled and shook her head.

"You'll want to hear this. We just got our first legit call in post-conference."

Emilia jolted up. She hadn't been *this* confident, but the adrenaline she could hear in Iverson's voice told her to pay attention. "Talk to me."

"Wayne Howard, a resident of Alexandria, called in. He says he drove across the bridge and saw Tony on it before he went over. And get this, he says a man matching Jacob's description was standing there with him."

CHAPTER 46
VERONICA

Night, March 11

I was about to turn the lights out. The kids had bathed, and we'd read another chapter of The Number Devil. I'd be damned if I waited until it was more "age appropriate," my kids are going to be math savants. The correct number of stuffed animals had been placed in each bed (five for Nico, eight for Maria).

My mother had gone home, after I'd convinced her that the ball was now in my court. Whenever I needed Ben to come back, he would. She was still furious with him, but they'd have to take that up later. I didn't envy Ben for the conversations he would be subject to during our next family holiday. He'd made his bed, though.

Creeeeek.

The unmistakable sound of our front door opening. That old door that either Ben or I mentioned we needed to fix every time we pushed it open when returning home.

I froze. The door was always locked. This wasn't someone accidentally breaking in, not knowing what house this was.

Protect the kids.

I quickly whispered goodnight, and pulled their door shut, reaching around to lock it from the inside. That would slow the intruder down if I couldn't. Hubris got you killed—I never assumed I could better an assailant. If all went well, I'd easily just pick the lock afterward to reopen the door.

I wanted to flip the hallway light switch off, but that would give away my position. I glanced down the hall, looking for the closest weapon. I used to hide them all over the house, but as every parent will tell you, toddlers will always find the most dangerous thing you have. Once the twins could walk, I had to scale it back.

Calm breaths. Deep breaths.

I could feel my heart thumping. I never told anyone, not even my birth father, but there was a reason I did all of my work for him during the day.

I don't do well at night.

Decades later, and I'm still haunted by the moment my brother died. And in that way that the brain does, a connection was made. Bad things happen in the dark.

I was not the same calm killer I was in the daytime. I looked down, because I could feel my hands shaking. Even though I had the light upstairs, this was still a battle that would be waged in darkness, I knew it.

I pulled a frame off the wall. *Sorry,* I whispered, looking at my kids' faces, smiling back at me in their kindergarten portraits. I smashed the glass against my knee, and carefully palmed the biggest shard.

I heard a loud crash downstairs. I flinched but didn't make a move. I knew the ploy. Draw the victim out.

That shit doesn't work on me. I make my own moves.

Just because I was frightened didn't mean I was helpless.

If it weren't for Nico and Maria, I would climb out a window, turn the tables around on the intruder. But I wasn't going to leave them unprotected, even behind a locked door.

I waited, listening intently. All the lights were still off downstairs, so if I came downstairs, backlit from the upstairs hallway, I'd be a sitting duck.

The light had to go off. By now he'd know I was upstairs anyway. I squeezed my eyes shut as hard as I could for ten seconds, to make the adjustment to darkness easier, and then swung my arm up and flicked the light off.

Without hesitation, I launched myself down the stairs, rolling over the banister as I got down to the bottom few steps and landing without a sound in the hall below.

I crawled to the living room, staying as low as possible. When your house is being broken into, surprise is one of your few allies. My eyes were still adjusting, and I knew I wouldn't be able to see as well as the intruder.

Make your disadvantage your advantage. Dad used to drill that into me. When I was young, my disadvantage was clear. I was a small and relatively slight teenage girl, going up against fully grown adults. That was an easy one to turn into an advantage. I could be invisible, and I would never need to engage in hand-to-hand combat. If you're a ghost, they can't hit you.

He would likely know where I was. But he wouldn't know I knew that. Second order knowledge—or lack thereof—was the deadliest weapon.

Make it your advantage.

He couldn't be in the kitchen. I'd seen enough as I hurdled the banister to know that. So that's where I'd go next. Draw him out.

Our townhouse was not big, and the only other egresses were out the back. Both sides were made of concrete and brick. The dining room was straight ahead as I snuck back to the main hallway, its door as of yet untouched. The kitchen was off to the left, with its own door exiting to the back patio. He wasn't in the kitchen, and no doors had been opened, so there was only one option. There were no hiding places in the dining room, so if he was waiting for me, he would be against the wall, just beyond the threshold. If this was who I thought it was, he would be to my right, because he knows I am right-handed.

If I were alone, I'd have the clear advantage. There were two exits, and with him still indoors, he could not cover them both. Once we were outside, it would be a level playing field, and no matter the darkness, equal conditions favored me every time.

That hand-to-hand fighting that used to be a weakness? No longer. Plus, I've gotten pretty handy with that knife throwing trick. I've never tried it with a shard of glass, but it's all about the balance of weight.

Even though I missed when Jeremy Wiles attacked me in my hideout in Yorktown last year, I was enthused to see I hadn't lost the skill.

I straightened up and turned into the kitchen, offering my back to the intruder. If he knew who I was—and how could he not? —then he would know that's not something I would ever do willingly.

And yet. It's a fatal human flaw. Everyone thinks that they're the one who will catch their opponent slipping. No matter how often it fails, how often others turned up dead in my past, the next guy always thought he could outsmart me.

He'd let me into the kitchen. A cardinal rule of breaking and entering: don't let your victim access deadly weapons. I didn't need the shard of glass when I could now reach the steak knives. Those would fly hard and true.

But I didn't want to kill him. I didn't want to maim him. I wanted answers.

I reached out in the dark, the moonlight coming through the kitchen door guiding me, and snagged a fileting knife. Easier to palm, just as dangerous when used right.

But for my purposes, any would do.

I froze in place, listening. No one realizes how loudly they breathe until they have to be silent. He was still in the dining room. Still waiting.

I started to tap the knife on the kitchen counter. A soft tap first, then growing steadily louder. He needed to know the situation he'd gotten himself into.

This is how you turn your other disadvantage into an advantage. I don't like the dark, I don't feel comfortable in it. But only I knew that. My birth father taught me long ago to internalize my disadvantages. They're a burden enough, he would say, without your enemies knowing them.

The backdoor swung open, and I turned and raced out of the kitchen. I caught a glimpse of the man, dressed in all black of course, with a balaclava covering his face. As I got to the backdoor, he hurdled over the fence and out of sight.

That was it.

I could run for days, and I knew I could have caught him if I tried. The younger, rasher version of me would have.

But I couldn't guarantee he wasn't alone. I had to protect my kids. I had to let him go.

I kept the knife in my hand, but I allowed the tension to drain from my body. I walked back inside through the dining room, turned on the light, and went past the kitchen, and to the living room. The front door wasn't broken, and I was going to check the lock for signs it had been picked, but my eyes caught a glimpse of something on the couch.

I tossed our cheesy Old Town Alexandria branded throw pillow away and found an index card. I flipped it over and read the handwritten note. *I don't want to hurt you, but I will hurt him.*

"Fuck," I whispered, picking up my phone. Come on. Answer the phone. Don't be asleep.

"V?" Ben said, groggily.

I breathed out a sigh of relief. "You have to come home, right now, Ben."

"What is it, V?"

He tried to hide his sleepy voice, but I could tell I had woken him up. It felt nice to know he wasn't out having a grand old time.

"The house was broken into, and they left a threat against you. Get here right now. Turn your phone tracker on so I can watch it as you come. Do it now."

Ben arrived half an hour later. I sat outside Nico and Maria's room the entire time, their door unlocked again, watching his progression on my phone.

Once he arrived, I came downstairs and opened the door, welcoming him in. He gave me a hug and I let him peck me on the cheek.

He went right to the fridge and pulled out a beer. He cracked it open on the edge of the counter. "What's going on?" He asked, taking a long swig.

I handed him the note. His mouth twitched as he read it.

"This—this is Jacob Jordan, isn't it?"

"I think it has to be. And that has to be a reference to you."

Ben leaned his head backward and looked up at the wood-beamed ceiling. "Jesus Christ," he breathed out. "This confirms it, doesn't it? Jacob is the one behind all of this."

"I still don't know," I confessed. "It definitely looks that way, though. What I'm not fully settled on is his involvement in the rest of what's been going on. His car was the one following Mikaela away from the scene of Tony's fall, and now he was here threatening me off. I've been working with Mikaela, so this still could all just be related to Tony. Remember, there's still nothing explicit connecting Tony to Bridget and Senator Billingsley. Maybe we're looking at two different things happening."

"What does Jacob have to do with Tony anyway?"

I rubbed my forehead. "I really don't know yet. My gut says something about Georgetown, but that's all I've got right now."

"Hey." Ben reached out and touched my forearm. "How are you doing, really?"

"I've been better," I admitted. I felt jumpy. I had a possible murderer—a man I once considered a friend—in my house threatening my family.

I studied Ben. He was hastily dressed in what he liked to call workleisure. Stretch-fit chino pants and a performance polo. He looked good, though. Well-rested, bright-eyed. That's what running away from your parenting responsibilities for five days will do for you.

"Look, we're going to have some shit to talk about, but for now, you need to be back here. You can feel as uncomfortable as you like about it, but I know how to protect myself and you don't. I'm not having you get killed just because you didn't want to accept my past."

He had the good sense to look chagrined. "Did Nico and Maria sleep through it all?"

"As far as I know."

"Then we can just tell them tomorrow. I'll explain again that I was away for work."

"Good. They don't need any more upheaval than they've already had. And Ben, I'm going to ask Francisco to tail you. If Jacob is serious about trying to harm you, Francisco will stop it. I'm not going to take no for an answer."

CHAPTER 47
EMILIA

Morning, March 12

"What's the connection? What ties it all together?" Emilia was back in front of her trusty board. The pictures of the three Belles who died in the car crash had been added. She pointed at them one by one. "Jacob kills a family, save for Miranda, who then is killed later. After he gets out, he kills a Senator and another Georgetown student, writing notes about something that happened at World's Edge, and he pushes another off the bridge, but there's no note."

"Something happened at World's Edge," Iverson repeated. "It could make sense—college kids there because of Tracy, a senator there because of the parents."

"Exactly. But where does Jacob fit in? What does he have to do with whatever happened?" Emilia rapped on Jacob's picture with her knuckle. "That's the key we're missing."

"He's what? Three years younger than the others?"

"Five," Emilia corrected. "So, he wouldn't have overlapped at all with them at Georgetown."

"Bridget and Tony both weren't from the area. If they were at World's Edge, then it stands to reason that it was during college." Iverson folded her arms across her chest.

Emilia nodded along. "Agreed, and the key here is why was the Senator there? Having your friends over at your parents' mansion near your school makes sense. From what we know of Ulrich and Yvonne, they sound like they would have let that happen. He cultivated a friendly and welcoming public persona, so no reason to think that wasn't how he was in private."

"Could Jacob have known Miranda?" Iverson pointed at the board, holding onto her to-go coffee cup with her other fingers. "We know she wasn't killed by Jacob, but she was the same age."

"Good point. Jacob also wasn't from here, but we should run that down. Maybe there's a connection. Look into his high school years."

"What are you going to do?"

"*We* are going back to Senator Billingsley's office. You're doing that Jacob research after. First, we need to find out what the staff know of his connection to the Belles."

"Uh oh," Iverson whispered, her eyes flitting behind them. A lumbering figure made his way down the hall.

"Almost made it out the door." Emilia raised an eyebrow and grinned. "I've been avoiding him since Branaman made the switch."

"You guys are still on the Billingsley case, aren't you?" Fahey stopped just a little too close to them.

"Of course," Iverson quipped, stepping in between Emilia and Fahey. "You can't possibly have forgotten that."

Protecting her own. Emilia felt like a proud teacher.

"What's the latest?"

He was trying so hard not to sound desperate, and somehow that had the opposite effect. Emilia couldn't believe she almost felt bad for him. "Running down leads, trying to piece clues together, you know the drill." She shrugged. "How are your cases going?"

"As if you give a shit about the Leonard Barry case."

"Where are you on that? We had only just started."

"You're not still trying to work that crazy Belle family angle, are you?" he asked, instead. A patronizing look down his nose followed the question.

Nice reminder why I shouldn't feel bad, Emilia thought. "As I'm sure you're aware, we are pursuing the possibility that it is connected, especially since their car accident was almost certainly murder."

"It was what?" He shook his head vigorously. "That's crazy! No one would kill them!"

A realization dawned in Emilia's mind. "Fahey, did you know the Belles?"

He grimaced. "I knew Ulrich, okay? He was a good guy, and I don't like his name being dragged into this."

There it was. Nothing annoyed Emilia more than biases in detective work. She reached up and put her hand on his shoulder and, mimicking his patronizing tone, said, "Fahey, I'm going to investigate this because that's my job. You know better than anyone I'm very good at it. I'd suggest you stay out of my way."

CHAPTER 48
VERONICA

Morning, March 12

I was always an all-or-nothing girl. There wasn't really any other way to be, the way I grew up. So now that Ben was back under our roof, I was going to move forward, and consider the whole situation done. If he wanted to keep sulking about the whole private detective thing, then that was on him, and he could talk to me about it whenever he wanted.

He was an all-or-nothing guy, though. He hadn't said anything yet, but I could see the way he looked at me, kept sneaking glances when he thought I wasn't looking. The kind eyes were back. The loving look. It was like he was seeing the full version of me, secret prologue and all, for the first time. A complete work, and he understood it.

"Question for you," I said, sitting across the kitchen table from him as we both drank our coffee. The initial excitement of having dad home had passed, and the kids were in the living room playing with magnetic blocks.

"Fire away." His face gave nothing away.

"I've got a ripped picture, where I can only see half a face. I know the other people in the picture but need to find out who the woman is whose face was ripped. How would you go about doing it?"

He stroked his chin and looked up at the ceiling. Men love that. It makes them think they look erudite. The societally acceptable possibility of hair growth there means only they get to do it, apparently. It just wouldn't carry the same gravitas if I did it.

"What's the context?"

"Three Georgetown students standing by a pool in someone's backyard."

"Okay, so likely the fourth is a Georgetown student too."

Such incredible insight. "Well, yeah, I'd actually made that leap too," I said, shooting him a side-eye.

"Okay, so did you look up their class roster? I think you can find that online in their archives, or you could talk to someone at the registrar who could get it for you, I'm sure."

"That's not a bad idea. I've looked through socials and can't find anyone who looks like her."

"Can I see the picture?"

I hesitated. He must have known we were talking about my work with Mikaela, but we hadn't spoken it outright.

"It's fine," he said, sensing my hesitation. "I know who this is for. I want to help."

"Because she's your sister, or because you've decided you're okay with my new venture?"

He waved his hand in the air, a vague gesture I couldn't follow. "A little bit of both, I guess? She was done dirty for so long by my family that I feel an obligation to help."

"And…?"

He smiled with a warmth I had not seen in weeks. "And I'm not willing to give you up that easily. I still have my reservations, but I'll work through them."

"Thank you," I said, handing over the photocopy that Mikaela made me of the picture.

He took it, studying it closely. "Isn't that—?"

"Tracy Belle?"

"Yeah."

"Good eye. She and Tony and Bridget—the woman murdered over in Burke—were all friends. I assume that picture is at the Belles' mansion. I need to know who that fourth woman is."

"Jesus Christ."

"I know. This thing is growing fast."

"Exponentially?" He smirked, anticipating my response.

I groaned. "I hate it when that is used wrong. Do people not realize that exponential growth starts slow and the fast exponential growth they always mean is after the initial part—"

"That t-shirt lying on the sun lounger behind them." He was animatedly pointing past the figures in the picture.

"What?"

"The shirt."

"What about it?"

"Take a look. Tell me if I'm wrong, but doesn't that look like the Alexander Hamilton Society logo?" He handed the photo back across the table to me.

I squinted and held it up close to my face. "I can't tell what it says."

Ben was one of those men who was blessed with perfect vision seemingly just for the fun of it. No cavities, great skin, all the genetic home runs. "Look at the top left. We've all seen *Hamilton* now, you're telling me you can't make out that profile?"

"We don't know whose it is, any of them could have been in it," I said. This was a good lead, though. Much better than anything I'd gotten to so far.

The Alexander Hamilton Society was a nonpartisan foreign affairs-oriented student group named for the founding father. With chapters at dozens of schools across the country, it helped guide students interested in foreign policy into fulfilling careers.

I pulled up their website, found the contact email, and fired off a quick note asking if I could see their list of members.

"Knowing that Bridget Lowe wanted to be a diplomat, I wonder if that's just hers," I said, feeling the adrenaline in my body evaporate.

"Could be, but nothing ventured, hey?" Ben said. "And who knows, maybe you're about to crack this whole thing wide open."

CHAPTER 49
EMILIA

Morning, March 12

Emilia took a seat and looked around the office. It was sparse, but often that was the case for Senators. This wasn't a campaign office, or any other outward facing space. This was the inner sanctum, where the sausages were made.

No one cared how many pictures of family, or college diplomas were hung on the wall.

Iverson shuffled in behind and pulled the door closed.

"We're glad you could meet us," Emilia said to the man behind the desk.

He had a tousle of brown hair, and his face retained the baby fat that only privilege begot. He wore a navy blazer with a pink bow tie. Since he didn't stand to greet them when they arrived, Emilia could not confirm her guess that his feet were covered by boat shoes.

"We in the Billingsley bunch always have time for law enforcement," he said. "If you want resistance, you'll have to go across the aisle." He sat back, smiling smugly at his joke.

"You are...," Emilia made a show of checking her notes, pretending she didn't remember his name. "Edwin March, chief of staff, is that correct?"

He momentarily deflated but quickly regained his composure. "That is correct."

"Mr. March, we were hoping you would be able to tell us about all the meetings that took place between Senator Billingsley and Ulrich or Yvonne Belle, including at the Belle household, World's Edge."

He smiled wide, a pasty and patronizing gesture. "Now, detective, that is a big ask. We have had lots of meetings over the years, as I'm sure you understand."

"Okay, let's start with an easier question, then. Can you show me the latest correspondence between Billingsley and the Belles, via email?"

March made a big show of slowly turning toward the computer. He clicked a couple times, typed in a word quickly. "I'm sorry, there is no correspondence," he said, shaking his head as if he, too, were let down by this news.

"Okay, then between you and the rest of the staff and the Belles."

"Nope, I mean there is no correspondence from our office at all to the Belles." A smug smile spread across his face.

"None?" Emilia blanched. "You're telling me that they never communicated?"

"That is exactly what I'm telling you."

"Unless someone deleted them," Iverson said, her index finger raised. "Is there any reason the Senator would want to delete them?"

March whipped his head toward her, his eyes blazing. "That is illegal, as I'm sure you know. Are you accusing us—or our *dead* boss—of a crime?"

"Oh, I'm sorry," Iverson said, her hands raised. "How silly of me, that would be the first crime ever committed by a congressperson, so I apologize for my mistake.

Love the sass, Emilia thought. "My partner is here for the same reason I am. We're trying to catch whoever murdered your boss and stop them from killing again." She gave a quick nod of encouragement to Iverson. "Our job is to be thorough, and I have been reliably informed your boss and Ulrich Belle were close. So, consider me puzzled that a titan of the city and a friendly senator wouldn't have ever sent an email to each other."

"I don't have anything to tell you."

"You know, Iverson, I'd say this is more suspicious than if he'd just coughed up those emails." She pointed a thumb at March. "I wonder if he knows that we have witnesses who place the Senator at World's Edge multiple times. So, it makes me wonder what their preferred method of communication was, and why they wanted to keep it quiet."

March's face was crimson as he pushed his chair back and stood up forcefully. "I will not stand for this, I have answered your questions, and now you need to leave immediately!"

CHAPTER 50
VERONICA

Midday, March 12

I read and re-read the Alexander Hamilton Society's alumni list. I poured through every detail of the pages of names. I had to find an answer that wasn't the one staring me in the face.

But I knew it was all wrong. It had to be her.

The response had come within a couple hours, and I had jumped up and ran into our backyard to read it. They sent over a list of everyone who had ever been accepted into their organization.I liked to be outside whenever I was on the phone or dissecting any information. Ben used to laugh at how I paced around our back patio when I'd be deep in thought during research projects.

I expected to see Bridget Lowe or Tracy Belle's names early on, and to chalk it up to another dead end. But neither of their names were present. So I read on, looking for any name that stuck out. It wasn't exactly a needle in a haystack operation, but I knew it was far-fetched. The likelihood was that I would have to comb through all the alumnae who overlapped with Lowe and Belle, searching online and in archives until I found a matching picture to the half-face I had.

Then I read the name.

It was a common enough last name, so at first, I thought maybe it was just a coincidence. But when I found nothing else about her online, literally nothing at all, I knew.

Janet was the other young woman in that picture.

Janet Jordan, Jacob's older sister.

The sister whom reporters and journalists searched for after his arrest. The sister who had seemingly vanished without a trace, the last sign of her a high school diploma and a local newspaper note saying she was off to Georgetown.

Jacob's parents hadn't spoken to any press, but a neighbor said he'd heard she found a boy and ran off west, never looking back. A tale as old as time.

Never in any of my years with him had Jacob mentioned his sister. I found out he had one the same time everyone else did, during the aftermath of the attempted assassination.

Georgetown's official records did not include her.

But this was proof. Here she was, in a picture with three Georgetown students, her picture seemingly deliberately torn in half. And her name in a list of members of a student society.

Was Tony the one who tore it? If not him, then who?

I had to go see Mikaela, but I needed more information. I picked up the phone and dialed.

"Alex, what's up?"

I knew Francisco had his own life, and he must have been on strict orders from my father to drop everything whenever I reached out, but I appreciated the reliability.

"Francisco, got another project for you."

"You know I'm not just your personal lackey, right?"

I heard the mirth in his voice. "Of course not, except isn't that basically what my father would say you are?"

Francisco laughed. "He might, this is true."

"Am I interrupting a busy schedule?"

"Well, it's a Tuesday morning, so I'm heading out for a long run and then off to whichever farmer's market is open."

"Look at you. You have gone native, haven't you? Next, you'll be telling me about your weekend brunch plans for one in the afternoon."

"I do love a good late brunch," he conceded. "But actually, you know I'm on standby to follow your husband as soon as he leaves your sight."

"Glad he's having a quiet day today, I'm sure."

"Makes my life easier. But what have you got?"

I filled him in on my discovery.

"Wow. So, you need to find her."

"Yes. I need you to find a ghost. This is right up your alley."

CHAPTER 51
MIKAELA

Midday, March 12

"Do you think Janet could be the real killer, then?" Mikaela asked, after several silent moments, her hand resting on her stomach. She read that there was no way she could feel kicks yet, but she could swear she felt them.

Veronica pursed her lips. Her raised eyebrows made it clear she didn't think so. "I don't know. It's hard to square that with the new press release the police sent out saying that Jacob was seen with Tony on the bridge."

"Okay, so maybe they're working together?"

"Maybe. Maybe that's why there were notes for Billingsley and Lowe, but then none for Tony. But nothing points that way, yet, at least."

Mikaela's eyes glistened.

"How are you holding up?" Veronica asked.

Mikaela didn't have a good answer to that, she realized. Just over a week ago, her entire life felt like it was in turmoil because she and Tony weren't having any success conceiving. But in the space of a few days Tony was gone and she was pregnant. On top of that, she'd now made contact with her stepbrother.

She remembered when she'd first seen the Walshes on television.

She'd known who Ben was, ever since she'd learned who her father was. She had thought about reaching out to him, asking for money or otherwise. His younger brother Caleb was out in Michigan, living day to day, so he wouldn't be much help. But Ben, he seemed like someone who had it all.

Until she saw his face on her screen, hounded by press as he tried to shuffle by quickly. The headline telling the world that his wife was a killer. That wasn't a guy to whom she could ask for reparations for her childhood.

To say it had come as a shock was too cliché. It wasn't a shock, so much as a thrill. Mikaela grasped onto the idea and mythos that was Alessandra Portillo. She read everything she could, devouring the think pieces and docudramas alike.

The chance that this woman could be related to her was mesmerizing. She didn't know what to do with this information, but as soon as Tony went missing, the thought came to her naturally. Of course, Veronica would be the one who helped her find him.

"I've been better. I'm conflicted, actually." she admitted, cocking her head and sighing. "I feel like hot garbage, because my husband is dead, and I still think I'm the one who drove him to go up onto that bridge. I can't shake the feeling that he was planning on killing himself over our infertility issues. But now I have this new hope, this baby. This part of him that will live on. So, he'll always be remembered. But then he'll never know. And how could I be happy about that? Plus, now I have you and Ben in my life, and that makes me so happy but then so guilty for allowing myself to feel any happiness, you know?"

"You're human," Veronica said, reaching out and gently touching her arm. "You're allowed to have feelings that don't make sense to you."

"I know I'm supposed to be making funeral arrangements, but I can't just get myself to do it, and they haven't released his body yet anyway. His family are all coming to town, and I just can't handle much more of the sadness. Does that make me a bad person?"

"I am more qualified than most to say this because I know grief well. No, it does not. When my mother died, I wanted the sadness to envelop me, I wanted to hold on to it as tight as I could. But when my brother died, I had the opposite feeling. I didn't want to grieve at all. I wanted to pack his stuff, all the memories, everything, into a little tidy box in my mind, kept behind lock and key. Only accessible if I absolutely needed to enter.

"I think it depends on what you need to do next with your grief. When it was my mother, I was a small child, so all I could do was swallow up all the sadness. When it was Kelvin, I didn't have the mental space. I didn't realize it at that moment, but that was when the Alessandra that became notorious was born. I had to step up. So, the important question is not whether you are a good or bad person based on how you grieve, but what you need that grief to do for you. How do you survive this grief? Whatever facilitates survival is always the right thing to do."

Mikaela nodded, dabbing her eyes. She could feel the dams were about to burst. "I've never had a friend like you, Veronica."

CHAPTER 52
EMILIA

Afternoon, March 12

Nothing could have convinced Emilia further that Senator Billingsley had a connection to the Belles than that performance by his former chief of staff. *No paper trail?* That just screamed that there was something there, off the books.

While it wasn't evidence, she was happy with the direction the case was going. Now she knew that all parties were connected, and she had a strong suspect.

"Detective!"

Emilia turned around sharply. Iverson was running toward her, holding a small Post-it note in her hand. Her strawberry blonde pigtails were flying behind her, and her eyes were wild.

"What is it?"

"I've been looking into Jacob's childhood, and I think I've got something." She took a deep breath. "What's the connection to the other Georgetown alums, right? That's the big question."

Emilia nodded.

"Did you know his sister got into Georgetown? Janet Jordan? And she's the same age as our victims?" She pointed at the Post-it. "The local paper announced that she was going to Georgetown. I called the registrar, but they said they have no information at all concerning anyone named Janet Jordan at Georgetown."

"Where is she now?"

"No one has seen her since."

Emilia felt a pit in her stomach. "That's it, isn't it? Something happened to her at World's Edge."

"I've got more."

Emilia had never seen Iverson's eyes more full of life. She realized that since this was the first real investigation she'd ever contributed to, this was likely the highlight of her professional career so far. "Talk to me," she said.

"So, like I said, no one has seen her since. But, get this, the Jordan parents did this big expansion on their house just a few months later. Why would they need to do that right after their daughter disappeared from college?"

"She moved back in with them." Emilia nodded, understanding.

"We need to talk to her."

Emilia was already rising. "Grab your things, we're heading to Valley Forge."

CHAPTER 53
VERONICA

Afternoon, March 12

"It's hard to find a missing person when I'm making sure your husband doesn't get killed," Francisco said as he reclined on our back patio.

Ben was inside, prepping some drinks now that the twins were down for some quiet time. They knew Francisco was a good friend, but I tried to keep him away as much as possible. He understood why.

"As I recall, you've always enjoyed a challenge."

"I haven't had much to test me in a while. Not since finding you."

"I'm still a little chagrined that it wasn't harder. But anyway, I think I might've jumped the gun about protecting Ben. I think Jacob was just trying to provoke me. Into what, though, I'm not sure."

A memory popped into my head of the last time I had to tell Francisco that I didn't need protecting.

He was twelve years old, just two years younger than me. It was a relatively quiet stretch, and I hadn't gotten her hands dirty in a couple months. I couldn't ever slip back into just being a child, but I was enjoying getting to do normal teenage things. Going to the mall, hanging out with friends.

We had a little group of four that stuck together. Myself, Francisco, and the Landaverde twins, Walter and Karla. They were the eldest of the group, a year older than me. Francisco was the runt of the litter, all wiry and gangly.

The four of us were drinking milkshakes and lounging on benches in a downtown park, dipping our toes in the fountain, and laughing as we splashed each other. Normal carefree kid stuff.

A scream echoed across the park. Walter and Karla sprang up, their guns already in their hands. "Stay put," Karla said to me and Francisco.

I tensed up, and Francisco mistook it for fear. I was actually just trying not to roll my eyes at the twins—the idea that I needed to stay back was laughable to me.

"Get under the bench," Francisco said, pulling out a small knife I didn't even know he carried.

"I... what?"

"Under the bench, I'll keep you safe," he insisted, holding up the knife that could have been from a child's toy kitchen set.

I was used to having to hide my secret identity among friends, but it hadn't gotten any easier. I stifled a laugh as I went along with it, crouching down on my knees to get underneath the metal bench.

This poor, chivalrous boy was trembling as he stood in front of me, holding the knife up in front of him.

I understood the importance of keeping my identity safe, I really did. What's that line every superhero says? *I have to keep my identity secret to protect the ones I love* blah blah blah.

I crawled out behind the bench and stood beside him, palming my own blade. "Alex, it's not safe!" he cried in a voice that was still far too high-pitched to carry any weight.

"Put the knife down, Francisco," I said, keeping my tone even and calm. "I know what you're doing, you're being tough and strong. But with you and me it's always us together, okay? If we have to fight, we do it side by side."

I was so close to telling him. He looked up into my eyes and I watched his own start to well up. The poor kid was ashamed he couldn't protect me. "Keep Alex safe," he mumbled.

"What?" I asked.

"Keep Alex safe." He sniffled and wiped his nose on the back of his hand. "That's what my parents always tell me. Every time I go out, they ask if you'll be there, and they make me promise to keep you safe."

As soon as the words left his mouth, I understood. Francisco's father knew my secret. But he couldn't tell his son, so Francisco was left to misunderstand the meaning. *Keep me safe*, because I'm the most effective asset this organization has, not because of some chivalrous notion that I need to be protected, that I'm too weak on my own.

What he must have felt when I went missing. I wondered how he reacted. Did he try to join the search party only to be told to stay home and wait? Agonizing hours that turned into days, thinking he'd never see his friend again.

I knew the last part was true because it was how I felt as well.

"Okay, you're sure Ben will be fine?"

I studied him, thinking about what a strong man he'd become. "Obviously no one is ever fully safe, but it's been a few days, and you've followed him to work, errands, all the hits. I think Jacob has bigger fish to fry—why would he even be interested in Ben? This all feels far more targeted."

Francisco gave a precise salute, which I promptly slapped down. "Consider the protection detail terminated," he said. "Full steam ahead finding Janet Jordan."

"Great, I appreciate it. But first, you and I have a task."

"Do we, now?"

"The police haven't figured out where Jacob Jordan is currently living, and I'm sure he's in enough of a disguise that neighbors aren't going to turn him in."

"That's where we come in." Francisco smiled. "Judging by your smile, I think you know where he is, don't you?"

I flipped over my hand to reveal the car keys in my palm. "Ben has the kids, let's ride."

Twenty minutes later, we pulled up in front of a shabby-looking apartment building just north of Georgetown, up Wisconsin Avenue.

"This place must have lived a long and glorious past life as a sleazy motel," I said. The prestige, money, and class of Georgetown abruptly ended as this building looked like it wouldn't withstand the next strong gust of wind. A small parking lot with uneven painted lines sat in front of the long and rectangular two-story building.

"I wouldn't have chosen this, but it could be worse," Francisco remarked.

I had explained to him in the car that I realized something I should have thought was obvious before. Wherever Jacob was staying, he wouldn't be so sloppy to use the same name. But the one thing I knew for sure about him was that he was brilliant and creative. And people who are that brilliant tend to have favorites. For him it was easy: Diophantus of Alexandria and Pierre de Fermat. Since he'd already used an alias referencing the first, I thought about what the second might be. He wouldn't try to translate the name fully, and pierre meaning 'rock' or 'stone' wasn't great as an alias anyway.

A first name that would be like Pierre, and a last name having to do with Fermat. Something to go on.

So, after a little time—okay, a lot—spent going down rabbit holes on the internet, I struck what appeared to be gold, and here we were, finally standing outside a one-bedroom apartment, rented to a Peter Close. There were no other Peter Closes living anywhere in the area. It was a stretch, thinking of Fermat as in the French "fermer," or "to close," and then just the most similar English name to Pierre, but it was exactly the sort of stretch I would take. I didn't teach him any of this horror he was putting so many through, but I was the one who taught him how to think, how to apply that innate intellect of his. I knew he would have been deliberate about picking a name that wouldn't catch anyone's attention but with an origin he would appreciate.

"Careful. Even if he's not here, he might have set some traps," I said as we exited the car.

Francisco gave me a pained look. Young Francisco lapped up every bit of advice I doled out. I was still getting used to adult Francisco. "Fine, sorry I said anything!" I said, holding my hands up in mock surrender.

We walked up the rickety metal stairway and down the outdoor hall. When we got to the front door, Francisco turned to me, shrugged nonchalantly, and knocked on the door.

We waited.

No answer.

"Lights are off," I said.

"Say no more." Francisco grinned.

I stepped back, bowing to his experience. I was always the one with the expertise, but I had been out of the game for a long time.

Twenty seconds later, I heard the familiar *pop!* as the lock was picked open. Francisco held up a hand, and I waited as the door slowly creaked open.

"No one home," he called, as he stuck his head inside. "Looks clear, too."

I followed him in. The apartment was a glorified studio, with an extra wall jutting halfway across the living room, providing a semblance of privacy for the 'bedroom.'

"Does… he actually live here?" Francisco asked.

The living room was immaculate. Not only clean, but empty. There was a single wooden chair and a coffee table, both lightly stained, but absolutely nothing else.

"Is this one of those things where math skills and OCD are closely related?" Francisco asked.

I shook my head. "No, I don't think so. He was always an incredibly precise person. He never used an extra word he didn't need, never exerted any unnecessary effort." I walked to the chair and leaned on it, listening to it creak.

We passed the divider and peeked into his bedroom. The queen-sized bed almost came out past the wall. At least here there were some clothes strewn around, a pair of dirty socks draped on the end of the turquoise duvet.

So, he was human, after all.

Short of catching him—and doing what? A citizen's arrest? —I wasn't sure what we were doing here anymore. This had to be his place, but it was clear we weren't going to find any proof. We could steal a dirty shirt and have the police check for DNA, but I didn't want anyone to know we had been in here.

"Time to go," I said, turning to Francisco who was studying the kitchenette. "Anything useful?"

"Nada."

As we exited, I gave one final glance at the place my best ever student was calling home. I didn't know, and hoped I never would have to find out, what it was like having a child commit a crime, but this was the closest I'd ever felt. I wanted to catch him, I needed him to stop, but most of all I was just struck by an overwhelming sadness. There would be no happy ending for Jacob, no matter how this turned out. I couldn't say he deserved one, but I wished I could go back to that bright young college kid and tell him his life didn't have to play out this way.

Francisco turned the lock, and we pulled the front door shut. "I think it's time to tell the police about this place," he said.

I sighed. "You're right. They'll pick over this place and find anything we missed."

"But…" Francisco led me with his eyes.

"But." I paused for a second before understanding. My mouth opened when I realized what he meant. "Of course. He'll know I was the one who tipped them off. No one else would have found this place besides us."

"I'm not here to tell you what to do, but do you need that in your life right now? After he's already broken into your house and threatened you?"

I shrugged. "I've got a better idea, then."

"Oh, come on," he groaned playfully. "I see that twinkle in your eye."

I raised an eyebrow.

Francisco let out a long, faux-exasperated sigh. "Yes, Alex, of course I'll stake it out. What do you want me to do when I find him?"

"Call the police, don't let him leave your line of sight. We need this to end."

I saw him turn his head sharply, and I instinctively knew.

"Shit!" I glanced down, seeing the car Francisco was staring at, pulling into the parking spot next to mine.

"Does he know your car?"

"If he's as smart as I think he is, absolutely."

The dark blue sedan jolted backward, and then hurtled out of the parking lot with a screech.

"Quick, go!" I yelled, as I ran toward the stairs. Francisco hopped onto the railing and launched himself down, landing with a frontward somersault and jumping back up in one motion.

Wow.

I felt conspicuously slow. Francisco had the car started before I even got there. I flung myself into the passenger seat, noticing he hadn't even changed my seat settings and was hunched over the wheel.

We sped out of the lot and turned north only to be immediately blocked by a string of cars waiting at a red light.

"This is not a city for chasing cars," Francisco lamented, banging his fist on the steering wheel.

I strained my neck, trying to get a glimpse of Jacob's sedan ahead. He wasn't at our light, and the visible lights ahead of us were all green. "He's gone." I exhaled loudly. "Fuck. All right, he knows we were here, so let's call the police and tell them. Who knows, maybe they will catch him and end this for all of us."

CHAPTER 54
MIKAELA

Afternoon, March 12

Mikaela wiped her mouth with the back of her hand and grabbed the mouthwash that had become a lifesaver. Damn this morning sickness. Why had no one ever told her that it's not just in the morning?

Who would have? No mother, and no mother figure in her life. No older sisters, no chosen sisters from foster homes who had kids to tell her.

She touched her stomach gingerly. This baby would grow up knowing love. He or she would not want for affection, nor wonder if anyone cared about them at all.

She took a deep breath, swallowed another bout of nausea she felt bubbling up, and came back out into the living room. "Sorry about that," she said.

"No apologies needed at all," Veronica replied, looking up from the couch and putting her phone back into her pocket. "I'm sorry I caught you at a bad time. I could've called, I know, but to me news should be delivered in person."

Mikaela felt her heart skip a beat. "Tell me."

"It should be over soon. We found Jacob Jordan's apartment and gave the location to the police. They'll catch him now."

Mikaela's face fell. Tears pooled in the corners of her eyes, threatening to break down the levies.

"I was told Detective Brown is out of town following something up, but that they'd put people on it right away." Veronica noticed her reaction and paused. "I'm sorry, are you okay?"

Mikaela wiped her eyes. "I don't know why that happened." *Why did she react that way? This was good news!*

Veronica rose and put a comforting hand on Mikaela's shoulder. "Did you hope that catching him would bring closure and some sort of —not happiness, per se—but acceptance?"

Mikaela gulped and nodded.

"And instead," Veronica continued. "You feel like your final tether, connecting you to a world in which Tony was still alive, is about to be snapped, and it will leave you listless and drifting?"

Mikaela gaped at her sister-in-law. "That's… exactly it. How did you do that?"

"My mother." Veronica's eyes misted over. "She had incredible emotional intelligence. She could tell what you felt before you even realized it. I try to do my best to emulate her."

"What was she like? I never had a mother figure."

"She was—" Veronica stopped, trying to come up with the words. "She was all-encompassing. I assume you know a bit about my father?"

"Yes. I followed your story when it all came out."

Veronica gave a self-deprecating smile. "Of course you did. I'm still not used to that. Anyway, he was the larger-than-life personality, and everyone assumed that was the case at home too. But my mom was the one who ran the roost. It was she who was gifted mathematically, she taught me things far earlier than I would have learned them otherwise.

"My grandfather had been in the organization too, so it was something of an arranged marriage for her. She could've done so much more with her life, but she took what she had and made the most of it. And she loved my father. I truly believe she would have left him, no matter the repercussions, if she wasn't happy.

"I remember where I was. I was ten years old, sitting in our living room reading, when she first complained to my father about her head. We didn't think much of it at the time, just a headache. She wasn't concerned, she just wanted some ibuprofen. Flash forward three months, and she was gone."

"That must have been awful." Mikaela could feel the tears silently sliding down her face now.

"I know everyone describes cancer as sucking the life out of a person. It's something of a cliché, but that's exactly what it was like. And all any of us could do was just watch. We were born into a family where boundaries and rules tended not to exist. Whatever we wanted we could get with enough effort or persuasion. I had never known what it was like to see my dad completely helpless. In hindsight, I now know that all the looks my mom would give him from her bed were her telling him with her eyes that she understood.

"We buried her in a small plot on the compound, close enough that we could just make it out from our house. Dad was stoic as ever in public. No tears, manly handshakes, solemn acceptance of well-wishers. But one night I heard a noise, around one or two in the morning. I crept to my window and watched him walk toward the plot, a single iris in his hand. I checked the next morning, and it was draped across her headstone. Every morning, I walked by and found a fresh iris there. I never told him I knew it was him."

"Was it worth it?" Mikaela asked.

Veronica's brow furrowed "What do you mean?"

"All that pain. Was what you had before worth it? Will my son or daughter feel this same pain eventually and wish they'd never had to deal with it?"

"Oh, Mikaela," Veronica said. "Love is always worth it. Whether you're given that love for a minute, or a lifetime, it stays with you forever. Your life is always better for having had love in it, no matter what comes next. Whatever phrase you want: love is eternal, love lingers, they're all true. Love is the greatest form of validation, when someone loves you, even if that person is now gone, it means the world."

———

"I can't take it. Can we go drive by to see if they got him?" Mikaela asked, pushing around her UberEATS Chinese food order. Why she thought she could stomach Chinese food was beyond her. She had visions of pregnancy cravings where she'd stuff her face with whatever popped into her head, not cravings so ephemeral that by the time the food came she would be disgusted by the mere sight of it.

"I guess it couldn't hurt." Veronica rose from her seat at the dining table. "I am curious, too."

Mikaela could feel her heart in her chest, thumping away loudly, as they drove, block by block, stop, start, stop, start. The predictable cadence of city driving. They entered Georgetown, navigating their way through floods of tourists crossing the M and Wisconsin Street intersection, before turning north on Wisconsin.

"Police cars." Veronica pointed ahead. "That's a good sign."

They inched closer, through the incessant Georgetown traffic.

"They seem very calm," Mikaela said. She thought of car accidents you see on the highway. Calm first responders is either a really good or a really bad sign.

Veronica's face clouded. "Shit," she muttered under her breath.

"So, that's not a good sign?" Mikaela asked.

Veronica shook her head. "I don't like the look of this."

They pulled into the small parking lot, immediately attracting the attention of an officer stationed by his car. He ran out in front of them and raised his hands. "Excuse me, ladies, you can't be here."

"Because this is Jacob Jordan's residence?" Veronica asked.

His eyes flashed, but he didn't take the bait. "This is an active police investigation, please leave."

"Okay, sorry, we'll turn around," Veronica said, and spun the wheel.

"Are we just giving up?" Mikaela whispered, her tone harsher than she meant to let escape.

Veronica just put her hand up. "Wait."

They pulled back onto Wisconsin avenue and drove south. Veronica didn't speak until she turned left toward Dumbarton Oaks, a Georgetown mansion now best known for its beautiful gardens. She found a parking spot at the end of a block and parallel parked.

"Come on," she said, grabbing the keys from the ignition. "We're going back."

"That officer is just going to turn us away again," Mikaela said.

Veronica pushed her door shut and responded over the car, "one, it's a public place, he legally can't as long as we don't try to trespass. Two, did you see the large detective standing behind him, just in front of the door?"

"No, should I have?"

"Not necessarily. But he's one of the detectives who was involved in my situation last year. He'll tell us what we need to know."

"Are you guys, like, friends now?"

Veronica smiled, a glint in her eye. "Less friend, more obsessed acquaintance who thinks I should be in jail." She turned and walked up the street.

Mikaela trudged after her. "I don't understand, how is this going to work?"

"You'll see," was Veronica's only response.

Detective Fahey was standing in the middle of the parking lot when they arrived. Mikaela wondered how Veronica would have convinced the other officer to let them by if he hadn't been.

"Oh, fuck right off," Fahey groaned as he saw them approaching.

"Nice to see you too." Veronica shot him a broad smile.

"Get out."

She put her hands on her hips "You missed Jacob Jordan, didn't you?"

Mikaela gasped and put her hand up to her mouth. How could they have missed him?

"What makes you say that?" Fahey glared at the pair of women disturbing his scene.

"You're desperate for good publicity, and you're standing outside his apartment decidedly not crowing to the world that you got him," Veronica said. "What happened?"

"You don't get to talk to me like that, murderer."

Mikaela watched as Veronica was about to respond but paused, and looked around, as if she'd suddenly realized something.

"Detective Brown isn't here. But you are. Oh boy, this is going to be bad for you, isn't it?" She shook her head patronizingly.

"What is?" Mikaela couldn't help herself.

Veronica turned to face her. "He heard about my tip-off about Jacob's residence, and I'm guessing—correct me if I'm wrong here," she flicked her gaze to Fahey. "I'm guessing he came in guns blazing without his partner, and let his big ego get in the way of an actual plan. So instead of staking out the place, knowing that Jacob would have to come back here eventually, he broke down the door, and lost the best lead we have."

Mikaela could tell from Fahey's face that Veronica was exactly right. After her initial hope earlier now all she felt was rage. "What the actual fuck?"

"Who even are you? I don't have to defend myself to some nobodies."

Veronica stepped between the pair. "This is the wife of one of Jacob's victims, so I'd back off right now. And you'd better hope to God that Detective Brown is having more success than you."

CHAPTER 55
EMILIA

Evening, March 12

The house was on a pleasant, shaded street, with a big yard in front and a basketball hoop at the end of the driveway. A brick chimney rose above the slanted roof, and black shutters contrasted with the bright white of the house exterior. A picture of suburban bliss.

Emilia parked on the street and made her way around the car to meet Iverson, standing on the sidewalk like a coiled spring. "Take a deep breath," Emilia said. "Whatever it is, whatever they say, it'll all be okay."

Iverson had spent the entire three-hour drive fidgeting, and Emilia was already exhausted and feeling overstimulated by the time they made it to Valley Forge. Her new partner went back and forth between impressing Emilia and driving her up a wall. She couldn't blame Iverson for her feelings, this was not going to be a pleasant conversation.

Emilia had decided against calling ahead, even though it raised the chances that they'd arrive at an empty house. She didn't want the Jordans to be prepared, with hours to rehearse their lines.

As they walked up the driveway, the dark wooden front door

swung open. A fit man, wearing a dark button-down and khaki pants, stepped out under the awning that shaded the front stoop, his feet bare. *A sure sign of someone who works from home.*

"We know what you want, and we have nothing to say," he called out, his voice trembling with anger, and Emilia noticed a hint of sadness as well.

"Hello, sir." Emilia waved and gestured to Iverson to keep walking. "I don't think you do, actually. My name is Detective Emilia Brown. I am a homicide detective from Washington, D.C. and this is my partner, Detective Iverson. May we come in and have a quick chat?"

"You cannot." His frame filled the entrance.

"All right, we can have a conversation about your daughter, Janet, out here then, if that's better for you?"

He folded his arms "We have nothing to say about Janet," he said, his voice stern.

Emilia raised her voice just enough to make him worry about it drifting over to the neighbors. "What about Janet herself? May we come in and speak to her? We know she's in there."

A woman appeared behind the man. She was stocky and short, her head peeking out just around his elbow. "Get inside!" she hissed.

The man sighed and glanced up and down the street with a resigned look. He moved out of the way and let the detectives pass. The space opened up into a wood-floored foyer, with stairs leading to the second floor off to the right. They walked through a large kitchen with a granite-top island holding a bowl of mangoes and settled down at the dining room table, the Jordans on one side, the detectives facing them. Iverson moved a large ornamental vase, seemingly adorned with diamonds, to the side so it was not obstructing their view.

"May I assume that you are Gavin and Camilla Jordan?" Emilia asked.

"Like you don't already know," Gavin scoffed.

"You've seen the news, I assume?" Emilia jumped right in. "Do the names of those killed mean anything to you?"

"No," Camilla said, and they shook their heads in unison.

"Just, no?" Iverson asked. "Nothing else to say?"

Emilia watched their eyes as Iverson asked. Both shifting away, attempting to make surreptitious eye contact with each other.

"If we came back with a warrant, which we could easily get since this is Jacob Jordan's childhood home and you're lying to us, what would we find?" Emilia asked.

Gavin's eyes flashed, and his fingers curled into a fist on the table. "No evidence that we're involved, that's for sure."

"But what might we stumble upon?" Iverson took over. "What might we accidentally find?"

"You already mentioned her outside, just spit it out," Camilla said.

"May we speak to Janet, please?" Emilia kept her voice calm and measured.

"No, you may not," Gavin said.

"Because she's not here, or because you're shielding her from us?"

"Because she's not part of this!" Camilla slammed her hand down on the table, rattling the vase. She lowered her voice. "She didn't deserve any of this."

"Any of what?" Emilia jumped on the concession.

Both of them quieted. They looked at each other, and Emilia saw Camilla's eyes narrow.

"Look, I'm guessing you know a thing or two about the victims here," Emilia said. "The Belle family, Senator Billingsley, Tony Alonso, Bridget Lowe. Do none of them ring a bell, really?"

"Of course, they do," Camilla snapped. "Do you think we're idiots?"

"Then talk to us. Help us understand," Iverson said. "Why did your son target these people? What happened at World's Edge?"

Emilia glanced at the vase again. She looked past it, her eyes stopping at the painting on the wall. A Picasso. "You're getting paid to stay quiet about it, aren't you?" she asked, her voice almost apologetic.

The Jordans fell silent. Iverson put her hand up to her mouth.

"I thought so. Was it the Belles? Is the estate continuing to pay, even though they're all gone now?"

The silence dragged on. Finally, Gavin spoke. "If we talk, the money stops. We can't afford for that to happen."

"Who is paying you?"

"They told us all. No talking," Camilla said.

Emilia glanced at Iverson. She could feel the tension in the room, like a muscle that had been stretched too far and was about to snap.

"Wait," Emilia said slowly. "What do you mean by *us all*?"

CHAPTER 56
VERONICA

Evening, March 12

I sat with Mikaela, holding her hand as she sobbed into her untouched gin and tonic.

"You know how…" Mikaela gulped down a sob. "You know how you have a horrible day but keep your cool until one little thing completely sets you off?"

I understood perfectly. Mikaela had been a trooper, taking it in stride that the police had botched the Jacob Jordan lead. We stopped by a nearby coffee shop, sat and talked, and I really thought she was doing okay. She asked if I could come back home with her, so I called Ben and made sure he was okay to be at home with the kids until I got back.

All was going as well as it could, until I went to the bathroom and came back to find her in the throes of gut-wrenching cries. She just pointed at the drink she had poured for herself, and I knew.

She'd forgotten she was pregnant. After a desperately long and trying day, she poured herself a nice drink before realizing she couldn't have it.

"I'm going to be a horrible mother, aren't I?" she sobbed. "I can't even remember I'm pregnant."

"Look, you've been through more in your first days of pregnancy than anyone should," I said, taking the untouched highball glass away and dumping it into the sink.

"It's all I've ever wanted. That's terrible to say, right? I tell myself that it's okay Tony is gone because I can have the baby we always wanted. Like it's some sort of devil's trade? I gave up my husband's life so I could get my baby."

"You tell yourself whatever you need to do, okay?" I came back and sat down next to her. "You now have an obligation to hold yourself together, despite it all, for this baby. He or she is going to need you, so you do whatever keeps you moving."

"I can't believe he's not going to see his baby. I mean, how cruel is that?"

"Heartless, I agree. That's what this world is." I'd seen more evil things—perpetrated a few, if I was being honest—than she would ever know, but despair and grief should never be a race to the bottom. Someone out there having it worse than you does not invalidate your own feelings, and the people who think that need therapy.

Mikaela suddenly rose and walked over to her dining table. She picked up the torn picture from the yearbook. "This poor kid," she said. "Look at him, standing there like the world is at his feet. Ten years later, and he's dead. Gone, wiped off the face of the earth. Cast overboard into the sea like some mutineer.

"He was a really good man, you know. He once drove all the way to Philadelphia and back for me just because I'd mentioned I missed a specific type of cheese I'd found at Reading Market. That was the type of guy he was. He would fall over himself to make a stranger's life just the tiniest bit easier. It was as if he had been handed a mission from up on high to bring the most good into the world possible."

I was listening, but I felt her words weren't for me anyway. As she continued talking, I focused on the printout in her hand. I heard every third word as she told a story of him making her favorite pimento grilled cheese each time they had a pregnancy setback.

"Mikaela!" I jumped up, ripping the photo from her hand.

Her shock rendered her silent. She stared at me, a confused expression cemented on her face.

"Sorry, I just—" I held up the picture. "This is ripped cleanly in half, right?"

"Um, yes, why?"

"These are three kids here, plus Janet Jordan. But this is only half the picture. This picture should be double in size. Look at it, it should be a full piece of printer paper. But it's only half. So that means that this girl is not the only one cut out of Tony's picture."

"Oh, no. Shit."

I nodded. "There could be three other people here."

CHAPTER 57
EMILIA

Evening, March 12

Camilla stifled a patronizing laugh. She and Gavin shared a conspiring glance. "You come in here acting like you've got it all figured out, and you didn't even know *that*."

"Then tell us," Iverson said, her voice rising.

"Well, it's pretty self-explanatory. The Belles paid others too." Camilla shrugged as if that was that.

"Who?" Emilia asked.

"Others."

"We need names. Now."

"Why?" Gavin asked. "Why would it matter now? What could possibly change by knowing the other poor souls from years ago?"

"Poor souls," Iverson repeated, an eyebrow arched.

"What happened?" Emilia asked.

Gavin huffed and threw his hands up. "Look, we don't actually know what happened, okay? None of us do."

"All right, fine. Let's do this," Camilla said. "But if the money stops coming because of something you do, I'm coming after you. We were eating dinner, in downtown Philadelphia, with Jacob, celebrating that he had just won a cross-country race. It was at the end of finals week, and Janet was staying a couple extra days after her last exam to be with friends before she came home for the holidays. I got a call on my phone from a D.C. number we didn't recognize and picked up. A detached, emotionless voice asked if I was Janet Jordan's mother and then just told me that our daughter was in the hospital in Georgetown, and we needed to come immediately.

"We grabbed our coats and took off. Gavin threw a bunch of bills onto the table, I don't even know if it covered dinner, and we just ran. The car ride down to D.C. was the longest drive of our lives. The three of us sat there in silence. Gavin drove, and I still don't know how he managed to keep us on the road with the speed at which he was driving. All I knew was that I had to be with my baby, my angel, as soon as possible."

Her voice broke, and she coughed into her hand. Gavin glared with red-rimmed eyes at the detectives. "She shouldn't have to relive this." He had barely made it through the sentence when his own voice began to break.

"No, Gavin, it's okay." Camilla patted him on the forearm. "We made it to Baltimore, and we felt like we were close. I'd forgotten just how damn far away Baltimore is from Washington. We finally arrived, and Gavin pulled up on the curb by the emergency room entrance. We couldn't give a damn about the parking ticket. We sprinted inside. Jacob made it in first, still in his cross-country uniform. There were only a few people in the waiting room. A small family, huddled around a little girl whose wrist looked broken. I remember that so vividly, because I have spent years wishing we were them. Just a normal family with a little girl who took a fall and broke a bone that easily heals."

"Not the family with a little girl who took a fall and broke everything," Gavin said, his voice barely above a whisper.

"Oh, fuck." The words were out before Emilia could stop them. Everything clicked in Emilia's mind. She knew what happened. "She was at World's Edge. That's where the fall happened."

Camilla shot Gavin an annoyed look. "Yes. As Gavin just so crassly put it, our Janet fell over the cliff."

Gavin snorted. Emilia glanced over at Iverson, who was sitting with her chin in her hands, her attention rapt.

"Yes, Gavin. I was getting to that." Camilla said, her voice now tinged with exasperation. "It wasn't just a fall. She was on a golf cart that went over the side."

Emilia waited for more, but Camilla fell silent. Emilia was prepared to wait them out, but Iverson jumped in "She wasn't driving it, was she? Who else was in the cart?"

"I'll never forget it, until the day I die," Gavin said. "We stood there in the center of the emergency room, and some lady came out from a hallway. She wasn't part of the hospital, so I don't know what she was doing there. But she took one look at us and said, 'oh shit, are you guys the family of one of the kids that died?'"

Emilia put her hand to her mouth.

"Wait," Iverson said. "Kids dying in a fall? We would have heard about that. How did we not?"

Camilla nodded. "You'd think so, wouldn't you?"

"Senator Billingsley," Emilia said. "He was driving the golf cart. Or at least caused the accident. And then he paid you all off to cover it up."

"Yes and no," Gavin said. "The Senator was there, and he was the driver of the golf cart. The dumb son of a bitch got too close to the edge and bailed out. He saved his worthless ass and left the others to die."

"But we don't know if he was the one paying," Camilla took over. "The Belles were there of course—it was their house. But we still think it couldn't have just been him. We've been getting ten thousand dollars a month for ten years, and we didn't have the worst of it, as horrible as that is to say. I looked him up, he didn't have the money for that."

"So, who else was involved?" Iverson asked, her pen hovering over her notepad, ready for action.

"We know which kids were there, and now every one of them except our Janet is dead. That group of seven, forever inseparable, I guess. But we never found out who else," Camilla said. "We never knew which adults were connected, or how many, and frankly, we didn't want to know."

"Can you tell us the names of the other kids?" Emilia asked.

Camilla shook her head. "I'm sorry, that's not our story to tell. But I think maybe it's time for you to meet Janet, if you'd like."

The Jordans led the way back to the foyer, and up the stairs to the second floor. They stopped just before a door covered with a child's art. Emilia looked closely and noticed they all had Janet's name and a date, stretching back to the late 1990s.

"She isn't normally locked away, I know how this looks," Camilla said. "This is her room, and we let her do as much as she wants in the house. The instructions we got about payments were very strict, though. They said no one could find out what happened, or else they would stop. You'll understand in a second. We needed the money."

Camilla gently turned the doorknob and pushed the door open. "Janet, honey," she called. "You have some visitors who want to say hi."

Emilia let Iverson step in first and followed behind as they entered the bedroom. The walls were all painted seafoam green, and the entire room was themed like a tropical getaway. Fake palm trees stood in one corner, their large leaves draping over a giant bed, forming a single-sided canopy. In the bed, under a large sandy brown blanket, lay a young woman.

"Oh, my goodness," Iverson whispered.

"Hi, Janet, how are you feeling today?" Camilla asked in a gentle voice.

Janet's mouth opened a fraction. Emilia thought she heard a tiny voice but couldn't make anything out.

"They call it akinetic mutism," Gavin said. "It can be caused by severe damage to the brain's frontal lobe. It is a combination of akinesia and mutism, so she basically can't move or speak." He turned toward Janet. "But she can still hear us, she can say a single word every once in a while, and we're lucky because she's still here with us. We watch movies, read her books, and spend as much time as we can making her life joyful and fulfilled, don't we Janet?" He squeezed his daughter's hand and tears welled up in his eyes.

"You said frontal lobe, so she hit her head in the fall," Emilia said.

"That's right," Camilla said. "It isn't a sheer cliff, it's slightly angled. There are trees and bushes. Along with the brain injury, she broke her hip, femur, collarbone, and six ribs. They tell us she was lucky because she was unconscious so if she'd landed in the water she would have drowned. They rescued her on the bank of the river."

"Come on." Gavin ushered them back outside, telling Janet they'd be back in soon. Once they were out in the hallway he spoke again. "We don't like talking about it in front of her, because she gets distressed. The reason she survived when the others didn't is exactly what Camilla said. The others were pulled from the water."

They walked downstairs, and moved toward the door, standing awkwardly, waiting for the detectives to leave. Emilia understood why. They didn't want to finish the conversation. She pointed at the living room. "Let's talk about Jacob," she said. "You know that he's why we're here."

Gavin shook his head. "We have nothing to say."

"Because you don't want to incriminate him?" Iverson asked. "Unless you have a signed confession from him, you're not going to do any more than tell us what we already have. We're not here for evidence, we're here to find out more about him, and then find him."

"You have to understand, Jacob worshiped Janet." Camilla barely got the words out. "He changed after the accident. You wouldn't have known it in public. He was great at looking the part. But internally he was seething mad."

"That's enough. We have no more to say." Gavin pulled the door open and ushered them out. When they were standing in the driveway, he spoke. "I don't know how he found out who else was there, and we definitely did not know what he was planning, but I can't say I'm mad about it." He paused and looked directly in Emilia's eyes. "Everyone there is guilty in my eyes."

CHAPTER 58
VERONICA

Night, March 12

I sat on the back patio, watching the twins playing in their mini jungle gym. Ben reclined next to me, a steaming mug of hot chocolate in his hand.

"This is nice," Ben said. "This is how it should be."

"This is how it always has been until last week," I shot back, raising my own mug as a toast to diffuse tension. I didn't care that he had his little sojourn away. Skeletons in the closets aren't normally literal skeletons. He could have as big a freakout as he wanted about all that.

But I did not like how he abandoned the kids. He would have to win back their trust, and I wasn't ready to give him any handouts in that regard.

But we were always going to be each other's end game. I believed that much would never change. As long as Ben could now move past his fears, we would move forward together, as we always had. A new normal, but one we could learn to be comfortable with. We'd be the duo with the best stories in the nursing home, that was for sure.

Plus, doesn't every guy deep down have a femme fatale fetish? Did I marry the one guy who didn't? I wasn't buying that.

"I have a name for the photographer who took those pictures of me and Mikaela, by the way," Ben said.

"Okay…" I wasn't sure how this was noteworthy.

"He followed me for days, I think. I'm going to find him and confront him, because how did he know?"

"Everyone here has eyes." I shrugged. This clearly meant more to him than it did to me.

"What do you think—"

I shushed Ben with a hiss. He followed my eyes toward the back gate.

I don't know how to describe it. An instinct, years of training, some finely honed skill? Whatever it was that let me do so, I was able to sense movement, a physical presence. Nothing had stirred, no tiny rustle that only my ears picked up. But there was someone there. On the other side of the fence, in the alley.

"Ben, how about we treat the kids tonight?" I said in a deliberately loud voice, waving him into action.

Nico and Maria whipped their heads around in unison, their hopeful eyes looking up expectantly.

"What if—" I paused, letting the tension build. They didn't have to know it was to give a quick listen to the surroundings while they were quiet. Nothing. Not a sound. "Dad makes some homemade ice cream?"

Ben shot me a pensive look, before his eyes widened with understanding. "Francisco?" he mouthed.

I jerked my head toward the back door in response. That wasn't a bad guess, but I didn't think he was right. I'd learned Francisco's tells. This was different.

"Mom, are you coming too?" Maria asked as she got to the door.

Kids. You can never trust them to understand operational security.

Whomever was out there now knew I was staying back. So they must know I had sensed their presence. The game was up. "Coming, sweetie, just grabbing dad's mug!" I called across the patio.

Once the door closed and Ben was inside with the kids, I stood up and calmly walked over and locked it, palming the key afterward.

I returned into the center of the patio and spread my arms wide. "If you can see me, you know I am no threat to you, Jacob. Tell me why you're here."

He responded with a rueful chuckle from my neighbors' pitch-black yard.

"Didn't think I'd know you were there?" I kept my voice light, but my eyes were scanning for weapons. You can never be too prepared.

"I have to hand it to you, Dr. Dub." He said, using the go-to nickname for me from Georgetown. I can't remember when it came about, but some student years ago thought that sounded more fun than Professor or Doctor Walsh, so it stuck among the kids who liked to think of themselves as rebels. The sort who acted the part but backed down at the first sight of trouble. "I had no idea what a professional we had teaching us. Is it really true you killed a guy with a pencil sharpener?"

"What do you want?" I kept my voice measured and calm.

"I want your help," he said matter-of-factly.

"My help? Come on, Jacob. Turn yourself in. End all this shit."

"I'd really rather not do that. I'm tired of playing in the kiddie pool. It's time for the big leagues."

Mixing metaphors was uncharacteristic for him. "What bigger league could you possibly want than killing a senator?" There was a stick on the ground that would do in a pinch. I reached down and picked up a small pebble. I tossed it over into our neighbor's yard on the opposite side, and when it made a noise and I knew it would draw Jacob's attention, I moved five feet to my left and grabbed the footlong branch that had fallen from our maple tree.

"Allegedly. Allegedly killing a senator. You're not going to catch me slipping with something that easy, Doc."

"Are you here to threaten me?"

"You? I know better than that. You'd chop me up and they'd never find my body. I'm not keen on that."

"Then why are you here?" I asked again, feeling myself getting exasperated. This was always a problem when I was young. I was patient, I knew how to play the game, when to strike, but I also got bored quickly. You want a tense standoff? Then give me some fucking tension, don't just lob softball answers over the wall like some peewee player.

Now here I was making baseball metaphors.

"You took away my home."

Ahh. "I found your home. The police raided it."

"You told them."

"You have this strange belief that, despite you threatening to kill my husband, we are somehow on the same side."

"Do you know why I'm doing this?"

"Something to do with your sister, right?"

"What was the story? Your brother was killed and in retaliation your father killed dozens, including a mother and a baby? And it was all deserved because that's what you do when your family is attacked?"

"One," I held up a finger, still not entirely sure if he could see me or not. "He did not kill a mother and baby. The woman there looked like she was holding a baby, but it was actually just a signal that the ambush was set. Two, you heard that story and believe my father was the hero? There were no heroes in that story. No one won, no one kept their soul. The answer to injustice isn't wanton violence."

"But what if there's no other way?"

I swore I heard his voice crack. "There's always another way, Jacob."

"Not for the rich. They just buy off people and throw money at things until it goes away."

"Jacob, what happened to your sister?"

This time I definitely heard him stifle a sob. A long silence ensued.

"Fuck this," he finally said. "I thought you of all people would understand, you would be a sympathetic ear. My favorite ever professor, who coincidentally also turned out to understand the effects of violence on growing minds. All right, then. When this all hits close to home, you have only yourself to blame."

CHAPTER 59
EMILIA

Night, March 12

"You don't think he's done, is he?"

Emilia looked over at her partner. Iverson was leaning her head against the window, watching the trees fly by as they drove back south toward D.C. "Do you think he is?"

"I mean, I was just thinking. You've got the driver of the golf cart, Senator Billingsley. He's dead. We need to find out who the other three students were, but Camilla said they were dead too. Then the entire Belle family, also now dead." She furrowed her brow. "Wait, are we sure he didn't have something to do with Miranda's death?"

Emilia cocked her head to the side. "That's not a bad thought, but I was there at that crime scene and Jeremy Wiles confessed. Jacob was still in jail, and he only had interactions with Veronica Walsh while there."

"What's her deal, then?"

Emilia looked down at the Susquehanna River far below as they passed over the Millard E. Tydings Memorial Bridge, heading south toward Baltimore. She couldn't cross a bridge now without thinking about Tony Alonso and what it would be like to fall or jump. She had never been afraid of heights, and always thought of it as an irrational fear. Afraid of heights? Just don't get near an edge and you're fine, nothing to worry about. Now Janet Jordan would forever live in her head too. What must she have felt, the moment she knew the cart was going over the side? Did she still think she could get out, or was she resigned to an impending death that never actually came?

"Umm, Earth to Detective Brown."

Emilia looked at her partner. "Do people still say that?"

"What?" Iverson scrunched up her face. "I don't know. You were completely zoned out looking over the side of the bridge, and that was freaking me out."

"Sorry, just thinking. What did you say?"

"I was asking about Veronica Walsh and what's up with her."

Emilia chuckled. "I mean, how much do you know?"

"I followed the whole situation last year— how could anyone not? — but really, I didn't keep up too much. How's she not in jail or deported for all that shit she did?"

"No political will," was Emilia's sober answer. "Democrats weren't interested in that sort of thing, and she basically gifted President Leishear a second term, so he wasn't going to go near her. Did you see that he commented on it?"

"No, I didn't. I don't follow politics too much."

"How could you not, of all people? You live and work in the capital." Emilia shook her head scoldingly. "Anyway, the President said that she was a true example of how immigrants can leave their origins behind and become real Americans. Some bullshit like that, that didn't at all wash with his politics surrounding immigration. The suggestion was someone on his team saw an opportunity to win hearts and minds, because as a country we all decided we were on her side."

"But why did we all decide that?"

"That's a good question. I think that 'woman who survived a horrible situation and got out' is a strong story. Maybe enough of us have fantasized about a little light murder? Who knows? However it happened, she's a sympathetic figure to most."

"But not enough, if she got fired?"

"I think it's the difference between the court of public opinion and the rest of her life. She might not be getting charged or deported, but that's not to say that she got off scot-free. Rumor is there's a groundswell of anger in San Salvador, too."

Iverson nodded and fell silent. Several minutes passed as Emilia drove through wooded northern Maryland. She could see that the wheels were spinning inside Iverson's mind, so let the silence play out until her partner was ready to vocalize her thoughts.

"Okay," Iverson eventually said, as they passed the Maryland House Travel Plaza. "What I'm getting at here with these questions is that we know Veronica Walsh and Jacob Jordan were very close, right?"

"Yes."

"And he's now on the run, and she has a background that means she's uniquely qualified to help in this sort of situation."

"No—" Emilia started to tell her partner not to go there, but the words died in her mouth.

"You see it, don't you?" Iverson waved her arm in front of her as if she were looking at something. "I think this is something we need to follow."

Before she had a chance to consider her answer, the car's dashboard came alive as Emilia's phone rang. She glanced down, saw the caller, and pressed the accept button. "Hello, chief," she said.

"Brown, is Iverson there too?" Chief Branaman's voice sounded weary.

"Here," Iverson said.

"Okay, minor update for you. While you were at the Jordans, we received a tip with the location of Jacob Jordan's current residence. I handed the reins to Fahey, and, to put this frankly, he blew it. He went in guns blazing without even checking if Jordan was inside. I did not expect that, and I am sorry I did not instruct him to wait until you two got back."

What the fuck? Emilia wanted to explode but kept her feelings inside her. "Did he at least find shoes that can match the Billingsley scene?" They had already established a strong connection to Georgetown, so the trace evidence had not proven as useful as hoped, but the print itself was still a possible match.

"No luck. If it was him, he's either wearing the shoes or got rid of them."

Shit. "Okay, thank you for telling us, sir. We'll handle this accordingly." Emilia took a breath. "On our end, we learned a great deal about his motivation and background. It all stems back to an accident his sister had when she was at Georgetown."

"I don't remember us ever discussing his sister before."

"You're right, they've kept her, and the incident, very quiet. We think our next course of action needs to be to follow up with the next most important figure in his life, Veronica Walsh. What did she know? Could she have even helped him?"

"Just to get to the bottom of this," Iverson added, causing Emilia to roll her eyes.

"Funny you should mention her."

"Why is that?"

"She's the one who called in to give up Jacob Jordan's address."

CHAPTER 60
MIKAELA

Night, March 12

What did Tony know? Why did he even have a ripped picture from freshman year of college? Was it a reminder of something?

Mikaela couldn't shake the feeling that there was someone else out there, holding on to the second half, ignorant of the danger he or she was in. Could that be the case? Or was it just Tony keeping the good memories and throwing away the bad?

She couldn't stand it anymore. All of a sudden, she had to get out of the house. She couldn't spend one more minute there without Tony.

She grabbed her coat and keys and charged out the front door. She climbed up into her jeep and started driving, without thinking one bit about where she was headed. She drove on autopilot, her thoughts racing.

How did it come to this?

The question she kept coming back to, the question she thought she knew the answer of the minute she was told. Why was Tony on that bridge? Was it really because of her?

Jacob Jordan had to have been there, since that's where he saw and chased her that first day. That witness then said he saw two men on the bridge.

Tony was on that bridge because he felt the overwhelming guilt of their pregnancy failures. He was up there because he couldn't take it anymore.

Right?

Mikaela realized where she was going as she made one final left turn and began creeping down the dark unlit road into Jones Point Park. The park just under the Woodrow Wilson Bridge on the Alexandria side. The closest spot on land to where Tony took his final breaths. She pulled into a parking spot just across from the basketball court. It was closed at night, but even though it was dark already outside, the park hadn't yet shut down. Moonlight shimmered off the Potomac, the waves gently lapping against the concrete barrier.

Mikaela remembered that she'd heard somewhere that a fall into water from more than eighty feet was akin to landing on concrete. But she—like most people, she assumed—couldn't judge distances like that. She looked up at the underside of the bridge. Was it more than eighty feet? Surely, right?

So, maybe he died instantly, rather than plunging into the waves still alive and the water, Earth's great life-sustaining force, holding him down until his lungs gave out. Mikaela fought a losing battle against the intruding thoughts running rampant in her mind. What happens on a fall like that? What are the injuries? How much do you feel?

She walked to the water's edge, and up onto the small fishing pier. She took off her socks and shoes, and plopped herself down, dangling her toes into the water.

"Little one, this is the closest you'll ever get to your dad," she said, putting her hand on her stomach. Her voice lowered to a whisper. "I promise you, my dear, that you'll know who he was, though. You'll know his laugh, and his love. And you'll know his heart, because it is yours too.

"He will be with you always, because half of what you are is him. He made you, and because of that you'll be perfect. I'll tell you every single day that you are the luckiest child in the entire world, because your dad was the greatest. Other kids will have present fathers, and it will be tough for you, I know. But they won't have what you have. Your father's soul living inside you.

"I'll take care of the external stuff. I'll get you dressed, I'll change your diapers, I'll teach you how to ride the swing and speak with confidence and when to cry and when not to cry. He'll be there for the rest. He'll teach you how to be a human being, my little Antonio or Antonia."

She paused and took a deep breath. "Yes, you'll also carry his name with you forever. It's you and me against the world, little one. But we've got your dad in our corner, and he wouldn't ever let us lose. We'll survive, and we'll thrive, because that's what your dad would want. He'd want you growing up, learning, loving, and living life to the fullest. And that's exactly what we'll do, my little one."

Tears streamed down Mikaela's face as she pushed herself up and turned away from the river.

Her mouth opened into a scream, but no sounds came out. She felt like someone had ripped out her vocal cords.

A figure stood in the dark, a dozen feet away. The unmistakable silhouette of a knife extended past the outstretched arm.

"I think it's time we had a little talk, isn't it?" Jacob Jordan said.

CHAPTER 61
EMILIA

Morning, March 13

"The way I see it, you have one clear task." Chief Branaman steepled his fingers and looked over the top of them at Emilia and Iverson. "You have to find and stop Jacob Jordan. Now, having said that, discovering who these other victims were, and the scale of this cover-up, could be the way to do so. I won't tell you how to conduct your investigation. I trust you, otherwise you'd have never been hired here. But what I need now are results."

"You got it, sir," Emilia said, rising from her chair.

"And Detective Brown?" The chief's voice was low and deadly serious.

"Yes?"

"Once this is over," he turned and pointed to Iverson. "If you haven't already, you both will be unearthing the cover-up. I assume you'd be looking into that whether or not I directed you to. Either way, it needs to be dealt with. Report everything back to me, no matter how insignificant it seems."

Emilia gave her boss a resolute nod and they filed out.

"All right, what are we missing?" She asked Iverson as they walked together. "What don't we know that we need to know?"

"Where Jacob Jordan is at this minute."

"Okay, yes, that is the macro concern. But how do we get there?"

"What do you mean?"

"We work up to that point. He sees that his apartment has been found. What does he do next?"

"Find somewhere else to stay."

"Exactly. Where would he go? Disguise or not, his options are limited."

"Seedy hotel," Iverson suggested.

"Sure, but that doesn't strike me as his move. He thinks too much for that. His existence for years has been defined by being the smartest guy in the room."

"So, he needs a clever solution. A friend who wouldn't give him up?"

"Not bad, but he doesn't seem to have many connections here, so hard to guess who would care that much about him that they wouldn't turn him in for murder."

"Someone else who was wronged, then."

"And we find ourselves back to square one." Emilia shot Iverson a wry smile. "We need to find those victims."

They returned to their whiteboard. "I don't think this should be difficult," Emilia said. "They would have tried to cover up this accident because it would have badly hurt the Senator's career, that's the assumption we're running with right now."

"But we must be the enemy of certainty," Iverson said, a broad smile growing on her face as she looked up to Emilia for approval.

"Right you are." Emilia saluted her junior partner. "Wonder where you first heard that one. My point being, they didn't need to hide it from prying eyes for all eternity, they just needed to pay off the right people."

"And by 'they,' we mean Senator Billingsley and the Belles?"

"Yes, and hopefully we can confirm that once we see financial statements, although there will probably be layers upon layers of obfuscation."

"Or shell companies."

"True enough. But what I think we can assume is that these were other Georgetown students. I doubt they went back and erased entire student histories, so I think our first step will be to compare the full student body from before to the one after. There will be graduations, transfers, all the normal things, but we should find students who just stopped attending for unknown reasons. Those are our targets."

They spent the entire morning closing down leads. By lunchtime the detectives had a list of five students unaccounted for: two freshmen and three sophomores who did not return for the next semester.

"All right, status check," Emilia said. "I'll start with the freshmen. Daisy Bruce doesn't seem right to me—her family is destitute, and she got in on a scholarship. If they'd been getting payoffs for years, they'd have more to show for it. I'm guessing she simply dropped out, and we can easily check that. The other freshman, Michael Cross, seems more likely."

"Good looking kid," Iverson commented, looking at the picture Emilia pulled up on her computer.

"That's part of it. A kid who looks like that is the sort you'd expect to be at a millionaire's pool. His parents lived in Michigan but have since moved out to Orange County."

"That sounds like the sort of thing you do when you want to escape the past, and have the cash to do so," Iverson remarked.

"I called and they didn't pick up, so we can't rule him out. Michael Cross is too common a name to check every adult one by one, plus I started doing so and just kept getting '*do you mean Michael Kors?*' in every search, and that's driving me nuts."

"Okay, so then the three sophomores. This is where I get confused. We're looking for three people, right?"

"There's always a chance the Jordans weren't honest, for whatever reason, but yes. Camilla said seven. Tony, Janet, Bridget, and Tracy are accounted for. That leaves three."

"Yeah, so then here's the thing. We have twins who both didn't come back to school, and then one single other. Three students total in that picture would mean it has to be the twins, but I don't think it's them. I found an obituary for their father four months after the accident occurred. It says brain cancer, so I'm thinking that's got to be a fast one, like a glioblastoma. They went home to help take care of their father, and then just stayed after he died."

"Okay, confirm that thought ASAP," Emilia said. "What about the other?"

"She's more interesting, and the one I think most likely of all of them due to her fame on campus. Erika Grant, a sophomore on the women's basketball team. She was a star high school player out of Florida, and her bio and stats are still up on the Hoyas' website."

"This is what I'm interested in. How do you keep something this big a secret from friends, coaches, teachers? This isn't from some pre-social media age, they couldn't just pretend the kid went home and left a note and that's all."

"I'll find the number for the coach at the time, see what they tell me," Iverson said, writing down Grant's name on a sticky note and putting it on the board underneath the photos of Tony, Tracy, and Bridget.

"Perfect, and I'll look into Michael Cross' history and find something to confirm it for me. I feel confident. These are two of our missing students."

"Iverson, look at this," Emilia said sharply. After hours of striking out, finding nothing at all, she had finally struck... well, not gold. But something.

"What is it?" Iverson rolled in her chair over to Emilia's side.

"Michael Cross's class schedule for that semester." Emilia pointed and Iverson leaned in. "Look at who taught him."

"Dr. Veronica Walsh," Iverson breathed out. "Well, we wanted to have a chat with her anyway."

"We did. Let's go." Emilia grabbed her notebook, and they hurried out the door.

"All roads keep coming back to her," Iverson said as they walked through the parking garage.

"I agree, and I hear you," Emilia said. "But I just don't see her having any actual involvement. From everything we know about her, if for some reason she had gone back to her teenage ways, then odds are there would be no easily trackable connections to her. I think this is solely fact-finding. If she remembers him, we might be able to confirm he was one of the victims."

"True, but best-case scenario, we do confirm this guy was one of them, but we're still missing another victim," Iverson said as she opened the car door and slumped into the passenger seat. "Someone's still out there."

CHAPTER 62
VERONICA

Afternoon, March 13

My favorite people. Who doesn't love a surprise drop-in from the police? It always goes well, and no one ever has negative things to say.

I rolled my eyes at their faux politeness and let the detectives inside. I needed to tell them about Jacob showing up here anyway.

"Hi, Ben, how are you?" Detective Brown smiled wide at my husband as he poked his head out of the kitchen, where he was hard at work concocting the perfect grilled cheese sandwiches for the kids.

"Splendid. Good to see you, Detective." He offered the full-watt smile back. Glad to see he was back to Team Police. As all straight middle-class white men tend to be.

"Let's not sit. I can't imagine you're staying long," I said, just as the little baby junior detective bent her legs above the couch. She shot a wary glance at Detective Brown and slowly rose.

"Veronica—"

"Dr. Walsh, thank you."

Detective Brown huffed.

"And before you start, Jacob Jordan was here last night." I kept my face perfectly impassive.

"He, what?" Baby Detective blanched.

"He stopped by." I shrugged nonchalantly. I couldn't help myself. I liked riling up authority figures.

Baby looked over at Detective Brown. "Like what we were saying..." she trailed off.

I cocked my head at her, dialing up a saccharine smile. "Oh, what is it you were saying?"

Detective Brown put out a calming hand. "That's not what we're here about, but we think he must have someone he's staying with now."

I couldn't stifle the laugh, so I had to cover my mouth with my hand. "You're kidding, right? Me, then? I'm your suspect?"

"You tell me," Detective Brown said. "You just told us he was here. Why?"

"That's hysterical you think this. I'm not even offended." I quickly recapped the conversation for them.

"Well, you can't blame us for thinking you'd be useful to him, considering that he did too," Baby helpfully pointed out.

"And you made the leap because I'm a murderous sociopath with a well-documented history, right?"

Baby stayed silent. Detective Brown held up her hand again, palm facing toward me. Some kind of cross between a "stop" and a "calm" motion. I wondered which she was going for. "This isn't what we're here for. We're here because we want to know what you know about a former student, Michael Cross."

That was not what I expected.

Michael Cross. I hadn't thought about him in years. Truth be told, I didn't think about him much when he was in my class. That's not what teachers are supposed to say, but everyone knows it's true. You can't fully care about all of them. "What about him?"

"He didn't come back to Georgetown the semester after you taught him," Baby said. "Do you know anything about that?"

"What is it you think I would know?"

"Any hints, suggestions, feelings? Did he say he was leaving?"

I shook my head. "No, he was a thoroughly average student. Didn't make much of a dent. Your average college kid had no interest in math. We rarely interacted besides the requisite."

The detectives shared a look.

"What is it?" I asked.

"No indication that he was planning not to return? None at all?" Detective Brown asked.

"She already asked that. You clearly are about to tell me something, so spit it out."

The detective hesitated, considering her next words. "You said that Jacob Jordan told you about why he was doing this? Just how much did he tell?"

Now it made sense. Why couldn't they have just said this upfront? "You think Michael Cross was another victim in the accident that hurt his sister, don't you?"

Detective Brown nodded.

"And you're hoping I can confirm that, with some tidbit of info."

Another nod.

"One of the other people from the picture, right? Is that what you saw too?"

Both their faces froze.

Damn it. I hate accidentally giving out information.

"What picture?" Detective Brown asked warily.

Not my story to tell, but what was I going to do?

"Mikaela found a picture in an old yearbook of Tony's. It was ripped down the middle and had three people in it. Tony, Bridget Lowe, and Tracy Belle. We looked closely at it and saw it was ripped directly down a fourth person's face."

"Don't tell me," Detective Brown said. "Janet Jordan."

"*Claro*."

Baby's stare told me she didn't know even the most basic Spanish. I raised an eyebrow at Detective Brown.

"We think that we've discovered the identity of two of the other students," Detective Brown said.

"How many others are there?" I asked. We had been running with the assumption of symmetry in that picture, but that was just a guess.

"Jacob's parents confirmed it was a group of seven," Baby Detective answered.

Seven total. Three more on the other side of the torn paper.

Symmetry after all. People don't realize how much they love it. It's at the core of our very species. We find symmetrical faces more attractive than asymmetrical. Symmetry implies goodness, whether we consciously realize it or not.

"We don't have anything concrete and can't get family members to talk," the baby continued. "But we're thinking maybe there's someone related to the accident who might be helping Jacob hide now."

"No." I shook my head. "That's not what he would do. Remember, he's the smartest guy in the room. He's not going to trust someone else."

"Well, what do you suggest then?"

"Hits close to home," I said softly, recalling Jacob's words. The realization struck me with the force of a hurricane. Close to home. Of course that was what he meant. There were very few people in the city that I would describe as such, and he wasn't dumb enough to mess with Francisco. Ben had just about zero interaction with his extended family.

Except.

"What?" Detective Brown asked, her eyes narrowed.

"I know where he is."

CHAPTER 63
MIKAELA

Afternoon, March 13

"You know what your husband did, don't you?" Jacob Jordan stood in Mikaela's reading nook next to the bay window, looking out into the street. The translucent drapes hung just in front of him, clouding the view.

"I know what you did to my husband!" Mikaela snapped from the couch, where Jacob had her sitting, arms crossed. "You murdered him, you fucking psycho."

Jacob turned back to face her. He pulled his switchblade out of his pocket and flicked it open and closed as he walked over toward her. "Want to know a secret about him?" He smiled and raised his eyebrows, like he was just about to divulge a piece of juicy gossip.

Mikaela sighed. "Look, I know something probably happened to your sister and you think it was his fault."

Jacob laughed and shook his head. "Oh, you don't know, do you? You don't know what his final thoughts were?"

"What do you mean?" Mikaela felt whatever color was left drain from her face.

"Your husband helped cover up a horrible thing, sure, but that was years ago. What made him drive and park at the bridge, though?"

"You did! You forced him there and you killed him."

"Did I?" Another arched eyebrow.

"Of course you did. Now tell me what the fuck you're doing in my house."

"Did you not think it noteworthy that there was no note?"

"No note?" Mikaela repeated.

"Well, you've followed along, I'm sure. What did I say about Bridget and our esteemed late Senator?" When Mikaela didn't respond, he clucked his tongue and continued. "I said they would pay for what they did. Isn't it curious that I didn't leave a note there on the bridge?"

"It's a bridge, it probably blew away. What are you even talking about?" Mikaela knew he was trying to get a rise out of her, and, despite herself, she could tell he was succeeding.

"There was no note because there didn't need to be a note."

Mikaela closed her eyes and shuddered. "Just, please, stop talking to me."

"What else am I supposed to do in this big house?" Jacob asked. "This truly is a great house. I mean it. Especially for the location. I mean, what is this, a million plus? No offense, but you must have gotten it for a steal. As far as places to hide out, I was ready to settle for much less."

"Is that what you're doing? Hiding out here because we found your apartment?"

"Of course. What else do you think this is? This is a means to an end, and I'd like to think you'd want to help me, seeing as I was the one there when your husband jumped."

Mikaela launched herself toward Jacob. "You killed him! He didn't jump!"

"Ah, ah, ah," Jacob admonished, his forearm raised in a blocking stance, and his other hand brandishing the knife inches from her neck. "No fast moves."

"What are you going to do, kill me like you did Tony? Kill an unborn child along with me?"

Jacob shook his head, his eyes full of disappointment. "Look, since you clearly aren't getting this, and I need to spell it out for you," he said, emphasizing each word. "I did not kill Tony."

"Then who did?" Mikaela shot back.

"When you first learned that he had jumped, did it surprise you?"

Mikaela hesitated. She wanted to say no, but hadn't she thought she was the one who drove him to it? Hadn't that been her immediate reaction when the cops showed up at her door?

Jacob nodded as he watched her contort her face. "That's right."

"But..." Mikaela couldn't get the words out.

"I was following Tony. I knew the students that were there that night—Janet's peers. Everyone was guilty in my eyes, but I still think there was something more going on." He waved his hand. "Anyway, I watched as he pulled over. He idled the car for a few minutes before he got out. I assumed he must have seen me, since I pulled over not too far away from him. But when he finally got out, he didn't look around at all. He walked straight to the side of the bridge and peered over. He was so deep in thought he didn't hear me get out, and only noticed me when I was about six feet away from him. What I noticed first was his eyes. They were red-rimmed and bloodshot. He was emotionally strung out, and very clearly about to jump."

"Why should I believe anything you're saying?" Mikaela asked.

Jacob shrugged. "That's all on you. You don't have to. I don't need to be telling you this. Why wouldn't I just keep my mouth shut rather than weaving a tall tale for you, instead? Look, I'm telling you this because of what Tony told me when he saw me there."

Mikaela gasped. "You spoke?"

Jacob bit his upper lip and shook his head. "We did, and he asked me to do something."

He stretched out the silence for several seconds. "What?" Mikaela finally asked.

Jacob's voice was soft, almost comforting, and his genuine smile took Mikaela by surprise. "He asked me to tell you it wasn't your fault."

Mikaela's hands flew to her mouth.

"May I?" Jacob pointed to the seat next to her. When Mikaela didn't respond he went ahead and sat down next to her. The knife was still there, on his lap, but he took his hands off it.

"I told him who I was, and he said he understood that I was getting revenge for Janet. He told me I didn't have to worry about him, though. He said the demons had won. He wanted you to know, though, that it had nothing to do with your struggles trying to get pregnant, or that you'd told him you'd rather be alone if you couldn't have kids. He understood it all and was willing to work through anything with you.

"What he couldn't shake was the incident. He told me he could have stopped it. He said every single day he wondered what would have been if he'd just had the strength to stop Senator Billingsley. He wished that he'd been the one to go over the cliff rather than my sister and their friends. He'd tried to tell them not to get on that golf cart, he yelled that they'd all been drinking too much. But he didn't stop them. And then he was too cowardly in the aftermath to do anything but go along with the cover-up."

Tears formed in Mikaela's eyes. Jacob saw them and gave her a small consoling nod. "That's why I didn't kill him. His own memories had been killing him every single day since then. I don't know what pushed him over the edge, maybe it was hearing that the good Senator was killed, but I was just a witness."

CHAPTER 64
VERONICA

Afternoon, March 13

I watched as they rushed out of the house, Baby Detective stumbling as she attempted to leap the two front stairs at the same time. How did that pairing happen?

It took all the restraint I could muster to stay home and not follow them as they raced over to Mikaela Alonso's house. Of course, they told me not to, but would that have stopped me? My family was here, though, and we needed more time to heal.

I had forgiven Ben, and the kids were fine too, but that just meant it was time to move forward. Remind all of us of what the best version of this family can be. And that didn't include chasing after police detectives just to be there in case their arrest attempt went awry.

They would tell me, or I'd hear one way or another, what went down. I hoped Mikaela was safe, but barging in myself at the same time as the cops wouldn't do anyone any good. I reminded myself that I spent decades away from danger. I didn't have to dive headfirst at every opportunity, even if it was to protect my newfound sister in-law.

"What I want to know is what doesn't Jacob know about that night?"

"What do you mean?" Ben asked.

"Well, his knowledge has been pieced together, right? His sister can only tell him so much. So does he really know what happened?"

Ben thought about it. "He must know enough," he reasoned. "Since if he didn't, he'd be trying to get the full story rather than just killing those involved. If we go back to the Belles first, he drove them off the road. That wasn't the act of someone who needed information."

"You're right. And you make a good point. Who did know? Obviously, the Belles and Senator Billingsley, but who else? If anyone?"

"I've been thinking about that," Ben said. "It doesn't make sense that it was only Senator Billingsley there, besides a group of college students. He clearly ended up around them, probably because he was a horny adult male and there were college girls in bikinis, but what were the Belles doing then? Were they just watching him? Because that doesn't seem to make any sense to me."

I understood what he was getting at. "You think there were two separate things going on. The kids out in the back, and adults somewhere else?"

"Exactly. Somehow, they must have blended together at some point."

"So, there were more people there who saw it. People who might have been meeting with the Belles and Senator Billingsley." I arched an eyebrow. "People who know the full story of what happened."

"Who could it be?"

"I might have an idea, actually," Ben said. "Let me go see. You good with the kids here for a bit?"

"No problem, do your thing."

"Love you, ciao!" He popped up, blew me a kiss, and headed toward the door.

Look at us go. Working together to solve cases. Maybe we should put out a shingle together. Walsh & Walsh, at your service.

"Babe, have you seen my wallet?" I heard him call from the entryway.

My brilliant husband was afflicted with a common ailment among men. A debilitating case of recurring situational blindness. I didn't even bother to respond anymore. The moment I acknowledge it is always the moment he magically finds what he is looking for.

I waited, listening as he rummaged around.

The door opened, and then closed a second later. Guess he found it.

As I walked upstairs my phone rang. I picked it up ready to make fun of Ben for forgetting his car keys, or misplacing the car itself, but it wasn't him.

"Veronica, it's Detective Brown."

Her voice told me the answer to my question, but I had to ask. "Did you get him?"

"No. No sign of either of them, but he was definitely here. You know him best of any of us, where would he take her?"

"If I offer my thoughts, will you pick me up and let me come with you, or will I have to follow in a car right behind you?"

A sigh, then a pause. "Fine, sure," Detective Brown said. "I don't care, whatever lets us find him as fast as possible."

Guess I was back to running headfirst into danger after all.

CHAPTER 65
MIKAELA

Afternoon, March 13

Mikaela saw him tense up, just for a split second. "What is it?"

"Someone's coming," Jacob said. "Come on, we have to go."

"Absolutely not."

Jacob rolled his eyes up toward the ceiling. "Do I have to spell this out to you?"

"All I have to do is make it hard for you to leave, and then the police will catch you. That seems pretty straightforward."

"I'm wanted for multiple murders. If they catch me, I'm going away forever, or worse. Do you think that I would risk that by not simply shooting you if you try anything?"

"You have a gun?"

Jacob reached down toward his foot and rolled a single pant leg up. He pulled a small handgun out of an ankle holster and held it out in front of Mikaela. "Just because I don't bring it out immediately doesn't mean it's not there."

Mikaela trembled. There was something about a gun that evoked that much more fear than a knife.

"Look," Jacob said. "I don't actually want to hurt you, contrary to my actions so far. I have no quarrel with you, and as it turned out, I had no quarrel with your husband, either. Now, we're going to go somewhere and when the police inevitably come, they'll be so distracted getting you that they'll leave me to escape. After that, you'll never see me again, I promise." He flipped the gun around, so his finger was off the trigger, and in one motion re-holstered it on his ankle. "Are we good?"

Mikaela didn't know how to react, so she just stood motionless.

"All right, good enough," Jacob said. "Let's move."

He grabbed her arm, and they raced out the back door. They hustled through the back yard and into the alleyway.

"You don't have a second car back here by any chance, do you?"

"I wouldn't tell anyway."

"Fair enough," he conceded. "Good thing I found this key fob cloner online. Just need a car new enough that it starts with the push of a button." His eyes scanned the alley until he saw a Honda Pilot several houses down. "Bingo."

They were in the car and got it up and running in seconds. Jacob put the car in drive, and they careened out of the alley onto the main road.

"Where are we going?" Mikaela asked.

Jacob didn't take his eyes off the road. "You'll see." His hands gripping the wheel were starting to lose color.

He's losing control, Mikaela thought.

"I can't get caught now," he muttered through clenched teeth. "There's too much still to do."

Mikaela could feel herself beginning to humanize him, and tamped the feelings down as best she could.

"What's your plan?"

"What do you think? A trap." He shrugged. "You're going to help me spring it."

"Veronica will figure it out."

Jacob shot her a patronizing look as they headed for the beltway. "You don't think that's exactly who I've planned for? The smartest person we know is going to be after me, so of course I have a plan for how to neutralize your sister-in-law."

"My… what?" Mikaela did her best to look confused.

"Don't try to pretend. I know who you are. I know your half-brother. I know everything."

Mikaela felt her confidence eroding. She thought having Veronica on her side would give her the upper hand.

Jacob sighed, and looked over at her, his face contorted into a grimace. "Look, I know you're pregnant, and you're scared. I swear, you are just part of a trap. That's all. Just work with me, and everything is going to be okay."

Mikaela didn't know what to say, so they drove in silence. She watched as Jacob flicked the turn signal and moved toward the exit lane. Now she understood.

Where else would they be headed?

CHAPTER 66
VERONICA

Afternoon, March 13

I appreciated symmetry, like any good mathematician. I liked a good story to end back where it started.

But more importantly, I knew how much Jacob Jordan appreciated symmetry. The semester he took my abstract algebra class, he was mesmerized by the idea of symmetries in the mathematical sense. All the permutations and combinations that can lead you back to the original element. That rotating a square ninety degrees is a symmetric mapping but rotating a rectangle isn't. He liked that idea.

So, why wouldn't he return back to where it all began?

Lucky for me, our grandmotherly neighbor Stella was available to come over on short notice and spend the afternoon with the kids, so I hitched a ride with the detectives, and we sped through traffic, heading out west toward World's Edge.

"What's the endgame?" Detective Brown asked.

I wasn't sure if she was asking me or Iverson—whose name I eventually decided to commit to memory—and not just thinking out loud.

"My question is are we sure we should be listening to her?" Iverson jerked her head back toward me. "What if we bring the cavalry and he's not there?"

"Then I'll have made a wrong decision, and we'll all move on," Emilia said. "Anyway, she's not wrong."

"How do you know?"

"Just look at her."

"You know, I'm really fucking tired of that."

Detective Brown raised an eyebrow. "Go on."

Iverson glanced back at me, and I flashed a peace sign and offered a friendly smile. I also wanted to see where she was going with this.

"Why does everyone in this town treat her as some fucking hero? You do realize she murdered people? Murdered. As in that thing that we jail people for life over. Yet somehow because she's hot and seems like a badass and *probably* hasn't killed anyone in this country, it's all just swept under the rug? This is why I didn't closely follow that case, if you were wondering. Because the fawning is ridiculously over the top." She turned around in her seat and pointed an angry index finger in my direction. "How many people did you kill?"

"Twenty-seven." No point in lying.

"That's what I'm talking about, Detective." Iverson's face was like watching a ripening tomato on fast-forward. "She is a psychopath who we all just pretend isn't one because her father is a bad dude. You know who didn't kill *twenty-seven* people? Kids of criminals all over the world. Abused kids. Affluenza kids. Why the actual fuck do we make excuses for her?"

Detective Brown raised her eyebrows and looked at me through the rear-view mirror. "You want to take this, or should I?"

"I'm pretty curious to hear your answer," I said.

"Look," Detective Brown said. "I get it. But I can only control what I think. I can't do anything about what the rest of the world thinks. And the one thing the people of this country might just love more than a hero, is an anti-hero. On top of that, if it didn't happen in the States, a lot of people just don't care, or really think of it as real life."

When it was clear that was the end of her answer, I figured I might as well add my own take. "Here's the thing. People love true crime, right?" I waited for Iverson to acknowledge, and she finally gave a tiny nod, her cute little pigtails bouncing once and returning to their resting place. "Why is that? Because they love the stories of the good cops saving the day? No. Because they crave stories of violence that are far enough removed from their own lives. Emotional gravitas that can't actually affect you. Same reason people engage with any sort of entertainment. You want to feel alive. And when your daily life doesn't provide that, what do you do? Books, television, sports, anything to feel more. True crime makes your heart pound, and isn't that sort of what life is all about anyway? So, when you want a good story, something true but removed, what could be better than mine? A woman who was violent from a young age but also someone we can watch from our couches with our comfy blankets and root for. You can make excuses for me and my behavior, and that's what people want. People who do, or did, bad things but have layers. You watch pure evil once, and you don't look again. You see someone like me, and you keep coming back. That's just how it works."

Detective Brown didn't say anything, but I could see in her eyes through the mirror that she agreed.

"Just for the record," I added. "You trust that I'm right also, or else you would be putting up more of a fight. You just don't want to admit it."

Iverson didn't respond.

I watched over the seat as she folded her hands into her lap. They were trembling slightly. "You two are awfully chatty for people heading into a dangerous situation," she finally said.

"We can deal with your feelings about me later, but the reason that Detective Brown let me come with you is because she understands what I can do. Am I a certainty? Not at all. But am I the best secret weapon you could hope for? Absolutely. We're going to find Jacob, we'll confront him, we'll get Mikaela and her baby to safety, and you'll arrest him."

"How can you be that confident?"

"What do you lose by being confident?" I never understood this question. "If you trust in yourself, why wouldn't you be confident, no matter the situation?"

"Because that's not how life works!" Iverson raised her voice. "You get beaten down over and over again and it makes you question everything."

I snickered. "How old are you?"

"Twenty-five."

No way. She didn't look older than fifteen. "What has beaten your life down so far?"

I saw Detective Brown avert her gaze, as if she knew what was about to be said.

"My family is a little bit... different, and not so understanding," Iverson said. "They are used to getting what they want and having much higher ambitions. They never respected that I always wanted to be a detective. They have a lot of sway and think that I'm not using the opportunities I was given."

"Who is your family?" I didn't know of anyone in the city named Iverson. And no matter how silky a basketball player he was in his day, she couldn't be talking about Allen Iverson.

"I use my mom's maiden name. It's easier than my actual last name. People don't stop and ask questions every time they hear it."

"Just tell her," Detective Brown said.

"My full name is Elaine Leishear."

"A relation to our esteemed president, I assume?" I said, trying to keep my tone even. *So that's how she's a detective so young.*

"He is my uncle." She paused. "And godfather."

"So, your hard luck story is being born into *too* powerful a family and them being upset at you for not wanting to wield your portion of said power?" I gave up on the even tone.

"You don't know what that's like!" Iverson protested.

Detective Brown did a small fake cough. "Sorry, partner, but she knows exactly what that is like."

"Look, it is what it is," I said. "We can chat about your president uncle later. We're about to get to World's Edge. Let's finish this."

CHAPTER 67
MIKAELA

Afternoon, March 13

Jacob pulled into the long driveway of World's Edge, and then slid the car off the road onto the strip of dirt alongside. "We won't need a quick exit," he saw Mikaela's questioning look and answered her unspoken question. "Come on." He waved his switchblade at her, gesturing for her to get out.

She allowed herself a quick glance into the woods.

He shook his head. "Don't bother. Too much underbrush, you won't get very far."

"But I'll get away from you."

He mimed a large yawn. "I'd shoot you and then while the cops search and you bleed out, I'd make my escape that way."

"Why don't you do it then?" Mikaela threw her arms out, exasperation masking her fear for a second. "Just escape. Leave me here and run and never look back."

"No. Can't do that. I need a captive audience. I need them to know. I can't do the rest of this myself."

"The rest of what?"

Jacob didn't answer. He pushed her along around the side of the house. They walked through the concrete area next to the infinity pool. Mikaela recognized it from the picture immediately. They continued until Mikaela realized Jacob wasn't slowing down as they got closer to the cliff's edge. She planted her feet into the pristine grass. "Hold on, wait wait wait," she stammered.

"Come on now, I'm not throwing you off the cliff." He struggled to keep hold of her upper arm as she pulled away. "Don't make me—" he leaned and pulled out his gun. "Don't make me use this."

Mikaela saw it. This was her chance. It didn't matter what he said, his claims that she would be safe. She had to get away.

She leapt up, dug her foot into the ground, and pushed off, running parallel to the cliff, the fastest path to the tree line. The tree line meant salvation. It meant obstacles, it meant obstructions. Branches and tree trunks between her and Jacob. She counted her steps. Only twenty more. Don't look back.

Only ten more. Almost there. She was getting away.

She felt a thump against the back of her head, and the trees, her lifeline, faded as she fell forward into blackness.

CHAPTER 68
VERONICA

Afternoon, March 13

I didn't want the detectives to hear, so I waited until we pulled to a stop behind Jacob's stolen car and got out. He hadn't hidden it very well, which Iverson immediately claimed was a good sign. Brown disagreed, and Iverson looked over to me as I was the tie-breaking vote. I walked a few feet away, just out of earshot, brushing off her question.

Francisco picked up after the first ring. "I was just about to call you. You won't believe the guy, Jamie—"

I cut him off. "Francisco, I'm at World's Edge with two cops. Jacob kidnapped Mikaela and brought her here. Come now, and don't be seen."

"Okay, but you'll want to know—"

I hung up. Whatever I wanted to know would have to wait. I didn't have space in my mind for anything else right now.

I knew I didn't have to give him any other instructions. He would show up, assess exactly what was needed, and do it. The police thought I was their ace in the hole, but they didn't realize their ace had her own hidden up her sleeve.

I was still relaxed. We would have to take whatever threats he was about to make seriously, but he didn't want to hurt her. As long as he didn't think he was in a desperate situation, we would all be fine. He was smart, he would have a plan. As long as he thought his plan was working, no one would be in danger.

I walked behind the detectives. They were discussing plans in hushed tones. I didn't need to hear. This wasn't my show. I wasn't so hubristic as to think I was in charge. They'd lead, they'd engage, I'd stay back.

Until I was called upon.

My mind wandered as we passed by the side of the house. I think that's what separates me from most people. I walk into danger and become calmer.

The one time I'd ever set foot inside a house this size was one of those stories Detective Iverson would be upset about.

Maynor Mejia's home. My first targeted killing experience. I'd killed that one man who broke in a couple years before, but that had just been instinct. I never even found out who he was. I was too young to be included in such matters.

Not for long, though.

He and his brother lived in a house that backed up into a small grove of densely packed trees. I think the security wasn't necessarily lax, just not creative enough. The trees were tall but thin, no one thought that they were climbable. They were right—for adult men.

Not for me. I waited until Osmin had left the house. I could see everyone coming and going from my vantage point at the tree canopy. Maynor was the threat. Osmin was rumored to be the sanguine twin.

When the coast was clear I launched myself down onto a balcony. There were still sentries and other security I needed to avoid. I hadn't made it to the highest balcony. I wasn't an Olympian. I had to get up one more floor, avoid being seen—or at least, avoid having anyone alert Maynor. Shimmying up the side of the house was easy enough, and a reminder to tell my father all our houses should have smooth exteriors with no spots that could be handholds. There was no one on the upper balcony, but I could see a man pacing back and forth along the hallway inside. I wasn't yet the machine I would become, so it was all on instinct at that point. Thinking back, it was a blessing in disguise that he was there. Otherwise, I wonder if I might have lost my nerve once I came upon Maynor in his bath inside. But having already had to kill a man, I knew there was no turning back. So, when the man turned his back to the balcony, I shot inside and dropped low, sliding toward him. I slashed his left Achilles tendon with my knife, and I slid by. As he began to howl with pain, I launched upward and plunged the knife right into his neck as he fell. It was over in the space of a couple seconds and, most importantly, no one was the wiser.

I moved quickly into the bedroom, a quick scan showing me that it was empty. The bathroom light was on, though, and soft music was coming out. Someone was going to find that man in the hallway at any second, so I didn't even hesitate cutting Maynor's throat in the bath.

Taking his finger back as a trophy was an inspired idea, if I do say so.

I still don't know what gave me the confidence. Confidence begets confidence, though, so once I'd delivered the finger back to my father, there was no looking back. But before that first go-round? I had sat in my room, thinking about what Kelvin would have done. Kelvin would have fixed things, that's what he was good at.

Only as I got older did I learn Kelvin never fixed things the way I did. But I believed that I needed to stop Maynor because that's what Kelvin should have been here to do.

I didn't think a lot about my brother anymore. That sounds harsh, but that's also just the truth about death. Death robs you of shared experiences, and when someone is taken from you that early, you have an entire life of experiences that weren't shared. Do I wish Kelvin could have seen what I have become? Of course. But do any of my core memories past the age of thirteen include him? Nope.

I wonder if he would have grown up to be our father. I liked to think not. Kelvin wasn't as heartless as dad. We both got that little bit of humanity from mom, no matter how human dad tried to be now. He'd be Francisco, but looking down to his little sister, rather than looking up like Francisco did.

A piercing scream brought me out of my thoughts.

The detectives had turned the corner and were looking out onto the expansive back lawn. I followed Detective Brown's gaze.

On the perfectly manicured lawn, the contrast was stark.

Mikaela lay, face down, inches from the cliff edge.

Shit. Maybe I was wrong.

CHAPTER 69
EMILIA

Afternoon, March 13

Emilia started running, her gun already out in her hand. She couldn't see Jacob, but he had to be close. "Iverson, eyes up!" she yelled, assuming her partner was right behind her. No use running toward a victim just to get killed in the process. This was why you needed trust between partners. No time to check, she hoped she could trust her. The scream Iverson had let off when she saw the body didn't help.

Breathe into each step. Don't lose your bearings for even a millisecond. She ran across the open lawn, trying not to think about the trees flanking either side, and what they could be hiding.

"Ambulance now, World's Edge!" she screamed into her radio.

She was close now. Only ten more yards. Football players made it seem so small. A quick slant to your slot receiver and you make up that ground in no time.

Then two things happened at once.

Mikaela rolled over, wincing and blinking her eyes.

And a cell phone rang, just a few feet to Emilia's right, lying in the grass.

She froze. A quick glance at Mikaela showed her that she was okay, so she dove toward the phone. "Who is this?" she asked as she sucked in air.

"Put it on speaker," a tinny, modulated voice said.

"No."

"Put it on speaker, or she gets shot and goes off the cliff."

Emilia sighed and pressed the button. That's the thing with directly interacting with perps. Before you learn anything about the person on the other end of the line, you have to assume they are deadly serious. And given everything she already knew about Jacob Jordan, he wasn't one to bluff.

"Can all four of you hear me?"

"Four?" Emilia scanned the trees but couldn't make any shapes out.

"I see two detectives, Mikaela Alonso, and of course Veronica Walsh must be nearby. She wouldn't miss this."

So, he didn't have a view of the entire yard. He couldn't see Veronica behind them. Good to know. "What did you do to Mikaela?"

"Oh, she was just resting. She'll be fine as long as you do as I say."

"And what is that, exactly?"

"Stay right where you are. If you move toward Mikaela, or if Mikaela takes a step away from the cliff, she gets a bullet that will knock her right off. And I bet you already know what that fall will do, don't you, Detective? What did good old Camilla and Gavin have to say? Or were they too busy counting their money still?"

"Okay, we hear you. No movement." Emilia ignored the last question. She made eye contact with Mikaela. *You ok?* she mouthed.

Mikaela touched the back of her head, contorting her face into a pained grimace, but nodded. Her eyes darted around wildly. She opened her mouth to say something, but Emilia shushed her with a finger to her lips.

"There's an ambulance on the way already, Jacob. You're outnumbered and surrounded, so why don't you just come out?"

"Nope. It's time for a chat. Hey! Mikaela, don't you move," Jacob said suddenly.

Emilia turned around and saw Mikaela crouch back down. *No clear view, but he can see her.*

She looked at Iverson and shrugged. “All right. Let's chat.”

CHAPTER 70
VERONICA

Afternoon, March 13

Jacob began to talk.

"This was her favorite place in the world. Did you guys find that out in your investigation? Every time she called home, it was all she wanted to talk about. She was friends with Tracy Belle, and she got to spend every weekend up here. The Belles didn't allow big parties, but there were a select few who could come hang out with Tracy. It was the most exclusive club at Georgetown, and Janet made the cut. They were inseparable, that group. The type who'd eventually get matching tattoos to commemorate their friendship."

"And then Senator Billingsley took it all away," Detective Brown said.

"Don't rush me!" came the angry response.

Of course, she was trying to move things along. But I was only half-listening anyway. I wanted to know the story, yes, but I was the one who was going to stop him. I had seen Detective Brown looking around, surveying. She noticed the same thing I did.

He couldn't see the whole scene.

I slowly stepped back. No quick retort from the phone. I took another step.

Still nothing.

Iverson saw what I was doing and glared. I pointed at the phone and mimed that he couldn't see me. That didn't placate her. Worth a try. Not that I needed her approval anyway.

He had to be in the trees. There was no other option. But which side?

The point was to stay hidden. He needed us to not be able to see him just as much as he needed to see us. Right or left?

My instinct said right. I couldn't describe why, but that seemed the better option in my mind. Something deep inside my subconscious picked up on some tiny piece of information. Because that's what instinct is. Your brain working on such a level that you can't consciously tell why you choose a thing.

But there's a problem with instinct when you're me. My instinct was that the woods on the right were the better option. If I were him, that's where I would have gone. But I'm not normal. I'm not the average person. So, would his instincts match with mine?

EMILIA

Emilia watched Veronica sneak away, and a pit formed in her stomach. Something wasn't right. How could someone so smart, so good at planning have this obvious blind spot? Was this the next part of a masterplan, or the last throw of the dice from a flailing young man? Neither option filled her with confidence.

"Janet said there were always 'adult parties,' as she called them, happening at the same time," Jacob continued. "A group of men and women in suits who would stay upstairs in the house. As long as they were there, the students were left to do whatever they wanted outside.

"The pool is heated, so every gathering was a pool party, no matter the time of year. They had two golf carts that they would drive around. Caused the groundskeeper all sorts of bother having to keep the lawn pristine after they'd had a night of fun."

Emilia glanced back toward the terrace. She saw just one golf cart and another piece of the puzzle clicked in her mind.

"Did they smoke a little weed? Sure, but they didn't act too crazy or anything. Not until Senator Billingsley first laid eyes on them. You've seen the picture, I assume. You know what those girls looked like. It was a who's who of the hottest people on campus. Janet mentioned he was around. He'd always hover nearby, his eyes lingering. Mom and dad didn't like that at all, but what could they do? They reached out to the Belles. Mrs. Belle listened and told them she understood and would make sure she was always watching.

"All seemed okay, she was having fun, and her grades were fine, so mom and dad stopped worrying. They trusted the Belles to keep her safe from hungry men of power. But when in human history has that really worked? One night Mrs. Belle was, I don't know, otherwise indisposed somehow, and the Senator came down to the pool. He said he wanted to take the prettiest co-ed he'd ever seen for a joyride. He'd been drinking, and possibly more. Janet didn't want to go, but Michael Cross and Erika Grant convinced her. And when I say convinced her, I mean they basically dragged her on. They both saw the Senator as their ticket to the halls of Congress. They jumped in the back of the golf cart and pulled Janet into the front. They joked that they were acting as good staffers, getting two parties together for an important meeting. Everyone else in the pool—Tracy, Miranda, Tony, and Bridget—ganged up on her too. They all jumped out and surrounded the golf cart, holding her in."

VERONICA

I could still hear him talking, and my heart hurt for the Jordan family. You spend eighteen years protecting your children and send them off to college with the assumption they'll still be protected. Sure, they're technically adults, but they still need help. RAs, advisors, teachers, they're all supposed to be part of that protection.

I couldn't imagine what I'd do if something happened to a child of mine. Ben would go nuts.

A small stick snapped under my feet as I did my best to avoid a low-hanging branch. Someone had gone to a lot of effort to make these woods impassable. The Belles, probably. Or, more likely, a group of underpaid workers directed by the Belles from literally up on high. The thick bramble cut at my ankles, just above my HOKA running shoes. I needed to be looking at the treetops, but taking my eyes away from the ground for a second would cause me to fall. I wasn't concerned about potential pain, just the noise.

I glanced back, despairing that I was only a handful of feet from the lawn. This was taking far too long. I needed to throw caution to the wind. Cuts and noise be damned.

I thrashed and powered through branches and vines, making an unholy racket.

Minutes passed, and then I looked up through the dark of the branches. I couldn't explain how I saw him. There was no reason I should have been able to do so. He was perfectly camouflaged, a dark brown and green blob, blending in with the leaves and branches, at least fifty feet up.

But I saw him, nonetheless. My father used to shrug and say, "just one of those things," when lieutenants inquired about my most recent feat of wonder.

Two legs, dangling either side of a small branch.

There was no way to contact the others, I was too deep into the woods. How he even had any line of sight, I could not understand.

Guess I'm doing this myself.

I veered left and started picking my way through the underbrush. Time to save the day.

MIKAELA

"He got her in the golf cart, and they did a few donuts on the lawn."

Mikaela strained to hear. She didn't dare move further. Her head throbbed and she could feel each pulse down her spine.

She didn't know how Jacob caught her. She was sure she was going to make it to the woods.

Next thing she knew, she was lying on the edge of the lawn, and cops were yelling and running in her direction. Until they came to an abrupt stop.

When she came to, the first thing she did was press her hands to her stomach. She knew she couldn't feel any kicking yet, but she told herself she'd know if something was wrong. After a few deep breaths, nothing felt wrong, and she had thanked her lucky stars.

She sat up and swayed woozily as she listened to Jacob telling the story.

"After that didn't impress her, he took it further and further. She liked the attention, but she didn't like this. Like I said, she was in the passenger seat and her two supposed friends were in the second row. The rest of those friends," he spat out the word. "They ran alongside, joining in on the fun. She started reaching for the wheel, and the Senator put his arm across to hold her down. They wrestled for control. She almost made it out, but Bridget pushed her back inside. It was still all a game to them. But the golf cart continued to veer, closer and closer to the edge."

Mikaela realized she was holding her breath. In all her years of hoping, wishing, waiting for a child, she had never thought about what it would be like to lose one. She had only considered what it would be like giving a child a loving mother. Providing for them, nurturing them, allowing them to grow into the fullest versions of themselves. She felt her throat constricting. *I will protect you always, little one,* she mouthed down, cradling her stomach.

"I think you all know what happens next. The cart toppled over the side of the cliff. Because powerful men manage never to see consequences, the Senator managed to land comfortably on the lawn, inches away from the edge. My sister and the others weren't so lucky. The only reason Janet is alive today, and not in a grave along with those cowardly so-called friends, is because she was launched from the golf cart at the first bounce. The other two remained inside, all the way down, until the cart plunged into the Potomac. There was no saving them.

"My sister, however, was 'saved,' if you can even call it that. She hit a tree jutting out horizontally, and it stopped her fall. She dangled there for hours, before falling further to the bank. They finally managed to reach her by boat. But it was already too late for her to have a normal life."

This was the time to try. While Jacob was at his most emotionally vulnerable. When he might take his eye off the ball. Mikaela jumped up and lunged forward.

For a second there was no reaction. She was going to make it to the detective's side. She'd be safe.

"Don't you dare!" Jacob screamed.

A second later, she felt the ripple of air as the bullet went by before she even heard the crack of the rifle.

VERONICA

I heard the shot, but there was nothing I could do. I just had to keep climbing. Climbing trees was about focus and composure. You had to trust your muscles.

I remembered standing on the ground, looking up at the trees outside Maynor Mejia's home. I was terrified. I had climbed trees in our compound many times, of course, but this was different. This was a climb for a deadly purpose. I stood there for several minutes, waging an internal war. The rational part of me said just turn around, go back home. No one knows you are here. Nothing will change. The irrational, or maybe instinctual, side said something had to change, and I was the one to do it. So, up I climbed.

I had lost sight of Jacob as I made my way up the tree. There was no way he had moved, though. I was about twenty feet from where the branch he was on connected with the trunk. I was doing my best to stay quiet, but that wasn't important anymore. I just needed speed.

As I climbed, I realized just how close to the cliff we were. There were only a few trees between me and the edge.

The shot clearly came from above me, so who was he firing at? Did he make good on his threat to kill Mikaela? Despite it all, despite the mountain of evidence, I still didn't believe he was someone who would attack an innocent woman.

It must have been a warning shot.

I willed myself to believe it as I climbed on. Branch by branch, getting closer.

EMILIA

"Are you hurt?" Emilia asked, tentatively crouching and taking a step toward where Mikaela lay on her stomach.

Mikaela whimpered but shook her head. She pushed herself up into a sitting position, rubbing her shoulder.

"That was your one warning," Jacob said.

Emilia hoped Veronica was close to finding him. Iverson had tried to step away, but he'd seen her too, so she and Iverson were stuck within eyesight of a killer with a rifle. Not the best spot she'd ever found herself.

"Anyway." Jacob's voice was beginning to sound more and more agitated. "That should have been that, right? A horrible tragedy, an accident by all accounts, and then a just punishment for the driver. But that's not how things work in this country. Instead, they engaged in the true American pastime. A cover-up. Not just a simple 'something tragic happened, no one can say for sure what or why,' but a layers-deep conspiracy theorist's dream of a cover-up. The accident didn't even happen at all. Janet dropped out, Michael and Erika left school under suspicious but distinct covers. And the rest of them went on like nothing ever happened. Tracy, Tony, and Bridget just went back to school. Probably told all their friends that they, too, were perplexed about their classmates seemingly dropping off the face of the earth, when they knew the truth that those classmates literally did *drop off the face of the earth*." Jacob was almost shouting now.

Tracy, Tony, and Bridget. Emilia thought for a second. That wasn't right. "Wait, Jacob, who was the other student?" she asked.

"What other student?"

"We know there were seven students involved. Your parents told us. But only six are accounted for now in your story. Where is the seventh student?"

VERONICA

Having seen blood dripping down my hands many times, I couldn't rid my head of the thought that the sap seeping through my fingers looked eerily reminiscent.

Was my sister-in-law's blood pouring out of her at this very moment? Was I too late?

What people who learned my story recently didn't realize was how little fear was part of my life when I was a teenager. My missions were mine, and mine alone. There was no worry about whether someone else would get hurt if I made a mistake. There was only me. And I never worried about myself. It wasn't until I met my adoptive parents in Mexico that I truly began to fear what would happen to those close to me. Years of it just being me and my father, who would scoff at the mere idea of someone fearing for his safety, had dulled those senses. I had to relearn how to be vulnerable about others. How to worry.

Sometimes, I wished I could turn it off.

Seconds stretched into minutes as I continued my ascent, muscles burning.

It felt like hours had passed, but I finally reached the branch. I allowed myself five seconds to take a single deep breath and check all my muscles could still work as advertised.

All systems go. Time to move.

As I inched myself forward like a worm, I considered my options. I had the high ground, per se, since I was between him and getting back to the ground. The only other way down was over the edge. Most importantly, this was Jacob Jordan. He wouldn't shoot me.

Part of appearing invincible is simply knowing your adversary. You don't go up against an opponent without already knowing their weakness. This was my area of expertise. Infiltrating, sneaking, and then snuffing out before they even had a chance.

Why was I always so confident? Because I knew the state of play and I knew the likely outcomes.

Jacob wouldn't shoot me. Once I was close enough to him, I'd call Detective Brown, and that would be that. He'd bluster and threaten, but he wouldn't be able to bring himself to do it. If the choice were jail or killing me, he'd choose jail. You don't fake true human connection.

I stopped about ten feet from him. My only unobstructed view was of his legs, dangling on either side of the branch. I could tell, though, that he was leaning forward and holding the rifle. Criss-crossing branches from other trees obscured my view.

I took a deep breath and forced my pulse down. Just another day.

"Jacob!" I called.

He whipped his head around.

EMILIA

"What seventh student?"

"Come on, Jacob, don't play games with us." Iverson spoke up for the first time. "Who aren't you telling us about?"

"You set this all up out here so you could tell us your story," Emilia said. "So, tell us."

"I have no idea what you're talking about. There were six Georgetown students there: Janet, Tony, Bridget, Tracy, Michael, and Erika. That's all."

"You're lying to us. There's a seventh, and you're hiding them because they're helping you." Emilia thought back to the picture. Sure, they could've just been lined up lopsided, but that didn't make sense to her. Why would the picture be centered on the fourth person if there were only six there? "Do you know the picture we're talking about?"

"The one of them all standing together by the pool? Yeah, of course. Tony ripped his copy so that it was just a picture of him, Tracy, and Bridget. He couldn't bear to look at the full picture."

"Well then who was on the other side?"

"Michael, Erika, and—" Jacob started to laugh. "Wait, you really thought you had some clue? That I left some big strobe light flashing out the truth? You found the beacon, pointing you to some larger understanding?"

"Who else was there?"

"No other *student* was there. You must be smart, Detective, figure it out. Think."

Emilia didn't like his patronizing tone.

Mikaela's voice was barely over a whisper. "Miranda," she said. "Miranda was the seventh, wasn't she?"

Emilia grimaced. Jacob was right. Of course she should have thought of that. How old would Miranda Belle have been?

"She was sixteen," Jacob said, as if he could read her thoughts. "A high schooler who always wanted to kick it with her older sister's friends."

"But you didn't kill her," Iverson said.

"He tried," Emilia responded. "Didn't you? That car accident was supposed to take them all out."

"I never had as much beef with her as the others," Jacob said. "But you're right, someone else killed her. If I recall, Dr. Walsh, wasn't it your husband who pushed the first domino that led to her demise? You've been oddly quiet."

Emilia shared a worried glance with her partner. Iverson's eyes were wide. She shrugged and shook her head.

"Doc, are you there?"

"She's here, Jacob, you just can't hear her, hold on!" Emilia blurted out.

"Shit," he said under his breath.

The line disconnected.

VERONICA

Time slowed as the man swung his gun around toward me.

I was face to face with a man I had never seen in my life. He was fully decked out in Columbia Performance Gear, with a large fisherman's hat shading his face.

Jacob wouldn't shoot me, but who the fuck was this? I had no guarantees anymore.

My heart thumped. This wasn't how I was supposed to react. I felt myself start to overheat.

I thought I recognized his face from somewhere, but isn't that what everyone says? You want to recognize someone, so you convince yourself you do. He was probably in his forties, very tanned. He had a thin mustache and goatee.

But I was struck most by what I didn't see.

Anger. Fear.

He was simply confused, his brain trying to work out what he was seeing.

But the rifle kept swinging.

I had a million questions. But I wasn't a survivor because I stopped and asked questions. I was a survivor because I always act.

I didn't have the freedom of knowing I wouldn't get shot. But I never banked on that a minute in my life anyway.

Play to your strengths.

The detectives would be mad at me. They would want all their questions answered. But a dead woman can't answer questions. They would say I should have found a better way. Iverson would say once a killer, always a killer.

But that's the thing about me. I'm not a killer, I'm a survivor. I always have been.

I don't think he ever realized what I was doing. He was just concentrating on his task. Swivel and shoot. Take out anyone who comes near.

So, when I leaned forward and put all my weight onto the thinnest part of the branch ahead of me, he didn't react.

It was only when he heard the crack did his eyes snap up and catch mine. I don't like the fear in someone's eyes when they know they're about to die. Maybe because of how long I've spent thinking about how I would look. It's not nice, and I think that's what separates me from the psychopaths.

A distinction likely lost on most people.

The branch snapped in between us and for just a split second I heard him start to scream, and then he was gone.

CHAPTER 71
JACOB

Evening, March 13

Fucking hell.

This had all been going perfectly. He had to move now. If Dr. Walsh wasn't within eyesight, then she could easily be on his trail.

At least he felt confident that she would try to find and stop the sniper first. Neutralize the threat. But up until now he had been quietly confident that everything was falling into place.

The detectives were stuck in place, watching Mikaela, listening intently to his story. Dr. Walsh was supposed to be there too, and while they all were together, safe in the knowledge that Jacob was nearby, he was slipping away unseen.

This play had two acts. He needed them to know that act one was only just finishing. He hadn't gotten to that part, yet.

They would call back. They had to. He could get another shot fired in Mikaela's direction. Something to keep them on their toes. Ramp up the fear.

He shot a quick text off. He wouldn't get a response, but he was still close enough to hear the rifle fire through the woods.

He turned around, facing back toward World's Edge, and waited.

The shot never came.

VERONICA

I shimmied down the tree with a complete disregard for the skin on my hands. By the time I touched the solid earth, both palms were raw and bleeding, the blood mixing with the sap to form a sticky coppery mess.

I didn't want to risk calling now. I didn't know what the state of play was back on the lawn. I ran—well, stumbled—through the trees as fast as I could. A vine whipped me across the mouth, and I tasted blood. Quick tooth inventory check. All accounted for. Adrenaline surged through me.

When I made it back to the lawn, I could sense the charged energy as soon as I saw them. Mikaela crouched, still hovering near the edge of the cliff. Alive. And unharmed. I breathed out a sigh of relief.

I turned my eyes toward the detectives. They both had fraught expressions, and Iverson was speaking rapidly into her radio.

"What happened?" Detective Brown asked as soon as I got within earshot.

I told them about the shooter, and what I had to do.

"Why didn't you get him to talk?" Iverson asked.

Saw that one coming. I arched an eyebrow. "When you're unarmed and have a man swinging a rifle towards you, I'd like to see your solution. Why are you guys not on the phone?"

"He realized you weren't here and hung up angrily. We've been waiting nervously, wondering what was happening."

"Well, call him back."

"What?" Iverson's brow furrowed.

"You want answers about who that was up in the tree, don't you?" I turned toward Mikaela and gestured her over. "He's gone. You're okay. You're safe now."

EMILIA

Emilia was surprised to see the number wasn't blocked. She touched the latest number in the recent calls list—the only call there—and put the phone on speaker.

Come on, Jacob, pick up.

"You know you can't actually trace me with this, right?" His voice was calm and confident.

"Who was the man in the tree?"

There was a long pause. "Was?"

"Tell me."

"Why should I? Ask him yourself." He was trying to project confidence, but his voice sounded rattled.

"That's... going to be a little tricky."

"Why?"

"The branch broke, and he fell over the cliff."

"Fuck me." Jacob breathed out a deep sigh into the phone. "This is why I didn't go up there."

"Dr. Walsh says he was older, so he couldn't have been a classmate of yours or Janet's."

"Goddamn. He didn't deserve that. He was a good man. The only one who actually cared about Janet. Len."

Emilia gestured for Iverson to take notes. "Len who?"

"Man." Jacob chuckled, disbelieving. "This really wasn't much of an investigation, was it? Maybe you should be asking yourself why it took me taking action for your department to actually learn a thing or two. How do you not know who Leonard Barry is and how he was connected to the Belles?"

"Leonard Barry?" Emilia had to repeat the name to make it make sense in her mind. "Missing and presumed dead Leonard Barry?"

Iverson gaped at her. "Wasn't he your case before you got pulled for the Senator?"

"He's been missing for three weeks."

"The fuck?"

"Len has been a, let's say 'off-the-books' groundskeeper for decades," Jacob said. "He's the reason the grounds look like they do."

"He was here that night," Emilia said. "But why isn't he one of your victims, then?"

"He was the only one who went after them," Jacob said. "The only one who tried to stop a tragedy. And what did he end up succeeding in doing? He got there just in time to grab the good Senator and haul him to safety before the golf cart careened over the cliff."

"He tried to stop it," Mikaela whispered. "Oh, my God. Tony used to always give toasts about how Lenny deserved to be a hero. I thought he was just talking some nonsense about Of Mice and Men."

"I knew there had to be someone else," Emilia said, mentally kicking herself. "You killed everyone involved before they had a chance to tell the story, right? Which means you already heard the whole story, and we know that Janet couldn't have given you that much detail."

"I found Len first. He's been hiding out for the past few weeks, helping me behind the scenes. We staged a little accident at his house just in case anyone came looking for him. They would assume I got to him first. He told me everything. Most importantly, he told me about the cover-up. Before they even pulled my sister up, before the bodies were dragged from the banks downriver, the wheels were turning.

"It had to be a big, secret operation, and it had to happen fast. They must have worked throughout the night, and they must have offered a fortune for the other families to stay quiet. My parents told me that we had to take the money, we had no idea just how much it would cost to take care of my sister after she recovered. They had no idea just how true that would be. Akinetic mutism is like torture. How can you be given the choice between justice or caring for your injured child and not choose your kid?

"But it wasn't just the Belles, it was—" his voice cut off abruptly.

Emilia strained to hear what was happening. A second later, she heard Jacob say, "hey, what the hell?" and the line went dead.

CHAPTER 72
JACOB

Evening, March 13

"Hey, what the hell?"

Jacob stared at the long, gangly man who had seemingly appeared out of thin air. This shaded dirt road was supposed to be deserted. In all his time staking out escape routes, he had never seen someone come down this little road. It didn't even show up on Google Maps.

No one should know about it. Nor the clunker car he hid under a red cedar tree, its branches drooping low. He tried to look past the man, to see if the car was still hidden, but it was hard to see beyond the gun held inches in front of his nose.

Jacob had never liked guns. He understood their utility, although he always believed that the idea that having one in your house made you safer was bogus. But when you decide that you might need to use one in anger, against a fellow human being, it's worthwhile to do a little research.

"I will shoot."

The tone chilled Jacob's blood. The man said it like he was ordering breakfast. A casual comment, with no great thought to it. There was no doubt in Jacob's mind that he meant it.

"Who are you?"

"You stepped up to the pros, kid. But I don't think you're cut out for it."

Cocky demeanor. Swarthy complexion. A polished, gleaming gun.

Fuck.

Jacob sighed. "You're that friend of Dr. Walsh's. The one that knew her when she was a kid."

"Francisco Orellana, pleasure to meet you." He accompanied the greeting with a wry smile. "You're in a real predicament here."

"I don't suppose you'd just let me go?" Jacob chanced.

"Not going to happen."

There was always a way out. Jacob just needed to find it. No one had ever outsmarted him. When in trouble, he always had his brain, and it had never let him down so far.

"I see you thinking," Francisco said. "So, let me answer some questions for you. One, yes Alex—Dr. Walsh, for your benefit—called me and asked me to come as soon as she knew you were coming here. Two, she did not know about this dirt road, but I did, and that's part of being the smartest person in the room, knowing when to delegate. I got here and searched for escape routes. You obviously weren't planning some grand suicide by cop, hailstorm of bullets, blah blah blah, so naturally you had to have a way out. A smart guy like you, you're not going to have only half a plan."

"Look, I can't stop now. There's so much more to this—"

Francisco held up his free hand. "Save it. I'm not interested in whatever manifesto you have." Keeping his gun trained on Jacob, he reached into his pocket and pulled out his phone.

Jacob knew he had just one chance. As soon as Francisco glanced down towards his pocket, he dove.

But not toward Francisco. He went headfirst into the underbrush, somersaulting down the shallow hill off the dirt path.

He heard an exasperated sigh behind him and felt the rush of air whizz by him before he even heard the bullet fly past.

"Don't test me! Next one goes in your knee!" Francisco called from the dirt road.

But Jacob didn't believe him. He hauled himself up and took off running, cutting left and right, trying to establish some distance.

Distance was his only salvation. If he could get away, then he could carry on.

He ran, losing his bearings, no idea what direction he was heading. It didn't matter. He huffed as he tried his best not to slow down. When he couldn't breathe, he ducked behind a tree and crouched down.

As he sat, his chest heaving, he couldn't help but think of the irony. This was exactly what Senator Billingsley had done. Run through the woods away from a man with a gun. Jacob glanced down at his gun, still holstered on his ankle. He didn't want to use it, but he would if he had to.

"It's endearing that you think you have the upper hand."

The voice came from the distance in front of him. Jacob whipped his head left and right and grabbed his gun out of the holster. "I will shoot!" he called.

"I know." Francisco emerged from behind a tree, only a few yards ahead. His gun was pointed at Jacob, but his expression was almost one of boredom.

"Don't come any closer!"

"If you swing that gun any closer toward me, I will shoot it out of your hand. I do not promise I will only hit metal."

Jacob despaired. How could he explain to this psychopath that he had to let him go?

"I meant it about the knee."

"What?"

"Your knee. I will shoot your knee," Francisco said. "I can shoot your hand, knee, wherever you like. I could even let you pick if you'd prefer. But I will shoot if you do not drop your gun."

"You have to let me talk to Dr. Walsh," Jacob blurted out.

"Oh, do I?" Amusement rippled across Francisco's impassive face.

"Look." Jacob took a deep breath. This was the only way. "If I drop the gun, will you let me talk to Dr. Walsh? Please?"

Francisco mulled it over, swinging his gun around in his hand. *He's begging me to test him and try a shot,* Jacob thought.

"Okay, we can make that work. But drop it right now."

Jacob tossed the gun off to the right and listened as Francisco called Veronica and told her where he was. This really was it. There was no final escape. No last hurrah. The perpetrators would go free. This wasn't supposed to be half a mission. All or nothing, that's what he'd told himself.

What was it all for then?

Nothing.

VERONICA

The four of us rushed to the car and Detective Brown followed Francisco's instructions back out to the main road and onto a dirt road so small I thought it must have been just a bike path. The detectives and I piled out of the car when we pulled up a couple minutes later. Mikaela stayed in the car, batting away all attempts to get her to go to the hospital.

Detective Brown rushed ahead, her handcuffs jingling in her hand.

"Asics, huh?" she remarked, looking down at Jacob's feet. "We'll be taking those later."

Francisco slowly stepped away, and only I noticed him toss his gun into a patch of knee-high grass nearby. He'd be back for that later, and it definitely wasn't something he wanted on him around any police.

Detective Brown marched Jacob back to the car, toward the back seat that I had vacated. Before I could ask what they were going to do with Mikaela back there, Francisco spoke. "Wait," he said in that authoritative calm tone that used to infuriate me as a kid. "He's got something else to say."

Detective Brown looked at me. I shrugged. My part in this was over.

"Go ahead," she said.

"Look," Jacob said, holding his handcuffed hands up, palms out. "The cover-up is real. Senator Billingsley caused an accident that killed two kids and severely hurt another. But think about it, in this day and age, would that really have destroyed his career? He would have given some money to the families publicly, said some contrite bullshit, and the rest of the country would have lost interest in weeks, I guarantee it."

"So what?" Iverson asked.

"So why the cover-up? Why did they need to hide the incident *so badly* that it was better to pay off families forever to pretend their kids just disappeared? What are they actually hiding?"

"I think you're about to tell us," Detective Brown said.

"There's something else going on. These gatherings Janet said the adults had. I think that a group of adults, including the Belles and Senator Billingsley, are part of something much much bigger. They needed to make sure no one came snooping. No police, no accident reports, nothing."

"You want them to find out why." I nodded. "That was supposed to be your act two, wasn't it?"

"Yes." His voice was tired and scratchy. He looked right at me, those eyes I knew well for so many years. "All of those people are responsible for what happened in the aftermath, and I think there is some scandal at play here. Promise me, Dr. Walsh, will you get them to look into it? Or you're a private eye now, could you?"

I didn't know how to answer in front of the detectives, so I just offered a resolute nod.

"You're not in any position to be making demands, Jacob," Detective Brown reminded him. "But I'll check a few things and see what I can find. I'm not going to look the other way just because of the source of the information."

"Why did you write that thing on my Facebook?" Mikaela blurted out.

I raised an eyebrow to Detective Brown, but she looked just as confused as me. "What thing?" I asked.

Jacob cocked his head. "Oh, you mean about how there was someone else on the bridge with your husband? Written by Bill Andrews?"

"Yeah, why would you do that?"

Jacob let out a short sigh. "I don't want to speak ill of him now, but that was Len. He knew I'd gone to follow Tony, and then after Tony jumped, we hadn't communicated for a little bit. He assumed that I had pushed him off and wanted to change the narrative away from suicide. No one follows up on a suicide, and the point was to get noticed. I guess he thought I left a note, but that it had gotten blown away or something. Look"—he held his hands up as best he could in handcuffs— "I told him immediately to delete that. He wanted to make you know there was something more going on, and I guess obviously he succeeded, but as we talked about, there was nothing I could do for him anyway in the end. I really am sorry."

Mikaela's face was cherry-red, and she took several deep breaths.

Detective Brown turned to me. "Veronica, can you take Mikaela home—or better yet, to an emergency room, despite her protests? She needs to see someone, and I don't want her riding in the back with him. I'll send an officer to the hospital to stand guard."

I looked at Francisco, who hadn't yet moved. "What is it?"

His eyes flitted between Mikaela and the detectives. "Not here," he said. "But we have to talk as soon as possible. There's something you need to know about the guy who took those pictures of your husband."

CHAPTER 73
MIKAELA

Night, March 13

Mikaela lay her head against the passenger seat headrest. She closed her eyes and tried to force out the dull ache and throbbing. Veronica gave Francisco a salute as she pulled his Corvette onto Georgetown Pike and they headed east, back toward the city.

"Will he be okay?" Mikaela asked without opening her eyes.

"Francisco is always okay." Veronica chuckled. "Don't you worry at all about him. I'll drop his car off later."

"He's a nice guy to have in a pinch."

"He sure is, and he'll do anything for me and my family."

"It must be nice to have people that care that much about you." Mikaela felt a single tear slide down her cheek. Pregnancy hormones were bad enough when your life was boring.

"Mikaela." Veronica waited until Mikaela opened her eyes to continue. "All my family. Including my sister-in-law."

Mikaela's mouth widened but she didn't say anything.

"You've been through a lot, and for a long time you didn't have anyone in your corner, believe me, I get that. But now you're part of our team."

Tears formed in Mikaela's eyes. "Tony was the only family I ever had."

"And you'll make sure he lives on in your stories and in your child's life. But first, we're going to the hospital. You're no use to your unborn child with an untreated concussion."

"I just… I can't believe he really did jump. I haven't had a chance to process that, yet."

"He jumped?" Veronica's jaw dropped. "I am so sorry, Mikaela."

Mikaela filled Veronica in on her conversation with Jacob from earlier.

"Wow. I think he truly must have been living with a terrible pain. And I know you lightened his burden, but maybe there are things that are just impossible to come back from."

"When I think about it now, his entire persona was based on being that beacon of joy, the person who radiates enthusiasm for every tiny little morsel of life. I always believed that just came naturally to him, was just the way he was wired. But now I think it was all an act. Well, not an act," Mikaela corrected herself. "But a conscious attempt to be that person."

"I think you're exactly right. If you're stuck in that moment, living forever within yourself, you have to try your hardest to get out. Like Thomas Hobbes said, life without society would be 'solitary, poor, nasty, brutish, and short,' and I'm just sorry for him, you, and all his loved ones that he wasn't able to find an escape on this side."

Mikaela gripped Veronica's hand. "He would have loved this. Me being here with you. He thought you were incredible. He said that your success at restarting your life and making it better was an inspiration, and I think now that he really meant that on a personal level."

Mikaela stepped gingerly out of the car when Veronica pulled into the hospital. She checked herself in, glancing around and noting an officer standing leaning against the wall nearby.

"Sit down here, my dear," a nurse said. "Do you have any family with you?"

Mikaela turned and looked outside, making eye contact with Veronica, standing next to the Corvette by the visitor's entrance.

Veronica waved and placed her hand over her heart. A lump formed in Mikaela's throat. Maybe her tears were finally turning. Maybe dancing was in her future. "Yes. Yes, I do."

EPILOGUE

One Week Later

"Yo, what the fuck?" The blond teenager raced ahead of his brown-haired pre-teen brother. "Do you see that?"

The brother looked in the direction he was running. "I don't see anything, what is it?"

"It's a body, Tim! Right there at the edge of the river."

"Holy…"

"You know who this is, right?" Joe said. "This is the guy they're looking for! It's got to be."

"That accomplice of the dude who did those murders? Quick, find his wallet." The two pulled the body up onto the bank.

"Careful! They'll get you with all that CSI shit and say you killed him. Don't touch anything."

"But the police will know we were here, we're going to call them!"

"Just… be careful, okay?"

Tim pulled the wallet out, shook the water out, and peered closely. Joe watched as his face fell.

"What? What is it?"

"It's some rando."

"Goddamn it." He dropped the wallet and kicked it away angrily. "We could have gotten a reward or something."

"Was there a reward for him?"

"I don't know! But sometimes they give you money or something for doing your civic duty. This is just some random dead guy now."

"Fuck. Okay, let's get out of here, then."

The teenagers turned back into the woods, away from the water. They trudged on, shoulders slumped, the adrenaline that had raced through their bodies now coursing away.

Tim stopped, leaning against a small tree. "You think we should call someone?" he asked.

"Like, even though it's not that guy?"

"Yeah, I don't know. It just feels a little bad leaving him there like that. Who is going to find him?"

"Okay, I guess so, but we should do it anonymously. I don't want to have to deal with the police."

"Once we're out of here. We'll find a payphone. They still have those, right?"

"I think so," Joe said, leaves and sticks crunching below him as he went out of his way to step on them.

"Then that's the plan."

They continued their hike, taking great pains to avoid the riverbank for fear of finding anything else.

"Hey, what was it?" Joe asked suddenly.

"What was what?"

"You know, the name of the guy?"

"Oh, yeah, sorry." Tim shrugged and shook his head. "A boring name. Benjamin Walsh."

THANK YOU FOR READING DON'T LOOK DOWN

We hope you enjoyed it as much as we enjoyed bringing it to you. We just wanted to take a moment to encourage you to review the book. Follow this link: **Don't Look Down** to be directed to the book's Amazon product page to leave your review.

Every review helps further the author's reach and, ultimately, helps them continue writing fantastic books for us all to enjoy.

For more information on Matthew Becker's books, check out his website: www.matthewbeckerbooks.com.

ALSO BY MATTHEW:
RUN
DON'T LOOK DOWN

You can also JOIN our non-spam mailing list by visiting www.subscribepage.com/aethonthrillsnewsletter and never miss out on future releases. You'll also receive three full books completely Free as our thanks to you.

Facebook | Instagram | Twitter | Website

Want to discuss our books with other readers and even the authors?
JOIN THE AETHON DISCORD!

Looking for more great Thrillers?

From desk agent to unexpected field agent. The safety of the world hangs in the balance. Kate Malone is an intelligence analyst specializing in Russian military and politics. When asked to debrief a Russian defector in Paris, she considers it just another routine assignment. Routine becomes chaos and leads to a desperate chase through the capitals of Europe... With no training as a field operative, Kate must learn the ways of a spy even as Russian agents hunt her down. Failure could lead to another world war, but success depends on survival. And in the world of international espionage, survival is never guaranteed. **Experience a gripping tale of international intrigue and espionage perfect for fans of Tom Clancy, L.T. Ryan, and Saul Herzog. Join Kate as she must leave the safety of her agency office behind and face the dangers of life as a field agent.**

Get Too Soon A Spy Now!

The truth shall set you free. But for one young lawyer, it might just cost him his life... A popular priest is accused of a horrific assault and tied to the murders of two other women. Jackson Price and his mentor race to uncover the motives of his accuser. At the same time, detectives uncover a checkered past of inappropriate behavior with women and mental health issues. The case may hinge on the truth of an apparition and the impact it has on everyone involved. As the case races through the criminal justice system, Jackson finds himself caught between reality and the delusions of a killer. One could end his short career; the other could end his life. Strap in and follow the investigation to the thrilling end! **The Apparition is a gripping psychological legal thriller with high stakes suspense and vivid courtroom drama. From debut author Marc X. Carlos, it's inspired by one of his real cases as a career criminal defense attorney with extensive experience in high profile crimes, courtroom technique and crime scene investigation.**

Get The Apparition Now!

For all our Thrillers, visit our website at www.aethonbooks.com/thriller

ACKNOWLEDGMENTS

Firstly, thanks again to my publishers Aethon Thrills, for providing this platform and allowing me to create this story.

Thank you to my agent Gina Panettieri, and the Talcott Notch team, for being a constant source of wisdom and expertise.

Thanks to all of you who read RUN and were so unabashedly loud about it. Special thanks to Robin Agnew, Lynda Dietz, Judy Collins, and all the rest of the booksellers and readers who used their platform to help me promote my books.

Thank you to my fellow authors, for encouragement, blurbs, book events, and the genuinely kind community you have all created.

Finally, thanks to you all who came back for more and picked up (or clicked on) this book. The book bloggers, the bookstagrammers, the offline word-of-mouth readers, every one of you. If you're reading this you've likely read both of my published novels by now, so I want to express my deepest appreciation that you returned. I hope you'll stick around because the Walsh family saga is ending soon!

ABOUT THE AUTHOR

Matthew Becker is a mathematician, and formerly worked as part of the national Covid-19 response. He has a doctorate in applied mathematics from the University of Maryland, College Park, and is published in the Bulletin of Mathematical Biology. Matthew currently lives with his wife, a U.S. diplomat, and their two children in Tashkent, Uzbekistan. Run is his first novel.

www.ingramcontent.com/pod-product-compliance
Lightning Source LLC
Chambersburg PA
CBHW020528310726
48979CB00014B/2246/J
9781964505121